DJANSHA

Black silence hung over the devastated town. Yet
something, someone was still alive. From among the
smoking ruins a young, slender woman appeared. Her
small breasts rose firmly upward, lifting the fabric of
her plain, linen gown.

Her face was oval with a pert nose and a mouth with
gentle curves. Under arched brows, her eyes seemed
enormous—silver-blue between smoky lashes.

As she neared him, Lucas could see her hands were
painted with blood. Her gaze ran up and down him,
from the tangled hair and broad face to the feet that
moved with a catlike sureness.

She stopped before him, glowing in the lamplight.
"You are a warrior," she whispered. "You have won
me. Now take me, Lucas . . . take me . . ."

ROUGUE SWORD
POUL ANDERSON

ZEBRA BOOKS

KENSINGTON PUBLISHING CORP.

ZEBRA BOOKS

are published by

KENSINGTON PUBLISHING CORP.
21 East 40th Street
New York, NY 10016

Printed in the United States of America

AUTHOR'S NOTE

Fantastic though they be, the adventures of the Grand Catalan Company did happen. Our main source of information about them is a chronicle by one of the members, Ramon Muntaner, but there are other contemporary records. In addition, I have, of course, consulted various modern authorities.

As for the aftermath, the Catalans never entered Constantinople, but they ravaged the hinterland freely until they had picked it clean and hunger drove them off. Proceeding west, they first occupied Thessaly and then, in 1311, overthrew the Frankish lords of central Greece. For the next seventy-five years they and their descendants misgoverned these territories. Finally the Peloponnesian baron Nerio Acciaiuoli expelled them and brought, for a while, better times.

The Knights Hospitallers captured Rhodes in 1309 and ruled it benignly until forced out by the Turks in 1522. In 1530 they received the grant of Malta from the Emperor Charles V, and reached their highest glory when they repulsed the great Turkish onslaught of 1565. As feudalism waned, so did their popularity and power, though technical jurisdiction over the island did not pass from them to Britain before 1814. Today called the Sovereign Order of the Knights of Malta, they are a charitable organization of Catholic noblemen.

Poul Anderson

England

Flanders

France

Holy
Roman
Empire

Bay
of
Biscay

Burgundy

Aquitaine

Genoa   Venice

Dalm...

Adriatic

Portugal   Castile

Toledo

Navarre

Barcelona

Corsica

Papal
States

Seville Cordova

Granada

Valencia

Sardinia

Naples

Naples

Kingdom of

Sicily

Mediterranean

The Mediterranean
and Black Seas
ca. 1306 A.D.

■ Areas important to story

Poland

Lithuania

The Golden Horde

Dnieper R.

Don R.

Hungary

Walachia

Serbia

Bulgaria

Principalities

Albania

Kaffa

Black Sea

Sinope

Trebizond

of Trebizond

Anatolia

Greece

Lycia

Antioch

Rhodes

Cyprus

Crete

Beirut

Acre

Sea

Alexandria

Jerusalem

Nile R.

Red Sea

PROLOGUE

As he sprang through the window, Lucas heard steel whistle at his back. For an instant, he wondered if the sword had reached him. Then he was falling through darkness.

He straightened in midair and hit the canal in a clean dive. The water shut thickly above his head. Memory stabbed: thus had he often gone over a certain low cliff, into the sea that encircled Crete. And when he came up, the waves had glittered, unrestful blue to the world's rim, and had laughed with him. Was it only four years ago?

He felt himself rising, and struck out underwater. When his lungs were near to bursting, he broke the surface. A piling was rough beneath his hand, supporting him in part. The house it upheld gave him a helmet of shadow. He felt the water warm and oily on his skin. It stank. No, he thought, Venice lies far from Crete.

Cautiously, he glanced around. Thin night-mists lay on the canal, unreal beneath stars and a bit of moon. The houses lifted sheer from narrow walkways, doors barred, windows shuttered, blind with sleep. Yards behind and above him, one square shone with dull candlelight. The bulky black form of a man leaning out filled most of it. A metal gleam jumped about in his hand. Fear vanished in mockery as Lucas thought: If he failed to skewer me, why must he vent his anger on the unoffending air?

Then the merchant began to shout. *"Custodi! Ho, custodi!"* Echoes clamored from wall to wall and back again, down the length of the canal. A squad of watchmen could not be far away; this city was well patrolled. Lucas bit his lip in returning unease.

Another shape appeared at the second-floor window. The candle-glow touched her body and her unbound hair. She screamed above her husband's bellowings, "Lucco, get away! He'll have you blinded—" Gasparo Reni snarled and shoved her back into the chamber.

Did torches bob as men came jogging along the walkway, somewhere off in the fog? Lucas didn't care to find out. Moreta was quite right, bless her soul. Bless also her eyes and lips and arms and . . . He reminded himself sharply of his peril. Worse, in a way, than before. If Gasparo had slain him and thrown him into the canal (who would ask that great merchant what he knew about the fate of a penniless orphan apprentice?) he would at least be dead. But now, if the watch arrested Lucas, Gasparo would take his revenge through the law. By all accounts, he was vindictive enough to demand the extreme penalty for this offense, when the offender could not pay substantial compensation: loss of a hand and both eyes.

Even if the judge mitigated the sentence, Venice

would be no place for Lucas the half-Greek.

But where, then?

He began to swim, quickly and softly. After he turned off along an intersecting canal, the window and Moreta were lost to him.

It became very still. Few people were ever abroad after dark. He passed a number of moored gondolas, but their poles were stored indoors. Anyhow, a naked youth had best travel inconspicuously. Seeing the mouth of an alley gaping just beyond a ladder, Lucas climbed up and slipped into its concealing darkness.

The air chilled his wet skin. He shivered, fought against a sneeze, and wondered with increasing desperation what to do. Sunrise would trap him as certainly as the men of the Signori di Notte. He had disreputable friends, here and there—no, he thought, not such good friends that they'd help one who was hunted. Especially if Gasparo Reni offered a reward.

His throat tightened and tears stung his eyes. O all you saints, he protested, why did you have to let this happen? What am I to do?

Bad enough being damned to dreariness here, among aliens, with no other prospect for my whole lifetime; but now this!

A thought struck home. Terror, loneliness, self-pity scattered. By Heaven, he realized, this may be the very chance I've prayed for!

He laughed aloud, and hurried from shadow to shadow, across the city to the waterfront.

But at the Sclavonian Bank, he had to worm his way across the docks. Often he stopped, his heart almost bursting through his rib-cage at the sound of footsteps. When he reached shelter, his exhaustion was such that he could have gone no farther, though the watchmen's pikes were to lift above him.

He cradled his cheek on an arm. Sleep came like a thunderclap.

A racket of shoes and voices, in the first vague light before dawn, awoke him. He tensed, instantly alert. Thank Heaven for youth, he thought in a wry corner of his mind; one needs the toughness to survive the consequences of the rashness. He was, in fact, only fifteen years old, of medium height but close-knit, well muscled for his age. His head was round, his face broad, with a freckled snub nose, high cheekbones and a wide full mouth, hazel eyes set far apart, reddish-brown hair.

The new arrivals were longshoremen, come to finish the loading of a fleet. Lucas had known a convoy would leave today, with woolens, iron, and timber for Constantinople. He knew every ship in harbor, where it was from and where it was going and when and with what. The knowledge had fueled all his dreams, while he toiled in Gasparo Reni's countinghouse. He waited for his chance. Simply stowing away was not likely to get him far. But something might turn up.

His hiding place was in a stack of marble pieces, looted from Eastern cities and awaiting the day that some new building required them. A fluted column was hard against his hip, a frieze of centaurs like a barricade before him. Past the warehouses, he could see the twin spires of the Palazzo delle due Torri, near the Doge's palace, and the top of the Campanile. All was dim and blue-black, under dying stars.

An opportunity came, sooner than expected. The laborers were busy stowing deck cargo, but not far from Lucas another man went up and down a gangplank, carrying personal baggage that he had fetched in a gondola. Obviously he was some passenger's servant. Yet his cheap brown mantle, of Venetian cut, and the general look of him, suggested he was no beloved old retainer but merely hired for this occasion. He seemed worth testing; if inquiry gave negative results, well, something else must be tried. Lucas waited catwise. The man stooped to pick up a bag of provisions, such as all passengers must carry for themselves—at an instant when the stevedore gang was preoccupied with several ships down the line.

"Hsst!" called Lucas. "You, there!"

"What?" The man straightened and approached. Seen closer, he was a scrawny one. Indeed, thought Lucas, feverishly excited, the saints are being most helpful.

He kept his tones low and cool. "Would you like a bit of sport, Messer?"

"What's going on? Where are you?"

"I have a sister. Young. Breasts like the dome of St. Mark's."

The stranger paused, a few feet away. Lucas raised his head over the marble blocks, grinning, and saw lechery. "This is no time or place," the man hesitated. "Against the law."

"True. But we've instant need of money, she and I, and there's too much competition in the regular quarter. Only two grossi, Messer, the tenth part of a ducat, for as warm a half-hour as you'll spend this side of Purgatory. And a good deal more pleasant, eh?''

"My work—"

"You've little left to do, I can see. Who's your master?"

"A knight of Aragon." The servant preened himself. "He engaged me out of a hundred others, to accompany him to Constantinople and back. I have to make this place ready."

"You'll be at sea for weeks, then. Perhaps a whole month. Heat, seasickness, crowding—"

"No, he's engaged a room in the deckhouse. He's too well-born to mix with common merchants and that ilk, sleeping in the open. I can spread my pallet at his threshold."

"—bad food, worse water, and wine turned sour. Hardest of all, uninterrupted chastity. You might even perish at sea. Then think of my sister, as you gurgle down to the bottom!"

"Two grossi is too much."

"Well, we can discuss that. Here, where no busybody watchman can spy us."

The man came around the barricade, in among the marbles, and saw Lucas naked. His mouth fell open. Before he could cry out, he was attacked.

Lucas whipped him around, threw an arm about his neck, put a knee in the small of his back, and rapped sharply with the other hand. The man gasped once, and sagged. Lucas eased him down and undressed him. It was hard, acrobatic work in this cramped space, with the ever-present fear of discovery. His victim stirred and groaned. Lucas ripped a hem with the aid of his teeth, tore strips from the shirt, bound and gagged the man. Then he tucked him, helplessly squirming, in an entablature. Hastily he donned the remaining garments.

"You can get loose before sundown, I'm sure," he said kindly. "I shall offer prayers for your welfare."

He went out to the piled baggage and began loading it himself.

All the galleys of this convoy were identical, as Venetian law required: high in poop and forecastle, low in the waist, with oars and a single lateen-sailed mast. Catapults were mounted for defense against pirates; a shelter stood amidships for officers and the most important passengers. Lucas soon found the knight's cubbyhole, the goods already there marked with the same emblem as those on the baggage he carried. He worked fast to get everything stowed before anyone paid attention to him. When at last he could close the door, he was all atremble. He unshuttered the little port, hoping the dawn air would clear his head. Now, more than ever, he needed nerve and wits.

If his gamble failed . . . best not think of that. Think what success would mean—a way opened to the fabled lands of his most gorgeous hopes!

Deck passengers bustled aboard. Sailors followed. Flags were hoisted, to flap brilliant in the sky above the vividly striped hulls. One by one, the galleys warped from the long quay. When all were clear, trumpets blew and oars rattled forth. They struck the water with an enormous noise, but fell at once into a steady *creak-splash-thud* as drums set their time. The ships formed convoy and stood out toward the Adriatic Sea.

Lucas watched from the cabin. He caught a final glare, where sunlight crashed on the great bronze horses atop the cathedral. Far northward, the mountains made a wan blueness. When the fleet neared the Lido, he discerned other craft, not only fisher boats but merchantmen which had lain at anchor until sunrise made entrance possible. They bore to Venice the goods of a hundred lands: from her own possessions in Dalmatia, the eastern Mediterranean and the Black Sea; from foreign countries from Iceland to Cathay. Saracen trade came here, despite all prohibitions of the Church. Even the hated Genoese came, though it did not seem that the uneasy peace between them and Venice could last much longer.

And I, thought Lucas with a leaping in his breast, am outbound.

The door opened. He whirled about.

The man who stood there was tall, and increased his height by soldierly erectness. His face was narrow, with a jutting beak of nose, gray eyes, thin lips framed by a pointed beard and mustaches. His black hair was cut short immediately below the ears, like most men's. His doublet and hose were likewise black, of rich material, but he wore a white blouse and red cloak.

His sword leaped forth. "What are you doing?" he barked.

Lucas bowed. "Good morning, Ser Knight." His voice was not altogether steady. Sweat prickled him.

The cavalier poised his blade. "Good morning to you, Messer Thief." He snapped out the Venetian patois with a readiness indicating he had been some time in the Republic, but with a distinct accent of Catalonia. "Where is my attendant?"

"Here, my lord, at your command."

The Catalan lowered his weapon, as blankly as hoped. "What? Have I entered the wrong—No! Where is Giovanni Moxe?"

Need proved a sharp spur. Lucas found himself able to laugh. "Was that his name, Messer? Are you certain? Myself, I wouldn't trust him to say a truthful Credo. Think! He abandoned his duty to go rest behind the marble heaped on the waterfront! Naturally, your effects could not be left unwatched, so I completed their stowage and assumed guard over them."

His educated vocabulary impressed the other, Lucas saw. "Who are you?" demanded the knight, but the creak and thrum of the ship overrode his words. He closed the door to the crowded deck and repeated his question.

"Lucas, my lord. They called me Lucco in Venice." With a rush of defiance, he tossed his head and declared, "Now I shall again be of my mother's people, and bear the name she gave me."

"Do you know your father?"

A calculated gibe. Lucas felt his cheeks go hot as he answered: "I know who he was, Messer. A younger son of the great Torsello family. He was stationed for a couple of years at the factory—the mercantile center—at Canea, on the island of Crete. Then he returned to Venice and died of sickness soon after."

"Leaving a discarded mistress and her by-blow. A common enough occurrence. But you have uncommon impudence, I must say. Do you know the penalties for illegal embarkation? There are worse ones for murder. Tell the truth, you! What did you do to Giovanni Moxe?"

The sword lifted again. A sunbeam, sickling in as the ship rolled, turned it to bright menace. Lucas gulped.

"As God is my witness, Ser Knight, I didn't harm him!" he protested. "Not enough to matter. I only left him tied. He'll get loose within hours. Need drove me. Are we not all commanded to preserve our lives as long as reasonably possible?"

The Catalan's weapon drooped once more. He stroked his beard and considered the boy with narrowed military eyes. "So?" he replied, smooth again. "Pray, tell me the whole."

Hopefulness brought Lucas' smile forth, and the words tripped from his tongue.

"Consider, Messer. I did not force Gasparo Reni's wife. True, I did not repel her, either. She is pretty, and not much older than I, while her husband is a sullen oaf who went to Eastern lands less than a year after he wed her and was two years gone. Meanwhile I was an apprentice in the countinghouse. She would come and visit it—ah, like a sunbeam in the strangling gloom! We would talk. On some holidays I was invited to the house, most decorously. At last I took to serenading beneath her window. One night she let a rope fall from her sill, down to my borrowed gondola. . . . Well, when old Reni came back, a few weeks ago, I thought a very sweet time had ended.

18

But yesterday she sent me a message: he was to be gone after dark, to an entertainment at the Rialto. Would it not have been churlish and ungrateful of me not to respond, Messer? Yet how could we have known he would return home hours before any man who has any sense of joy in life should, and enter without the simple courtesy of knocking?''

Despite himself, the Catalan could be seen to fight an answering grin. To the haughty nobles of Iberia, a merchant's honor was of no account. "So you chose this means of escape," he said. "Well, I can understand Venice is no longer healthful for you." Harshly then, as the thought smote him: "But you were craven to abandon the woman to his wrath."

"Oh, no fear for her, Messer. Donna Moreta is of the Grimiani, and you know how powerful that family is. He'd never dare use violence on her. In fact, now that there is no object for his revenge, why should he make himself ridiculous by saying anything at all of what has happened? Better to keep the whole affair secret, no? Wherefore I did her the best service by fleeing."

"A rascal is never at loss for a reason. But can you give me one for not handing you over to the captain, that he may return you to your just punishment?''

"I can give you many reasons, Ser Knight.'' Lucas throttled his fear to speak glibly. *"Imprimis,* Our Lord bade us forgive the wrongdoer. *Secundus,* I have done you no harm, except to rid you of a servant so lazy and stupid he would leave his work to talk with a pimp. *Tertius,* you would be without a servant if I was arrested, which is not suitable to your dignity. *Quartus,* I am a most excellent servant. Besides menial tasks, I can read, write, and do sums; speak flowing Greek, with more than a smattering of other languages; sing rather well, play on whistle or cither, compose poems in all approved forms, sail a boat, fight, spy on your enemies, advise on affairs of the heart, and learn anything else my master cares to teach me."

"Ah, so." With a sudden gesture, the man put sword back in sheath. He was getting more than a little interested. "Where have you gained these marvelous abilities?"

The story was soon told, however much Lucas yielded to the temptation of embellishment when he saw his persuasion succeeding. After her Venetian lover departed, his Cretan mother had gone back to her own fisher people and married one of them. Lucas learned the handling of small craft from his stepfather. But an uncle of his mother, a monk, saw uncommon possibilities of another sort and educated the lad in the Greek and Roman alphabets. Likewise he learned the speech both of the Cretans and their unloved Venetian overlords. His mother died when he was eleven and her husband, with an eye to making good connections, inquired about his natural father. Pietro Torsello turned out also to be dead. But under Venetian law, no child could be totally disinherited, and Lucas' paternity was demonstrable. So another of the Torselli undertook, grudgingly, to make provision for him and brought him to Venice. Here he was apprenticed in the countinghouse of Gasparo Reni.

It suited him ill. He became the wildest of his

fellows, always ready for a fight or a frolic—and the Queen of the Adriatic offered both, in rich variety, to those who explored her byways. Though often in trouble, the boy showed such a potentially useful talent for languages that he was never severely punished. Simply by spending time in that polyglot city, he had become able to get along in half a dozen tongues. As for his warlike capabilities: he had been in more than his share of rough-and-tumble encounters; and early this year, on reaching his fifteenth birthday, he was enrolled in the arbalestiers like any other Venetian youth.

At the end of the tale, the knight said weightily, "If half of what you claim is true, you'll indeed be more valuable to me than that Moxe fellow. But since I plan to return through Venice, you must be left in Constantinople when I go."

"I shall find others who can use my services," cried Lucas, all ablaze. "Have no fears, Signor. I'll reach Cathay itself!"

"I wouldn't doubt it, if God doesn't weary of such a scamp," said the man dryly. "Well—do you know who I am?"

Lucas cocked his head. "Plainly, Signor, you're from Catalonia province, in the Kingdom of Aragon. Doubtless you've spent much time in the Sicilian War. From your bearing, you must be a *rich hom.*" He used the Catalan phrase, "great man," meaning a scion of those baronial families which enjoyed extraordinary powers. And he continued in the same language, haltingly and ungrammatically but understood:

"Yet forgive me if I suggest you are wealthier in

21

birth than gold. Your baggage and accommodations are not those of a moneyed lord. Was your estate perhaps devastated when the French invaded Aragon seven years ago? Ah, well, I'm certain you fought valiantly and had much to do with expelling them.''

"Know, I am the knight Jaime de Caza, traveling in the service for my namesake the Lord King of Aragon.''

"At your command, En Jaime.'' Lucas dropped to one knee.

His use of the Catalan honorific was pleasing. Most Italians would have said ''Don Jaime,'' as if the visitor were from the Kingdom of Castile. The nobleman nodded in a friendly way. ''My mission is not secret,'' he said. ''Now that Aragon has a new king, I am sounding out the attitude of certain powers concerning the war for Sicily that still drags on. Having been in Venice, I am bound similarly to the Byzantine Imperium. Since I talk no Greek, I admit that your instruction en route would be welcome; and afterward I can certainly make use of a confidential amanuensis. So be it, then, as long as you remain faithful. You shall have whatever pay you are worth, and I will not mention to anyone that you are not my original servant.''

It was more than Lucas had dared imagine. ''Blessings upon you, my master!'' he shouted, bouncing back to his feet. Gaiety torrented from him. ''I must go to work at once, to prepare a suitable midday meal. I confess I'm not expert in the kitchen, but I know what tastes good. So by adding a leek here and a smidgen of cheese there, a dash of vinegar and enough olive oil, I'll feel my way toward a dish not altogether insulting. And, oh, yes, Messer, I must see what clothes you have along, brush them and—Would you like entertainment? I can tell you the most scandalous stories; or chivalric romances, if you prefer, or a ballade or sirvente—" Hustling about the narrow cabin, laughing, singing, chattering, he soon crowded the other out onto the deck. And before him there shone the vision of Cathay and new horizons.

CHAPTER I

Fourteen years had passed when Lucas, called Greco, saw Constantinople for the second time. That was in April, in the year 1306.

He stood in the Augustaion, waiting for Brother Hugh de Tourneville to meet him as they had agreed. This was the heart of the city. On one side rose the wall about the Imperial grounds. Mailed Varangian Guardsmen with axes at their shoulders stood on the top and on the gates; their helmets flamed in the late afternoon sunlight. Above the parapets could be seen the roof of the Brazen House, their barracks, and a shining glimpse of the Daphné and Sigma Palaces. Behind Lucas, over flat intervening roofs, soared the domes of St. Sophia; around a corner bulked the Hippodrome, crumbling with age, its arches a shelter for beggars, prostitutes, and bandits by night.

Old and corrupt the Byzantine Empire might be, but nonetheless, here it surged with humanity. The citizens themselves, in long dalmatic and cope, dark, curly-haired, big-nosed, more Anatolian than Greek by blood, and styling themselves Romans; a noble in gold and silken vestments, looking with jaded eyes from the palanquin in which four slaves bore him; a priest, strange to the Western mind in his beard, black robe, and brimless hat; foreigners, English, Flemish, German, French, Iberian, Italian, Turkish, Arabic, Russian, Mongol, half the world poured down the throat of New Rome. Their voices, the shuffle and clatter of feet, the ring of hoofs and rumble of wagon wheels, made an ocean-like roar. A smell of dust, smoke, cooking oil, sweat, sewage, horse droppings, rolled thick across the grumbling and grinding city. High overhead, sunlight caught the white wings of sea gulls.

Lucas shifted his stance, ill at ease. His memories of his first time here were still bright; but today he saw how much of that glamour had merely been his own youth. He shook his head, denyingly, for it was wrong that a man not yet thirty should feel old. He could not have changed so much. Could he? His bones had lengthened and his muscles filled out. His face, which he kept clean-shaven as part of an inborn fastidiousness, had become a man's rather than a boy's, flat-cheeked and square-jawed, with deep lines from nose to lips. The sun and wind of Asia had darkened his skin, lightened his hair, and put crow's feet around his eyes. But he was stronger in every way than he had been then, wiser (or at least shrewder), with a thousand experiences both violent and subtle to prove he could rely on himself.

Perhaps, he thought, that was what he had lost. Fourteen years ago, Cathay had lain ahead of him; now it lay behind.

And scarce a ducat to show for it all, he added

ruefully. His clothes—blouse, breeches, hose, shabby leather doublet and stained cloak, faded red bonnet—were a goodly proportion of his entire wealth. From time to time he had known riches, but . . .

"Ah, good evening, my friend."

Lucas bowed. "Good evening to you, Brother Hugh." They spoke in Genoese, the dominant Western tongue hereabouts, though both were also familiar with Romaic Greek. A chance encounter yesterday had led to mutual liking; both had considerable free time, and the city was well worth their joint exploration.

"Did your business speed?" asked Lucas.

"No," said Hugh. "After cooling my heels in an antechamber, from morning until almost now, I was told the official could not see me yet. Oh, the underling was most polite, but his glee was plain."

"Aye, they'd enjoy baiting the representative of a Catholic brotherhood, in this most Orthodox capital. I would do them a mischief, were I you."

Hugh smiled. "If I lose my temper, will they not have succeeded in their aim? I can be patient; sit there as many days as need be, thinking my own thoughts. In the end, I'll outlast their delayings." Sadness crossed his countenance. "After all, they do have good reason to hate everything Western."

They began to walk, off the forum and down narrow streets between high walls. Daylight should linger long enough for them to visit the famous Mangana building. Afterward they would share supper. Hugh limped, the result of an old wound, and leaned on a staff; but his leathery frame did not seem to tire. He was tall and bony, with England

27

plain to see in his long face and long straight nose. Against the weather-beaten skin, his eyes were a startling blue. The grizzled hair was cut short, and he wore a close-trimmed beard. His dress was the humble garb of the Knights Hospitallers of the Order of St. John of Jerusalem: over plain clothes, a black mantle with an eight-pointed white cross on the breast.

But that organization of warrior friars held lands across half Europe. Hugh himself had fought at Acre, when the Moslems drove the last Christian dominion out of the Holy Land. Since then, the Knights of St. John had found refuge, like their Templar rivals, with the Frankish King of Cyprus; but their wealth and power remained. They acquired warships to guard the Christian and harry the infidel by sea, and lately they nursed some larger plan. What that was, Hugh kept secret. However, this gentle, drawling second son of a Lincolnshire baron had risen to the rank of Knight Companion of the Grand Master. He would not come hither to interview officials of the East Roman Empire, subtly probing strengths and weaknesses, for nothing.

"What have you heard about the trouble at Gallipoli?" he asked.

"Little enough truth," said Lucas. "I can relay any number of rumors, if you like."

Arrived here from Trebizond, he had sought passage farther and engaged a place easily enough. The Golden Horn was filled with galleys, westbound after trading in the Black Sea, and more were arriving every week. But that was because war had broken out at the mouth of the Sea of Marmora, between the Byzantines and a rebellious troop of foreign mercenaries. They held the area of Gallipoli, and the Imperial forces were besieging them. While the fighting lasted, no prudent shipmaster would risk passing through the narrows.

"I expect the trouble will soon be over," said Lucas.

"I am not so sure," mused Hugh. "Perhaps you haven't realized how enfeebled the Empire is. Whole provinces torn from her, her master a venal government under a vicious dynasty. . . . Well-a-day, it need concern you little. Did you say you were bound for Negroponte? You'll be safely distant from New Rome and her woes."

Lucas nodded. Negroponte, the Venetian-owned island of Euboea, lay just across a narrow channel from the Duchy of Athens. He dared not go directly to Venice, until he had cleared whatever old charges still stood against him. If the result of discreet inquiries proved discouraging, he could escape to the Greek mainland and take service with one of the Frankish nobles who ruled there. Not that he expected much trouble. After fourteen years, who would care? But those same years had taught him caution.

"I meant to ask you," said Hugh, "if you ever met a certain countryman of yours, one Marco Polo? He reached the same places in Cathay as you've mentioned. I chanced on him in Trebizond some years ago, when I was there on my Order's business and he on his way home."

Lucas shook his head. "No. I heard of him at the court of the Kha Khan in Cambaluc, but I came later."

29

Briefly, the recollection of graceful red roofs, willows and arched bridges above garden ponds, a philosopher who had been his friend and many gentle beauties who had been his loves, rose up to blot Constantinople from his awareness. And there had been music in violet nights when the cherry trees bloomed, and a certain mountain seen through clouds, and temple bells that rang in his dreams just at sunrise . . . what had driven him back to the filthy West?

They walked on in silence for a while. When they resumed their talk, it was with Hugh describing the state of affairs here in Europe. That was no hopeful subject in these years when one realm after another fell to pieces and anarchy raged through the ruins. But at least, for Lucas, it was impersonal; and that fact reminded him joltingly how rootless he had become. In the end, he had returned to the Occident because (however much he sometimes wished and tried) he could not change himself into an Oriental. So let him now seek out Venice. It might be a shoddy home for him, but a home, anyhow, perhaps.

The sun sank low. A small cold wind seeped down from the hills above Galata and across the Golden Horn, to blow dust through the darkening streets of Constantinople. The two men found themselves passing through a desolated section.

When the Crusaders gutted this city a hundred years before, they left ruins which the weakly restored Orthodox Empire had never repaired. Here the burned-out shell of a tenement stared down on a dirty lane filled with sunset shadows. The rains of a century had not whitened those charred beams;

weeds grew thick where the floor had been, and rats
scurried from human feet. On the opposite side were
inhabited buildings, sleazy flat-roofed structures rising several blank stories. A few ragged people went
by: a robber, openly armed in defiance of the law; a
sly-eyed old moneylender and his hulking body-
guard; a beggar, loathsomely crippled; a thin-legged
child who coughed. At sight of the child, Hugh
reached into his mantle for a purse.

"No," warned Lucas. "Give him a coin and
you'll bring the whole quarter screeching down on
us. The end could be a riot. I know these Asiatic
towns—and this section is not of Europe any
longer."

Hugh clenched his staff tightly. Lucas recalled
that the Knights of St. John had begun as a nursing
order and still maintained hospitals. "Yes," he said
after a moment. "I suppose you are right." They
continued.

Just ahead, another street crossed this one, a
broader way running toward the Venetian district. A
party of four was coming toward them. As if to
erase the child from his mind, Hugh stopped to look
at them. "Ah, your countrymen, Lucas," he said.
"They do make a brave sight, do they not?"

Lucas paused with him. There were three men in
the group, all bearing swords, by special license, no
doubt, since they would be abroad after dark. Two
were young, their garments a shout of red and blue
against the dingy walls. They carried unlighted
torches, for use when the last sunset glow had
vanished above the roofs. Plainly they were attendants of the third, an older man, heavy of body but

firm of gait, clad in rich green fabric. The fourth went wrapped in a hooded cloak, with bent head and dragging feet—a woman.

Hugh peered into the deepening shadows. The wind flapped the hem of his mantle. "Where are they going at this hour?" he wondered.

Lucas spat. "Can't you see? Look how the girl walks. She's a slave, and they're delivering her to some purchaser—a brothel keeper, or maybe someone giving a feast—who wants her this very evening. I've seen that sight before."

"I have . . . paid less attention." There was a thinness in Hugh's tone that brought Lucas' gaze back to him. The knight stood rigid, pale about the nostrils. "In my weakness," he said, "I averted my eyes from an abomination I could not fight."

"Do you feel thus about slavery?" asked Lucas. "Well, then you can understand why I'd rather not dwell under a tyrant."

He, himself, had witnessed so much cruelty that this delivering of a maiden like an animal looked mild enough. Since Brother Hugh stood unstirring, he held his ground, too. The little band came up to them and the leader stopped.

"Fellow Catholics!" he exclaimed. "God's providence! You know not how glad I am to meet you!"

There was something familiar about him. Lucas stepped closer. The man spoke Venetian in a harsh basso. His clothes and full purse showed him to be wealthy. He was of medium height, his black eyes about level with Lucas' hazel ones; his frame was stocky and muscular, turning fat in his middle age.

But as yet only a large belly impaired him. His hair was black, thinning atop the massive head; his shaven jowls were blue, his nose lumpy, with small broken veins. But he was not altogether ugly. There was a bear-like impressiveness about him.

"We're seeking the house of the nobleman Georgios Dalassenos," he explained. "Near the forum of Amastrianon. D' you know the way? We seem to have lost ours. Not much. We can find the place, even if you can't help. But I hate to ask one of those oily Greeks. Can't trust 'em. Good to see real Christians." He offered a furry hand. "I am Messer Gasparo Reni of Venice, with offices at Azov and Cyprus, and I'd like to invite—"

He broke off. His mouth fell open. He took a step backward. Even in the dull yellow light from the sunset clouds, Lucas could see how the blood mounted in his face.

"Lucco," he choked. "By all the devils in Hell—!"

Then, with a roar, he drew his sword and plunged to attack.

The training given by many desperate encounters saved Lucas. Before the other man's blade was clear, he sprang aside. The thrust went past his ribs.

Off balance, Gasparo lurched forward. Lucas put out a foot. The ponderous body crashed to the cobblestones. Lucas snatched forth the Persian dagger from under his tunic.

"What's the meaning of this?" cried Brother Hugh in outrage.

Gasparo struggled to all fours, bloody-nosed, and reached for his fallen sword. Lucas grinned. Suddenly the murk was gone from his head. He felt young and full of swagger. He kicked the blade away. "Naughty!" he said.

"Kill that gallows' bait!" bawled Gasparo.

Lucas turned a little, crouching, the knife poised in his hand. He saw the Venetian guardsmen hesitate, one sword half out, the other drawn but lowered, uncertainty on both countenances. "Don't listen to this hideous man," he advised.

"God's mercy, has a demon seized the fellow?" said Hugh.

Gasparo got to his knees. His head swung from Lucas to his companions, like a bull facing dogs. It rattled out of his throat: "Kill him, I tell you! A hundred ducats for his life . . . and my protection. Are you men or puling Greeks?"

The slave girl moved back until a wall stopped her. One hand lifted to her mouth, stifling a scream.

Gasparo threw himself forward. His arms closed about Lucas' knees. Lucas felt himself toppling. There was no time to think. The Ch'an Buddhist monk who had taught him a little of the way to use the body as a philosophical tool had also shown him how to fall. With every muscle loose, he hit the street and was unhurt. Gasparo scrabbled across him and regained his sword. Lucas glimpsed a triumphant baring of teeth as the merchant rolled clear with weapon in hand. He pounced. His dagger struck into the man's upper arm, and downward.

Gasparo howled, "Two hundred ducats!"

Lucas saw the attack from the corner of an eye. As one of the guardsmen's swords whipped toward his neck, he made a frog-leap jump from his crouched position. The blade pierced his cloak and rang on a stone. Lucas heard the cloth rip as he pulled free. He waited, knife in hand, ready to jump either way. Both men were stalking him, from right and left. In the thickening gloom, their faces were blurs. But their swords flashed bright. Lucas backed up and was brought to a halt. A solid wall lay behind him.

He heard the slave girl moan. Through all the pounding of his pulse, it seemed to him, dimly, that her voice held more sorrow than fear. His eyes flicked from his inadequate knife to the two broadswords. Their points were now a yard away. He remembered the chivalric romances he had once loved, a single knight against a thousand paynim. However—

"The name is Lucas, not Lancelot," he said, and threw the knife.

One Venetian yelled. His blade clattered to the ground and he fumbled at the steel in his shoulder. Then Brother Hugh came from behind, to snatch the other man and whirl him about. "In the name of God," commanded the Englander, "desist!"

Two hundred ducats raised the Venetian sword and thrust it against his chest. "Stand back." The guard had understood Hugh's Genoese well enough. "Back, friar, or I'll spit you, also."

Hugh skipped from the point, raised his staff, and struck at the other man's head. The fellow brought his glaive up barely in time to ward off the skull-cracking blow. Then they were at it, wood banging on steel, up and down the dusky street.

The wounded Venetian slumped with a groan.

Lucas went after his fallen sword. When he had it, he saw Gasparo Reni stumble toward him, blood running from the slashed arm but weapon gripped in the left hand. Behind the merchant, a crowd had formed, boiling from tenements to watch and yell and strip the fallen.

"What are you doing?" protested Lucas. "Who do you think I am?"

"Lucco, the Cretan bastard." It was a hoarse and horrible wheezing from that half-seen bulk. "I'm going to kill you."

Lucas raised sword, wondering frantically what to do about a disabled man who wouldn't stop.

Brother Hugh smacked his opponent's blade with a twist that sent it spinning from the hand. "Now," said the knight with renewed cheerfulness, "for the good of your soul and the purging of noxious humors, here is medicine." A few brisk whacks landed on head and shoulders. The Venetian wailed and ran. Hugh approached Gasparo and disarmed him with one deft blow of the staff.

The crowd moved closer, jabbering. Lucas saw them as a single mass in the chill, quickly falling twilight. Here and there a tattered individual stood out at the forefront. Then somewhere behind, loud, imperious, a voice shouted, "Make way!" and there came the iron tramp of fighting men.

Gasparo sat down and covered his eyes.

Hugh glanced at Lucas. "The Varangians," he said. "My mission would suffer if they arrested me."

"I wouldn't find it very useful either," Lucas leaned on his newly acquired sword and panted.

Hugh clasped his shoulder. It was hard to see, night was so near between these high walls, though the sky was still pale above; but Lucas thought the Englishman's look was searching. "We must talk further about this," Hugh said. "Best we separate now, I think. Do you remember where my lodgings are? Come there tomorrow after the hour of nones. Until then, *Dominus vobiscum.*"

His staff thumped loudly on the stones as he limped off, melting at once into the crowd.

Lucas swirled his cloak around so it hung from the left shoulder and concealed the sword he bore in that hand. Sidestepping Gasparo Reni, who sat shuddering with unpracticed sobs, he moved down a street opposite to the approaching watchmen. Bodies fetid with sweat and garlic resisted him, as if he breasted a river. Finally he broke free, turned a corner, and stopped to catch his breath.

A slender form in a hooded cloak paused beside him. He realized with astonishment and some dismay that the slave girl had followed. And then . . . why not, he thought, the headiness of victory still upon him. He took her hand. It felt soft, trembling a little but closing fingers tightly around his own. "Come," he muttered. "This way. I don't know these alleys, but I'd hazard this is our general direction."

They groped through lanes which became pitchy as night approached. Finally they stumbled into a courtyard with enough starlight to show heaped trash and low buildings. By standing precariously on two barrels, Lucas was able to chin himself onto a roof. There he looked across a city turning from black to gray and white, as the moon rose out of

37

Asia. From the North Star and the gleam of water, he got his bearings. As he sprang down again, the girl huddled close to him. *"Rhomaizeis?"* he asked. When there was no response, he inquired if she spoke Venetian, then Genoese.

"A little, Messer," she said to that. Her voice was low and pleasant to hear.

Lucas was relieved. The two patois were not so different that he could not be fluent in both, even after a lapse of years. He continued merrily, humming a bawdy French *chanson*. With a sword in his hand and a woman at his side, he felt able to deal with any number of robbers whom the noise might attract.

But there was no incident. He got lost a few times, in a tangle of streets two thousand years old, and after an hour they reached his hostel. Avoiding the walled quarter which the Venetians of Constantinople inhabited, he had found a cheap place in the slums of the Phanar district. There he passed himself off as a sailor from the Morea: admittedly under a Frankish overlord, but nonetheless a Greek. Venetians were so hated here that he would probably have been murdered if the truth were known. They had brought about the sack of the city, a hundred years ago, and the establishment of that Latin monarchy which it had taken a lifetime to overthrow. Nor had their subsequent behavior endeared them to the Empire. Only four years back, the fleet of Giustiniani had come harrying to extract an indemnity. The Genoese showed equal arrogance, having even turned Galata across the Horn into a fortified city of their own; but they remained Byzantine allies, anyway.

The inn was a mean building, crouched under the mountainous ancient wall of Constantine, but the moon stood high now and somehow gave it beauty. A few oarsmen were drinking by firelight in the common room. Lucas stopped to borrow a lamp and buy a crock of wine from the landlord, then went on to his chamber with the girl. A good-natured cheer followed him.

He closed the door behind them. The room was a mere cubicle, with cracked plaster and moldy straw on the floor. From the Cathayans Lucas had learned that it was not unhealthy to sleep with open windows. He put the lamp on a shelf, threw back the shutter and let in the moonlit air.

Only then did he look at the girl. She had drawn her cloak tight and she shivered as they came in. Now her back straightened. With a movement of decision, she flung off the garment.

His lips formed a soundless whistle.

She was young, perhaps seventeen or eighteen, but tall. Later she would gain the fullest form of womanhood; as yet she was slender in waist and flanks, long in the legs, her white neck almost childlike. But the small breasts rose firmly upward, lifting the fabric of a plain linen gown. Her face was oval, with a pert nose and a mouth with gentle curves. Under arched brows, her eyes seemed enormous, silver-blue between smoky lashes. Auburn hair, streaming thickly past her shoulders to her waist, glowed in the lamplight.

Impulsively, Lucas swept off his bonnet and bowed.

A ghost of a smile touched her. "No, Messer,"

she demurred in her lame Genoese. "I am the one who should—" She was about to prostrate herself before him. He caught her around the middle and held her. A slow blush went upward from her bosom. He let her go again, but felt a delighted grin crease his cheeks.

"Well, this proves virtue is indeed rewarded," he said. "Assuming that I have been virtuous. Who are you, besides the Queen of Elfland?"

"Djansha." She began to tremble once more.

"That sounds Circassian. Are you?"

"So you call us." Quick pride lifted her head. *We* say the Adygei. My father was Aoublaa of the Chipakou."

He knew those wild mountaineers in the Caucasus had long furnished the most high-priced slaves. To calm her, he said merely, "I am Lucas Greco, of nowhere in particular," and filled a cup for her from the wine crock. "Welcome, Djansha."

She gulped thirstily. He refilled the cup, took a few swallows, gave her the rest, and sat down on the floor, looking quizzically up at her.

"I'm not certain of the best thing to do," he said. My impulses have often gotten me into trouble."

She spilled half the wine, staining her dress as if with blood, and cried, "You will not give me back to him?"

"Um-m-m . . . there's a question of the law, you know." Lucas scratched his head. "Where were you going?"

She stared out the window. "He said to a feast. And afterward, he thought, a brothel." She drained the cup in a draught, picked up the crock, and shakily helped herself.

Lucas nodded. "A vile business."

She said something in her own language. He raised inquiring brows. She snarled the meaning. "May Shible the Just smite them with thunderbolts!"

"But you knew why you were being transported," he said. "I never heard concubinage was accounted a disgrace among your people."

"It is not." She spoke more quickly now, slurring a trifle as the wine took hold. "But I had hoped— My father was an *uork,* Lucas. A noble, you would say? My brothers warriors. I thought I would go to a Turk. Or a . . . a warrior. A man to give me children . . . and my sons would be free warriors again—" She emptied her cup and dashed it to the floor. "A brothel!" she yelled.

Lucas rose. She flung herself against his breast and wept. He held her close, stroked the bronze hair and made promises that no reasonable man should have uttered.

Until at last she stepped back and laughed up at him through the tears. She fumbled with her girdle. It fell, and she pulled the dress over her head and stood naked.

"You are a warrior," she said. "You have won me. Take me."

CHAPTER II

The room which the visiting Knights of St. John
shared, near the Church of the Holy Apostles, was
long, clean, and airy. An open window overlooked a
descending hill covered with houses, multitudinous
domes, and finally the Bosporus, sparkling blue
under a sky where the wind chased little white
clouds. Blue as Djansha's eyes, thought Lucas
dreamily.

"My brothers are out on their business," said
Hugh. "We can talk in private."

"Eh?" Lucas regained awareness with a start.
"Oh. Yes."

Hugh studied him carefully. "Before I say
anything more," he continued, "I must know why
Gasparo Reni sought your life."

"Only God can tell!" The steady gaze speared
him. Lucas' ears grew hot. "Oh, very well. The same
reason which drove me from Venice in the first instance. He found his wife and I were lovers, and
took it ill."

"As well he might," said Hugh severely.

"Was it such a great matter?" Lucas defended
himself. "Affairs of that sort are taken lightly

enough by most Venetians. And I was a mere boy. And name of God, that was fourteen years ago!''

Still Hugh watched him, until he squirmed. At last the knight nodded. "Well-a-day, I believe you," he said. "Christ Himself did not find that sin unforgivable. Would you be prepared to make amends, in the interest of a reconciliation?''

"Why should I?" Lucas turned sullen. "If he couldn't manage his own household better, whose fault is that?''

"Cain spoke in much the same way," Hugh reminded him, unrelenting. "Are you a Christian man or not?''

"Um-m-m . . . well . . . so be it then. I did wrong him. Yes, I'd offer amends, if I had enough money.''

"The florins are only a token. Would you humble yourself before him and beg his forgiveness?''

"But he tried to kill me!''

"You have not answered my question.''

Lucas looked away, clenching fists in anger. "How is this any concern of yours?''

Hugh sighed. "I had hoped for a somewhat different response from you. But I fear my calling is not to preach repentance. So I may as well admit, this morning I made inquiries. After several months here, one does learn where to get information. And . . . at present it would only benefit your own soul, to confess yourself at fault. He is like a wild beast about you. The sole reason he alleges is that you attacked him and made off with his slave, but he swears he'll have you killed.''

"He knows I didn't begin the fight! Is he possessed?'' Lucas crossed himself. The bright afternoon suddenly seemed cold.

Hugh shook his head. "No. I cannot imagine why he is so wrathful. It seems out of proportion to your offense, especially after so long a time has passed. Perhaps he let it rankle in him all these years; hatred is a cancer of the soul. But he's not a madman. I've been told by the Venetians whom I asked that he has always been valiant and able, if not overly scrupulous. They say he fought with rare courage throughout the Genoese War, though one of my informants winced to recall certain deeds of his. Since then he's been away from home most of the time, building a rich trade among the eastern Mediterranean and Black Sea countries, both Christian and paynim. He maintains a headquarters on Cyprus. I myself never encountered him; but then, the merchants there center in Famagusta, and deal chiefly with the Frankish nobles. He also has an office here, and one in Azov at the mouth of the Don River. Since Azov is a Genoese colony and Messer Gasparo a Venetian who did particular harm to Genoa during the war, you'll realize that he has uncommon skill as a diplomat, too.''

"Do you know anything about his wife?" asked Lucas, chiefly because he felt Hugh expected it. Moreta was another shadow to him; not his first woman, and very far from his last.

The image of Djansha returned, crowding out all others. She had been a novice to love, but ardently eager to please him. She waited for him at this moment. . . . Lucas barely noticed the knight's negative answer. But the next words snapped him to attention:

"This feud may prove an obstacle to your return home. You can imagine what might happen if an important signor makes an effort to bring the law down upon you. Fortunately, Messer Gasparo is going on to Cyprus from here. Maybe there I can persuade him of his Christian duty to forgive his enemies." The leather face flickered with the briefest grin. "I am not without influence in my Order, which is not wholly impotent in Cyprian affairs. But as for yourself—well, I can see no harm in your proceeding to Negroponte. Be careful, though! Walk warily and look for powerful friends."

"I came back hoping to be my own man," said Lucas with bitterness.

Hugh's mouth tightened. "Do you know why I'm intervening so much on your behalf?" he asked in a rough tone. "I've already done far more than the rule I live under would approve. But . . . I find that Gasparo Reni is one of the largest Venetian traffickers in slaves."

"I know," said Lucas, without gauging the implications.

Hugh swooped upon the words. "How? Who told you?—Yes. That woman they had with them, the slave Gasparo charges you with stealing. Did you?"

Lucas ran a hand through his unruly hair. "She fled with me," he admitted.

"I thought so." Hugh paused before he went on, dispassionately: "You need not fear arrest if you stay out of the Venetian compound. The quarrel took place beyond the Bailo's jurisdiction, of course, and the Byzantines are happy to torment him by refusing to act on the case. What's happened of late around Gallipoli—Well, that makes them all the more spiteful toward Latins. So I'm less worried about you than the girl. Do you still have her in charge?"

"Yes," said Lucas.

"She's not a Christian, is she?"

"Why . . . I think not . . . No, she called on a heathen god or two. She speaks Genoese. She was taught that in Azov, to enhance her value."

"I felt sure she had not been converted. I suppose you know that Holy Church has forbidden Christians to sell their fellow believers. Therefore slavers are at pains to withhold the Word of God from their poor pagan victims. You've taken a heavy responsibility, my friend. I cannot help her, being obliged to respect all secular law which does not conflict with the interests of my Order. So you must be the means of saving her soul." Tactfully, Brother Hugh did not mention her body. He smiled, though. "Which gives me my only logically valid reason for aiding you, you scamp. So that you may bring her to Negroponte and see that she receives Catholic instruction. Thereafter—" He sobered. "I beg of you, be kind to her."

Lucas hitched one leg onto the broad windowsill and half sat, half stood, looking down at his hands. But I only wanted a night of pleasure! he thought.

And then, wryly: I had it. Also a forenoon. And the rest of this day, when I leave here. Why not be her guardian? Her passage money won't be too much for me, nor will her company prove burdensome. At Negroponte . . . well . . . no doubt I can

46

make some provision for her. She may wish to join a charitable sisterhood. Or I may find her a husband. Something will surely happen to aid me. It always has.

"I'll do what I can," he said.

Hugh nodded gravely. "I believe you," he answered. "You've had a harder life than most, I gather. That freezes the souls of some men, but teaches others the value of mercy."

"Well, I've seen a bit of the world," said Lucas, embarrassed.

Hugh began to speak about those foreign parts. Piece by piece, under adroit and sensitive questioning, the younger man's life was brought back. His boyhood in Crete, his apprenticeship in Venice, his escape to Constantinople as the attendant of an Aragonese knight. He spoke of the Venetian merchant Niccolo Banbarigo, whom he had met here and who had engaged his services in turn, of their sea voyage to the Crimean port, Soldaia, which Venice maintained. The caravan inland, over plain and desert to Bokhara and Samarkand, where Mongol power dwelt beside ancient Islamic scholarship. The eventual return, to discover that the war had broken out between Venice and Genoa and that the Genoese, dominant in the Black Sea, would likely seize them and their goods. The fighting between Soldaia and the Genoese colony of Kaffa; the capture of Lucas Greco, who had no wish to rot in an enemy prison and therefore managed to escape eastward. The Tartar merchant whom he came to serve, as fighting man and clerk and—through his gift for readily learning languages—interpreter. His

47

stays in Sarai, Karakorum, Khan Baligh, the gracious towns of Cathay, until at last homesickness came upon him, not so much for any one place in the West as for the daily ways of life and of thinking which he remembered. His early aimless, often dangerous wandering back across many nations, until he came to the Turkish Black Sea port of Sinope. The Turk there who became not only his employer but his friend, as they traded and fought and intrigued through the turbulent emirates of Anatolia. And at last, the friend slain in a senseless encounter with bandits, and Lucas Greco's lonely trek to Trebizond.

Not that he told Brother Hugh everything. There had been too much. Nor was he proud of it all. In countries where the only law was the sword, he had lived by that law. Often had he foresworn himself, or swindled a slow-witted chieftain. The women he did not regret, though he had long ago lost count of them. Some remained entirely clear in his memory—one of rare beauty and learning in Bokhara; a tall Russian girl with hair like ripe wheat; a dark and skillful Kazakh, a Mongol wench as hot as she was unwashed; tiny Mei-Mei who sang to him in the dusk of the Heavenly City—a few such, the rest nearly forgotten, lost in a waste of years and miles.

He said merely, "I fear you'll think I've been too much in the company of unbelievers."

"What else could you do?" responded the Englishman. "I've known Turks whom I wished were Christian . . . and, in all honesty, certain Christians whom I would have preferred to be Turks."

Lucas did not press the matter. He had fallen out of righteous ways. How long since he had even heard a mass? He could not in his heart feel deeply concerned about it. On him, whose childhood had been marred by the clash between the Catholicism of his father's people and the Orthodoxy of his mother's, the Cathayan belief that there were many roads to God, or else none at all, had fastened powerfully. Only in the last few years, as he approached an age where the meaning of things overshadowed the things themselves, had he wondered—more and more often—what God truly wanted of men. Nowhere had he found a reasonable answer.

"And now you're tired of roving, and would return to Venice, eh?" Hugh's tone grew wistful. He leaned back in his seat and looked at the ceiling with blind eyes. "I can understand that. Sometimes I dream I am in England again, when the hawthorn blooms. I wake laughing. But it is only a dream. Well-a-day, men have offered greater sacrifices than exile."

Lucas shook his head. He didn't know why he had thus opened himself to a chance-met foreigner, unless it was that all this had been caged in him unendurably long and the serene slow voice made talking easy.

"That's the best I can think of to do," he said. "But I was never happy in Venice. Merry, sometimes, but not happy. I look back and remember all the faces as being hard. And now I hear the signors have closed the membership of the Grand Council and hanged Bocconio who dared protest. So the Republic is become entirely the engine of

49

the merchant princes." He paused, then blurted, "I can never forget how they oppressed my mother's people."

"Perchance you'd rather go to Crete, then?"

"A penniless adventurer, trying to make his way under that outland tyranny?" Lucas' laugh exploded like a Cathayan firecracker. "Also . . . I am not a Greek, either. I'd be even less at home among dull fishermen and peasants than—Oh, let's talk no more of it. I seek a house to call my own, nothing more. But I will not raise my sons to lick the boots of some overlord, nor my daughters to be carried off as slaves when my home is sacked. Tell me where to find a country with strength and justice."

Hugh stirred. A shiver went through his gaunt body, his lips moved. Something strong gripped this military monk, Lucas saw, something he wanted to say and could not. The knowledge sent prickles down the younger man's backbone. The Knights Hospitallers had been a mighty force. For one brief moment, after Acre fell, they alone of Christendom had made a strange alliance with the Tartar Ghazan Khan, and regained Jerusalem. Hugh himself had stood watch at Our Saviour's tomb. Then they were driven out again. But they were not men who ever really yielded.

"No," said Hugh, "there's nothing in this part of the world to satisfy you."

Seeking easier conversation, Lucas asked, "What's this tale you mentioned, about the fighting around Gallipoli?"

"Oh, yes." The turquoise eyes sharpened. "The news came this morning, early. The Catalans—"

"What?" Lucas glanced up, surprised. "Are the mercenaries Catalonian? I heard of them while I was wandering through Anatolia, of course, but they were called simply Giaours or Franks."

Hugh shrugged with a touch of humor. "We Europeans are not so important that the rest of the world troubles itself much about telling us apart. Yes, the Grand Company is chiefly Catalan. Do you know their history? No? A tale of increasing discord between them and their Byzantine employers. Finally Michael Paleologus, the co-Emperor, had their leader assassinated and laid siege to them in Gallipoli. So they sent envoys to declare formal war—their eight thousand against the whole East Roman Empire! And Emperor Andronicus had these ambassadors, who had been promised safe conduct, murdered and quartered on their way back. At the same time their admiral and all his people were slain in this city.

"Even with the Alanic horsemen at their walls, the Catalans in Gallipoli sent a small fleet up the Sea of Marmora. It took Perinthos town, butchered the inhabitants, and started back stuffed with gold. But a Genoese convoy heading for Trebizond captured those ships and brought their commander here, where he still lies imprisoned. Meanwhile the force attacking Gallipoli was strengthened." Hugh's quiet voice took on a metallic ring. "Cruel they may be, but by the Rood, those Catalans are men! They scuttled the last of their own vessels so there could be no talk of retreat, and stood fast!"

"I've heard a little of all this, but paid scant attention," said Lucas. "The matter didn't seem important. This Empire is as full of local strife as a rotten apple is of worms. What was today's news?''

Hugh smiled grimly. "Upsetting. Outnumbered and ill-nourished, the Grand Company marched forth against their besiegers. They slew some thousands, with trifling loss to themselves, and the rest were put to flight.''

Lucas whistled.

"Well, we shall see what befalls," said Hugh. "Rather, I who must remain here for some weeks yet will see it. You, I think, will soon depart. The merchant convoys will make haste through the narrows now that fighting thereabouts has ceased for the moment.''

"Christian against Christian," said Lucas. He rubbed his eyes, feeling weariness rise in him. "That's nothing new. But after all my years among aliens—''

He looked out at sky and water, and murmured,

> "I had not thought the world would be so wide,
> Nor known all other folk would be so strange.
> When seas uncloven met me like a bride,
> I had not thought the world would be so wide
> And yet so poor in places to abide.
> When I returned to my familiar range,
> I had not thought the world would be so wide
> Nor known all other folk would be so strange.''

"I've some acquaintance with minstrelsy," said Hugh, "but yon triolet I never heard before.''

"No doubt, since I composed the thing. I'm sometimes a poet, for my own amusement.'' As if he had released the darkness within himself by speaking it, Lucas felt a return of mirth and strength. Or the cause might simply have been that he remembered Djansha was waiting for him. "I can also name the stars, recite numerous maxims of K'ung Fu-Tze, ride a camel, and remove cockleburs from milady's spaniel. Now, Brother Hugh, I must go back. But you've been a true friend; so, since you've told me your besetting vice, you may first trounce me in a game or two of chess."

CHAPTER III

The Venetian merchant skippers did indeed seize this chance to depart. At sunrise of the second day following, they rounded Europa Point and stood out to the Marmora, a combined fleet whose member convoys would go off toward their separate destinations on the other side of the strait.

All that day they rowed. Constantinople slowly fell behind, first the walls topped by her many domes, and a ringing of bells which followed the ships far across the water as if sad and anxious to be remembered; then a smudge on the sky; at last, nothing. To port the waves glittered and chuckled, a gay noise under the creak and chunk of the oars. To starboard rose the Thracian hills, green in the young year. Towns and villages were passed, elegant estates, castles, farms and plantations; this land seemed richly at peace.

But the only sail was a strange red one in the distance, which had the look of a Turkish pirate. Every villa stood empty. Armed men paced all castle battlements. Late in the afternoon, Lucas spied smoke rising thick from a ridge. Something had been fired—by Catalan raiders?

"This wind is good," said Djansha. It whipped a loose lock of her braided hair across the broad clear brow. "Why do they not raise the sails? There were sails up most of the way from Azov to Constantinople."

"But that was a single convoy, in which all ships were exactly alike," Lucas pointed out. "Here are many sorts together. Given sail, the lighter and faster craft would outrun the heavier, and we'd all become subject to attack.'' He wrinkled his nose. ''The breeze is useful all the same, to keep the air somewhat fresh on deck. I'd hate to be downwind of our oarsmen.''

She laughed, even at so poor a jest, and squeezed his arm. He let his own hand slide down her back until he clasped her waist. She leaned against him. Wide-eyed, she continued to stare at the passing scene.

Their two days together in Constantinople had been happy, Lucas thought. Not that they could talk much, since he knew no Circassian and she had little Genoese. But she was quick to learn from him—even though he was also working to convert her to the Venetian dialect—and already he could speak with her about more than the simplest things.

Anyhow, there were other languages than words. The way she cleaned and packed his gear, stood up at his entry until he pulled her down beside him, made a wry face at the hostel food and thereafter brought him meals she had prepared herself: this told him a great deal. As they walked about the city, her awe and pleasure, her sheer delight when he bought her a few cheap dresses, needed no explication. And finally, when they returned, her supple, fervent body in his embrace was enough to think about.

There was more than the famous handsomeness of the race to make Circassians much sought after on the slave market. Those tribesmen raised their daughters to be the opposite of their own fierce selves: sweet-tempered, skilled in every household art, submissive to the man who got them. But not spirit-broken. Unwed girls were merry, flirtatious creatures, and no doubt the wife of many a blustering warrior was the real power in the household. Well aware of the demand, Circassian fathers often sold their girls, though chiefly for Turkish harems. Djansha herself, however, had been captured when the *Pshi*, petty prince or warlord, of the Abbats, swooped down upon her own Chipakou in one of those tribal wars which the slave trade helped stimulate. She had seen her father and a brother slain, but they had fallen, sword in hand, with dead men at their feet. She was brought to Azov and sold to the Genoese, who kept her over the winter and then resold her to Gasparo Reni.

But all those dealers, Abbat, Genoese, Venetian, were after gold rather than girls. An unscarred virgin Circassian was worth far too much for anyone to molest her. She had been instructed in language to increase her value, but nothing else happened. In that long winter's dullness, she had formed friendships with other slave girls; then in spring, she was taken from them. She had expected to continue to Cyprus and end as the concubine of a Frank or Turk; the latter, she hoped, for they were better liked in the Caucasus and Islamic law gave considerable freedom to any woman who had borne a child. Instead, a sniggering Byzantine dandy looked her over and arranged for her delivery to his house; and Gasparo had told her that afterward she would probably be resold to a bordello.

Small wonder, thought Lucas, that she turned so

willingly to him. Half her ardor must be a flight from nightmare. And yet it was an honest passion. Once, when she thought he was still asleep, she had knelt, smiling, on the pallet and very gently stroked his hair.

She looked about the crowded galley deck. The passengers who milled and chattered, waving their arms, hawking and spitting, cracking fleas, swigging from leather bottles, snoring in the scuppers, were chiefly Levantine. But that meant a hundred nations, from thick-bearded Armenian mountaineer to shaven Athenian trader, from half-savage Vlach to half-civilized Bulgar.

"Will we be long at sea?" she inquired.

"Two or three weeks, I should guess," replied Lucas.

She grimaced. "Never alone?"

"Does that matter?" he asked, a little surprised. Since leaving Cathay he had almost lost the habit of privacy: which was uncommon in all events, even in Venice.

"Well, you and I—" She flushed and hurried on, "I mean, at home . . . the nights were still . . . and trees, many trees, green everywhere—" Her vocabulary failed her. But Lucas could imagine.

He too had seen her mountains, though from afar, their snowpeaks floating high and holy in the sky. He had also traveled beneath leafy arches, and watched sunflecks dance among anemones, and heard a living quietness ended by birdsong. He had visited sacred groves, where a rill tinkled into a pool that gave the sky back its color and its clouds, and sunlight went like laughter through the birches. He remembered a clifftop overlooking vastness; and he remembered rough, warm hospitality among mountaineer tribes. And then he remembered the hut of his boyhood, and his mother crooning over the newest baby's cradle.

He looked away from her. After a while he said, "Yes, you are right. If possible, someday, would you wish to return home?"

She drew a gasp, and her answer was delayed. "You are kind, my lord. I have no words to thank you. It would be good to see my land again. But only to see it. My clan are scattered, their power broken. At best I might hope to become the second wife of some *hokotl*." Tossing her head: "My father was an *uork*. No. I will dwell where you go, Lucas."

He felt a little taken aback, though for the present such a desire made enjoyable traveling. However— She saved him from further thought by facing aft, raising her arms, and chanting in the Adygei language. When he asked what that was for, she answered naively, "I called upon Seosseres to give us good winds and smooth waters, that we may soon reach the place you want to be. I will give Seosseres a sheep if he helps us. Will you buy a sheep? We can eat most of it ourselves. The gods only want certain parts. If they're too far away to have heard me, though, then you must call on the gods living closer by. I do not know their names."

"Holy saints!" Lucas crossed himself and looked around to make sure she had not been overheard. "Ah . . . such things are more difficult in these parts. Best you say nothing about gods. I'll have a priest explain things to you at journey's end."

"What? Can you venture out to sea with no sacrifices? I did not know my lord was so great a wizard!"

"Let's teach you some more Venetian," he said hastily.

At sundown the ships dropped anchor. So large a fleet could not very well sail these waters after dark, even though the moon was nearly full. Also, however often they took relays, the oarsmen were exhausted. They came up on deck for supper and air: mostly Sclavonians, hired from Venice's Dalmation possessions, dark half-naked men who shimmered with sweat and sat staring empty-eyed until they soon went below to sleep. The deck passengers composed themselves where they might best fit, rolled in their blankets among bollards and coils and their own disorderly belongings. They were a dense, noisy mass. Lucas was kept awake for a long time.

In part, that was due to annoyance. He had already had more of a fancy for cleanliness than the ordinary European, and his stay among well-scrubbed Cathayans had reinforced it. He would have to live like a pig on this voyage. The best he could do was change his day clothes for a robe. All his garments were shabby. In prosperous moments, he thought wistfully, he had worn rainbow-colored silks. Yes, and enjoyed some noble foods and wines. He had conversed with philosophic men; hung his chamber with calligraphic scrolls or a delicate ink-wash drawing; ridden horses so beautiful that the sight of them caught at his throat; enjoyed some darlings of concubines—well, on that score he had no present complaint. But poverty and exile were acrid in the mouth. Was it not worth kowtowing to Venetian grandees and forgetting how they dealt with their Cretan subjects, to have a house of his own?

I could have stayed with the Cathayans, or the Turks, or the wise Arabs in Bokhara, he thought. They all liked me. I might have accomplished great things among them. But they were never quite my people. So I came back, and found that here they are not my people, either. Not any longer.

Djansha lay gently breathing by his side. Gradually the grumbles and snores of the others faded, until at last he could almost listen to the silence. He got up and walked to the rail.

The galley was dark, barred with moonlight. He could see how the moon made a trembling bridge on the water; but that was interrupted by the other ships. The lanthorns hung at their poops burned like strewn stars. A couple of lights moved on the water, somebody going from one vessel to the next in a tender. The shore was blackness shouldering against a deep purple sky. Immensely far off, a watchfire made a single red spark. Lucas wondered who sat beside it. The moon drowned out many stars, but he recognized old friends, Arcturus, Vega, Polaris, the Twins, and white Venus.

Sharp as a sword, he remembered ibn Yakoub in Bokhara, gray beard and kindly eyes, the ruinous tower where a grandfather *imam* and a Christian boy forgot all else as they tracked the planets across heaven. Dear God, he had been young then! And, for those few months, drunken with discovery! If he could get a house, he would build a turret on it and go up there at night with quadrant and astrolabe, a silly little ant happily peering toward the throne of the Maker.

But Venice's air was thick.

Wind lulled in the rigging, the timbers creaked and wavelets went lap-lap-lap against the hull. A louder noise recalled him to earth. Squinting across the water, he saw that the rowboat had left one galley and proceeded to another. Voices drifted to him. He couldn't quite make out words, but he gathered that the man being ferried wanted a Jacob's ladder let down so he could come aboard and see the captain. The captain was not to be awakened, sir. Oh, yes, he was. . . . In the end, the man climbed up and stillness returned. Lucas yawned, incurious about what message went traveling from ship to ship. He was a mere passenger. His own vessel—a pleasure boat, at least—yes, someday he would have that too, if only— Well, he should be able to sleep now.

He fumbled his way among sprawled bodies to the place near the poop that he had claimed for himself and Djansha. Here it was totally lightless. He crawled back under the blanket they shared over a straw pallet.

She stirred. One hand reached forth and touched his face. "Oh!" she whispered. "I was afraid— Where did you go?"

"My errand could have been less ethereal," he chuckled, "but I really did go to look at the stars."

He thought from her movement that she must also have glanced up at that glittering sprawl. "*They* are still like home," she said.

His lips brushed her cheek. She threw an arm

61

around his neck, drawing him close. He hesitated an instant. But the devil take it! Everyone except the lookouts was asleep. . . . His mouth sought hers.

In the morning the fleet continued. Lucas stilled hunger, like the other travelers, with a bite of hardtack; he looked forward to the midday meal Djansha would prepare, even though the fire hazard caused frying to be forbidden. His fellow passengers had become individuals to him, rather than an ill-smelling horde, and he fell into agreeable talk with a native Euboean. The man had a small harp with him, which Lucas borrowed. His singing and playing drew a crowd and he was offered refreshment from many wineskins. The wind held fair, promising a fast transit beyond Gallipoli; whitecaps danced on the sea. It was remote, of no real consequence, that they passed a fisher village lately burned to the ground.

The tender resumed its errand, patiently weaving between the ships, and finally reached this one. Lucas leaned far over the side, clinging to a shroud, to watch. Overhauling from behind, the boat called for a towline and was drawn alongside. Rather than accept a sailor's hand to pull him up the low freeboard at the waist, the passenger stood on his dignity and insisted on a rope ladder. It was dropped from the poop deck, beneath which the boat was then tethered, and he climbed up: a young man in good Italian clothes, sword at hip, who addressed the captain in Venetian.

"I have a message and a warrant from the Bailo in Constantinople. It has to be executed before this fleet passes the narrows and goes its various ways, for otherwise action may come too late. I have been going about all day yesterday, far into the night. A private talk—"

The captain led the way down to the main deck and into his cabin. The crowd broke up, buzzing with curiosity. Lucas reseated himself on the barrel he had been using and strummed the harp absentmindedly, scowling.

Djansha curled herself up at his feet and rested her head on his knee. "Is something wrong, my lord?"

"I wish I could be certain," he muttered. "A warrant from the Bailo. This has a bad look. I've never heard of the like."

"Must we turn about?" The Euboean wrung his hands. "Oh, horrible! If I don't get home soon I'll have no chance whatsoever to buy my olive oil wholesale. The saints forbid!"

"Offer them candles," suggested Lucas. His mind added: Or else a sheep. Alarmed, for such thoughts were said to be caused by invisible fiends, he smote the harp and broke into a ballad of Roland.

Presently the captain leaned out of the door and summoned four sailors by name. He talked to them inside. They emerged and went below. When they returned carrying pikes, silence fell over the deck.

Lucas wet his lips. "No," he said through the noise of his own heartbeat, "I do not like this at all." He slipped a hand under his doublet. The requirement had been reasonable that he, a commoner, leave his sword with the captain; the dagger he concealed in its place was little comfort.

I'm borrowing trouble, he told himself. This has nothing to do with me. I hope.

The captain and the Venetian stranger emerged. The latter held an unrolled paper with an official seal. The captain signaled to his pikemen. Barefoot, the sailors moved across the deck as quietly as tigers. The passengers made way, crowding to either side, unspeaking, frightened. Lucas nudged Djansha toward the poop. He looked for a ladder, if—

The captain saw him and pointed. "That's the man." The quarterdeck voice rolled across the muffled drumbeat timing the oars. "Same looks as you told me, and he calls himself Lucas Greco."

"Then arrest him," said the newcomer, "in the name of the Republic of Venice!"

CHAPTER IV

Djansha cried out and snatched Lucas' hand. He shook her off without taking his eyes from the messenger. A mumble swept through the packed watchers, like the first sough before a hailstorm.

"No!" Lucas shouted. "This is some connivance of my enemies!" He had no idea what he would say next, but the vision of fetters raised his tones to a roar. "Captain, arrest that imposter!"

"What?" The skipper blinked. "But, but he's from the Bailo."

"He says!" Lucas forced his mouth into a sarcastic grin. "What's his touchstone?"

"This." The messenger held up the paper.

"Can you read it, Captain?"

"N-no," stammered the mariner. "D' you think me a priest? But he told me—"

Dim as one star seen through a winter tempest, his plan came to Lucas. He shot a look around. Between him and the others was a clear space, perhaps two yards wide, with the passengers and idle crewmen foward of it. Behind him rose the poop. He pushed the girl a little aft. He himself moved toward the messenger.

"I have enemies," he stormed. "I didn't imagine they'd be so bold as to take the name of the State in vain. Yes, and falsify an official seal! O God of justice, strike down this knave!"

Going red and then white, the Venetian sputtered, "I have never heard such impudence in all my life! All men know me, Zorzi da Carrara, assistant to his excellency the Bailo. This wretch dares—" He became incoherent.

Lucas snatched the paper from him. "Do you call this a warrant?" he sneered. Zorzi opened his mouth. "Silence, you lying rogue! Let me show you, Captain, how clumsy a forgery this is. See here—"

All the while, he scanned the writing. A chill fastened upon him. This was indeed a properly secured document, demanding the arrest of Lucco or Lucas, nicknamed Greco, natural son of the late Pietro Torsello, on several sworn accusations. Assault and robbery did not surprise him. It followed almost as a matter of course that he should be charged with breaking the confines, fleeing the jurisdiction in which he stood accused, even though he had not been notified. What brought the blood draining from his heart was the count of desertion. Which was stated to be a capital offense!

Venice had not been at war when he fled. Nor was there then a death penalty for bolting from armed service. It must have been decreed subsequently, during the long conflict with Genoa. But that made no difference to his case: not in Venice. At least, not if so powerful and vindictive an enemy as Gasparo Reni were to ask for the severest judgment.

The fact remained, he had left the arbalestiers

without permission. The boy had given that matter no thought; the man would be hung in an iron cage and starved to death.

Gasparo, beyond question, had wrought this. Without his urging, surely no one would have troubled about such ancient peccadillos. A fine might have been set. Or, quite likely, no punishment at all. But Gasparo, thought Lucas, each realization streaking across the clamor in his skull, Gasparo had gone to the Bailo, made out an affidavit (perjuring himself about the alleged assault, but that was safe enough; who could reconstruct a street brawl with certainty?)—he had used his influence, possibly a substantial bribe as well, all to destroy one penniless wanderer.

The insane malevolence of it shook Lucas as much as his own danger. The man must be possessed!

Zorzi da Carrara took the warrant back from lax fingers. "Captain," he said frostily, "if you are foolish enough to heed this rascal for one moment, then there are worthy men aboard my ship who can identify me and my office. He is to be taken in irons to Venice and held until his accuser—"

What he must do came back to Lucas, driving out that horror of Gasparo which had crawled under his skin.

His performance had only been to divert attention. There was no chance, there had never been any, to escape by cunning. But he stood next to one of the pike-bearing sailors. They were all agape, staring at the Venetian signor.

Now!

Lucas gauged the spot on a bare, hairy stomach.

Just under the breastbone. He seized the pikeshaft with both hands. His foot came up, into the solar plexus. The wind went from the seaman. He reeled backward.

Lucas recoiled in the other direction, grasping the pike. The captain yelled. Lucas swept the heavy weapon in an arc. It clopped on the captain's temple. He tumbled to the deck.

"Djansha!" said Luca. "Up the ladder! Climb!"

He had no chance to see if she obeyed. Another pike was thrusting toward him. He swayed aside, letting it pass. His own lowered shaft went between the wielder's legs. The man tangled with it. Lucas shoved on his end of the improvised lever. Man and pike flipped across the planks.

A third steel point threatened Lucas. He evaded that one, too, bouncing directly up to the sailor. The man rasped an oath and drew back one fist. Lucas kneed him in the groin. As he doubled over, Lucas hit him on the neck with the edge of one hand. He fell like a mealsack.

The Mongols knew how to fight!

Stooping, Lucas snatched the fellow's pike and cast it. The fourth sailor bellowed and sat down, blood running from a gashed shoulder. The second one was getting up, reaching for his own dropped weapon. Lucas got there first. The mariner fled him.

Messer Zorzi drew sword and lunged. Lucas gave him the butt of the pike in the pit of the stomach.

Mere seconds had passed. The crowd, now in a shouting turmoil, would hinder the crew for another minute or so. But then a score would attack him. Lucas bounded up the ladder.

Djansha stood on the poop, hands clasped together, calling her gods for help. The steersmen cursed at their oars. But when Lucas appeared with pike in hand, they squalled and scuttled off to the main deck. Lucas yanked Djansha over to the taffrail and slapped her. She stopped wailing and stared at him, open-mouthed. He pointed to the Jacob's ladder. "Go down that and be ready to jump into the boat," he snapped.

Tucking the pike under one arm, he hauled on the towline with more strength than he had known was in him. The rowboat bumped against the galley stern. Lucas went over the side. He slid down the cord. The two sailors there demanded blasphemously to know what was wrong on deck.

Lucas scrambled past them to the stern, wheeled about, and poised his weapon. "I'm bound ashore," he said. "Sit down! Start rowing! The first one who makes trouble will get this in his guts!"

"What in Satan's name—!"

Lucas jabbed a thigh, drawing blood. He whipped the shaft back before it could be seized. "Row!" he spat.

Djansha stepped from the ladder to the foresheets and cast off. A gaggle of faces appeared at the galley rail. But God be praised, they were still in utter confusion up there! Lucas braced himself as his captives took their oars. One bold sweep could knock him overboard. His eyes caught those of the nearer sailor; he grinned and jerked his pike. Hastily, the man put oars between tholes.

"You'll come to no harm if you get us ashore," Lucas promised them. "But they'll be shooting at us

69

with crossbows and ballistae before we're out of the fleet. I can swim, but I know how few seamen have mastered that art. So crack your thews, lads!"

The boat sprang forward.

"My lord, what is happening?" choked Djansha.

Lucas managed to grin. How her hair shone in the sunlight! "Certain persons wish to make me a prisoner," he said. "But, as that would take me away from you, I shall fight them with the strength of a hundred bears."

Even then, she reddened, and her long lashes fluttered.

The galley fell behind. Another loomed close. Its captain leaned over to shout: "What's the trouble over there? Where are you headed?"

"After help!" Lucas called. "A gang of mutineers are trying to seize our vessel. I think they mean to run it aground for the Catalans to plunder. Go give help, I pray you!"

He left chaos behind, which was carried ahead of him by stentorian lungs. Despite everything, he laughed.

A splash of the water ended his jollity. He looked behind. The nearest of the several ships he had passed was coming about. Up on the forecastle, a team of men rewound a stone-throwing ballista. So . . . the fleet officers had at last gotten the true story. Now they must put on speed, and make pious vows.

"Row, you sons of noseless bitches! Row!"

He heard the snap and clunk of the ballista, and another missile hit the sea, close enough to drench him. "Djansha," he asked, "can you swim?" She stared mutely. "Can you—oh, curse it—can you keep yourself up in water? Like a fish?"

She shook her head.

Well, thought Lucas, if the boat was hit, that would be the end of her. It was best, he supposed. Better than Gasparo's patrons, anyhow. . . . He looked at her again, and she offered him an uncertain smile. By all her heathen gods! He could not swim off while she drowned! It wasn't possible. She would come back to him in dreams, with weeds growing from her mouth. No, let him try to carry her along, and if he failed, let them drink the sea together.

What lunacy had ever made him lead her off in the first instance? He groaned.

Another ship lay ahead: a cheland, lighter and swifter than the galleys. Its oarsmen churned the water white and it moved across his bow.

"Starboard! Hard a-starboard!" Lucas shook his pike and threw Arabic obscenities at the other vessel.

An iron point smote the side of his craft. Was he really in crossbow range? The cheland didn't look near enough . . . Oh, yes, it was monstrously near, almost on top of him. He would crash into those centipede oars in one more minute— A quarrel buzzed before his nose.

He swallowed until enough spittle came back for him to talk. "You see, lads," he told the sailors, "I was right. This is no healthy spot, so don't linger. Here, I'll set the time for you. Thus: aSTERN of us are UGly men. Our LIVES they will not SPARE. Our HANDsomeness has STRICKen them quite GREEN. They KNOW that if we MAKE our port

71

beFORE they've blundered THERE, the HARbor girls will SWARM o'er us and TREAT us very FAIR: to wit, igNORE those UGly men and KISS us everyWHERE. But IF you eat a CROSSbow bolt you'll NEVer hug yon QUEAN!—"

The boat went astern of the cheland, so near that their wakes crossed. For a moment it sleeted quarrels. Several struck deep into planking. The foremost sailor whimpered and lost the stroke, as one shaft buried itself in the thwart inches from his hip. "Row, I told you!" bawled Lucas. "Are you deaf?" The boat surged shoreward again.

And then, as if struggling out of a fever dream, they cleared the convoy. Lucas snatched another glance behind. Ships were strung out far over the blue water. But they were not pursuing him into the shoals. Two boats had been manned and were after him. He saw sunlight wink on a helmet, a quarter-mile off.

The shore ahead rose abruptly from a narrow beach. A row of cottages lay near, but there was no sign of man or livestock, nor any boats drawn up under those poles where fishnets were meant to dry. Orchards and crop fields stretched untended beneath the still, shimmering sky. All the people had fled.

Lucas realized he was atremble with reaction. His own sweat stank in his nostrils. He made himself sit at ease, contemplate serenity, as the Cathayan monks advised; he drew a few long slow breaths in place of gasping. All his strength would soon be needed.

"Djansha," he said, "spring ashore the moment we ground."

Her murmur carried to him through the descending quietness: "Oh, my lord, you overcame them all!"

"That's a pleasant way to phrase it." He nodded at the sailors. "I thank you, my lads. When the boat goes ashore, push the oars out, hard. You'll understand I don't want you clubbing me. But still I thank you for your trouble, and if ever we meet again, I'm not the one who won't stand you a flask of good wine."

One man gave him a dull glare, but the other laughed.

The bottom grated. Djansha waded up onto the grass. The sailors thrust their oars from them. "Farewell," said Lucas, and followed his girl. The two men slumped an instant, then splashed after the oars. They were much to tired to attempt his capture.

Others would do that. Lucas trotted inland with Djansha. "Quickly," he warned. "We must be out of bowshot before those two boats arrive. I doubt the men will chase us far, though. This is too hazardous a place."

"For us also?" she panted. Her slippers were hardly suitable cross-country footgear. But hurry she must!

"Less so than what we've escaped." He gave himself to his jog-pace. Thought continued: I may well be a liar. What do I know of the company ravaging this land? Or we may meet an Imperial army. . . . Even if we elude all those perils, where can we go?

Where would I even desire to go? he asked himself wearily.

They hastened by the smokeless huts and onto a rutted dirt road, which wound upward as the land rolled higher. Lucas cut directly across the bends, over fence and hedge and field. Before long Djansha was exhausted, her gown torn, her ankles scratched and muddy. He gave her an arm, choking down anger. She could not fairly be blamed for lacking a man's strength, yet she dragged on him and slowed him. When he looked behind, he glimpsed four or five tiny figures in pursuit.

But they were gone from view once he had topped a ridge. In a way that was comforting. Yet it would have been still better to know with certainty that they had given up. Well—

A broad olive orchard came into sight. Lucas led Djansha over the fence rails. "Carefully, now," he said. "Leave no traces of our passage. . . . Good enough, if the saints are kind. I invoke especially St. Ananias. Come!"

The air was cool under the trees. The land brooded silent, except for the birds who were happy to be no longer molested. Nonetheless, when she emerged from the other side, Djansha was lurching on her feet.

"I think we can rest awhile," said Lucas.

She lay down on the grass and shuddered.

He sat chewing a straw. The sunlight beat on his shoulders. God's wounds, but he was hungry! Only now did he notice. But his stomach was one cavern of hunger. Across the fields he saw a poplar-shaded house with its outbuildings, doubtless the center of this plantation—but empty as the fisher cabins. He wondered if he dared stop long enough to break in, on the chance of finding some bread or a cheese overlooked in the flight. Or even silver; he would need means of purchase. He shook the girl. "Up," he said.

She raised eyes gone pale. "I cannot."

"Up, I say!" His temper snapped. "Or I leave you here! Haven't you been enough of a burden?"

She buried her face in the grass and lay unmoving. He started off. After a few yards, he looked around. "Well, are you coming?" he said.

She climbed to all fours and then, slowly, to her feet. He went on ahead, fuming.

The clatter of hoofs burst through his preoccupation. Too late! He stood slack-jawed, near the door of the house, as a dozen horsemen galloped around a bend in the road and up toward him.

For one instant he thought of escape. Then Djansha came out onto the path. An exultant yell reached his ears. He shook his fist at the saints, hefted his pike, and went to stand beside her.

The horsemen reined in with a clang. There were six Turcopols, armored in light mail over flowing shirts and trousers, with spiked helmets on shaven half-Asiatic heads. They rode their ponies high-stirruped in the nomadic fashion; their weapons were saber, ax, and a powerful double-curved bow.

Five other men were also light cavalry, but in Western gear: breastplate, flat helmet, sword, dagger, and lance. Boots were drawn over trunk hose and round leather shields banged their horses' cruppers. Their features were equally European, tanned, bearded, and hard.

The leader was Occidental too, a full-armed

knight. Cuirass, brassards, elbowpieces, tasses, and greaves were added to the hauberk that protected his neck and arms, the ringmail on his thighs. A red cloak fluttered at his shoulders and a plume on his conical, visored helmet. There was a coat of arms on his oblong shield and a pennant on the mastlike lance he gripped in one gauntleted hand.

Teeth flashed white through his beard. He said in Catalonian: "Keep away from that pike of his. Put an arrow in him, Arslan. Be ready to catch the girl if she runs, Ferrando. We'll take her into the house."

Catalan traders were nearly as ubiquitous as Venetian or Genoese. Lucas had gained fluency in their tongue while he was working out of Sinope. "Wait!" he cried. "In God's name, Micer, what is it you do?"

The knight reined back his big gray stallion. "I thought you a Greek," he said. His tone was rough and unschooled. "Well, then, what are you?"

Lucas hesitated. How had the story gone—? Oh, yes, the Genoese had seized the ships of the Catalan Company. "Venetian."

"All alone here?" The leader raised shaggy brows. He was a hulking figure of a man, with a heavy and deeply pocked face. His nose had been broken in the past, a few teeth were missing, a scar zigzagged past one brown eye. "How does that happen?"

"A petty misunderstanding. If Micer Knight will let me explain at length—"

"If you're an outlaw, you've no value. Be off!"

Death-white, Djansha looked from one rider to the next. A Turcopol leered at her. "Leave the woman, Venice dweller," he said in bad Catalonian.

76

"On second thought," said the knight, "he would make trouble later. Kill him, Arslan."

It leaped forlornly to Lucas' tongue: "Wait, I say! I have a message for En Jaime!"

"Who?" The leader gaped. The archer lowered his bow.

"The *rich hom* En Jaime de Caza, of course." Lucas stamped the butt of his pike on the ground. "I suppose you can take me to him. Do so!"

"Hold!" rapped the knight to his followers. "Hold off, you whoresons! Back there. . . . Uh. Your pardon, Micer de Venezia. I didn't know. As soon as we've stripped yonder house, I'll be glad to bring you and your lady before my lord."

CHAPTER V

The house in Gallipoli had belonged to a noble of
Byzantium. Now En Jaime and his staff occupied it.
By day, boots racketed across mosaic floors,
weapons clattered and horses tramped in the formal
garden, a cowed servant corps waited on unwashed
men-at-arms with a kick and a curse to speed them.

This evening, however, the knight baron used a
dining room whose riches of carpet and tapestry had
escaped such treatment. Between slender columns,
candles in silver brackets lit the stiff depictions of
East Romans many centuries dead. A glazed window
overlooked a steep downhill view. Here and there a
light glimmered from some other house, or the bobbing torches of a sentry squad. There was more il-
lumination beyond the city walls, at the waterfront:
not only the moon but a pharos, high on one of the
cliffs, revealed a few ships tied at otherwise empty
docks.

En Jaime nodded toward the harbor. "Those
vessels brought men to enlist with us," he said.
"Certain Turks—and Greeks, who hate their
degenerate overlords so much they'll shave their

heads and join us as Turcopols. They have come, and we've sent envoys whom we expect will recruit many more such allies.''

The years had changed him little in outward appearance. His hair was slightly gray at the temples, and the narrow hook-nosed face bore deeper lines. But his bearing was as soldierly as Lucas remembered, his elegance of white linen and black velvet as unpretentious. He turned about, hands behind his back, to give Lucas the old thin smile. ''Enough of the future,'' he declared. ''We have many yesterdays to learn about. It seems to be my destiny to pull you from one fire of your own lighting after another. But good to see you again, you scapegrace!''

Lucas lounged back in a carven chair. Good to be here, he thought, with a well-cooked meal inside him, wine goblet in hand and luxurious plum-colored garments (looted from the Genoese factory) on his skin. Djansha lay between silken sheets in the room given them, and he preferred to let her sleep and talk to his friend, instead.

Or his lord? That was no easy question. Even in those few months of his service, before En Jaime went back from Constantinople and left him, the fugitive boy and the proven man had been something more than master and servant. Lucas owed much of his skill in swordplay to En Jaime's teaching. For his part, he had instructed the knight in Greek and shown him how to write his name. Lucas had been impudent as a sparrow—but the Catalan had allowed it, without loss to his austere dignity.

When they parted, Lucas had wept a little.

Now, he thought, matters were not quite the same as before. The knight who found him, Asberto Cornel, had lent spare horses and accompanied him here. That had been a wild ride, bursting doors and seizing what they would, sleeping one night in a Byzantine villa and the next night on the ground! Arriving late today, Lucas had been well received by En Jaime; but the *rich hom* was preoccupied with the Company's affairs, as it finished plundering the camp of its recent besiegers. This evening had been their first opportunity to speak at length, in private. They were still feeling their way with each other, the awkwardness of long-interrupted acquaintance upon them.

"You mentioned having traveled as far as Cathay," said En Jaime.

Lucas nodded. "I set off for the Orient soon after you departed, Micer. Only this month have I come back to Europe."

"You must have much to tell." The gray eyes lit up. "Did you learn anything of Tartar military practice?"

"Somewhat. I'm unsure how much could be adopted by your light cavalry—what's the word?—your *jinetes*. Doubtless your Turcopols have already learned a great deal from the Mongols in Persia and elsewhere."

"We shall see." En Jaime stroked his pointed beard. "You retain your clerkly skills, I hope? Excellent. We've need of men who can read and write. If they can also wield a blade, why, we'll make counts of them!"

Lucas stirred uneasily. "I know not if I—"

En Jaime went on without noticing: "You've kept other gifts, too, I observe, such as finding beautiful women and causing trouble." He seated himself and picked up his goblet. "You've told me how you escaped from the galleys, and intimated why. I gather you're outlaw in every Venetian domain. Well, then, here's your country!"

He flushed a trifle at the ring of his own words, which did not accord with aristocratic reserve. "We are glad to enroll any worthy man as a soldier of the table," he said with more dryness. "I can make immediate use of you on my own staff. That starts you high. I am on the Council of Twelve which the Company has elected to govern them under our new commander, En Berenguer de Rocafort. Good service on your part cannot go unnoticed; you may hope to be knighted before long."

Lucas stared into his wine cup.

"Well?" said En Jaime.

Lucas jerked. "Oh . . . yes. You're most kind, Micer. But—"

He was remembering how Asberto's troop had been ready to kill him like a beetle and drag Djansha into the house they intended sacking. And he remembered, even more vividly, another moment on the ride hither. The approaching horses had flushed a Thracian peasant from the brake in which he huddled. He ran down the road, his tunic flapping about skinny shanks. A *jinete* galloped after him, pricked him in the rear with a lance point, again and again, until blood soaked his gray tunic. At last the peasant collapsed in a faint, if his heart had not burst. Asberto Cornel rocked in the saddle with laughter.

"I know so little about the Grand Company," faltered Lucas.

"What? You've traveled in Anatolia and not heard of Roger di Flor?"

"Not by name, Micer. You understand how distorted such news is. In the eastern emirates, we heard only that a band of Giaours had brought God's wrath with them."

"Which was not so ill put," En Jaime agreed in a satisfied tone.

He crossed one leg over the other, raised the glass to this lips, and looked cordially across it at his guest. "Our tale has many ins and outs," he said. "I would need years to relate all that has happened to every man of us. And *desperta ferres*, more will happen in the future. But I can give you the bare bones of the story at once.

"So. Where shall I begin? The Sicilian War was a long one. But in the end, with God's help, Aragon was victorious and King Fadrique mounted the throne of Sicily. That was three years ago. Now, during that war, he had hired many troops. Good, skilled, valiant lads, every one of them. However—" a touch of sardonicism—"as is not uncommon, the Lord King found his coffers not quite deep enough to pay them.

"The mercenary captain, En Roger di Flor, had distinguished himself in the war. He had had a gallant career even before, as I must someday relate to you, until his enemies caused his expulsion from the Templars and he ended taking service under Aragon."

Lucas reflected that anyone cast out of so

notoriously lax, greedy, and violent a brotherhood as the Knights Templar must have been a bandit indeed. It would be most impolitic, though, to voice his suspicion. Judging from what Asberto Cornel and others had let fall, Roger di Flor was regarded by his company as a martyred saint.

"After the war," said En Jaime, "seeing the danger King Fadrique was in from his own troops, En Roger broached a plan which the king was very willing to assist. You doubtless know in what poor condition the Empire here was, with the Turks gobbling up one Anatolian city after the next. En Roger offered to lead a strong Catalan force to the Emperor's aid. This was gladly accepted. In September, three years ago, we reached Constantinople in a fleet of thirty-six sails, six thousand men, many of whom had their families along, as well as the thousand cavalry and thousand infantry who carried En Roger's private standard."

"Ah," laughed Lucas, "you say 'we.' That was the thought which saved my life: wherever Catalans were fighting, my old master was likely to be."

En Jaime's smile was a warm response. "For a time," he said, "it looked as if we'd get no fighting, except riots. Body of Christ! I'd not dreamed a government could be so corrupt and effete. No provisions whatsoever had been made for us. Yet Emperor Andronicus did at once, before we had so much as lifted a halberd, issue four month's wages. With idle soldiers and mariners lounging about the streets for weeks on end, brawling with the Greeks and with the Genoese of Galata—why, in one such riot, the Grand Drungarios himself was slain, as his troops tried to halt it. But those Greeks are worthless, the merest yellow mongrels. . . . Your pardon. Of course, I don't include Cretans.

"Meanwhile Andronicus sought to curry favor with our officers, adopted En Roger into the Imperial family, named him Grand Duke, wed him to the Emperor's granddaughter Maria. At last we were removed to Asia, where we cleared Cyzicus and Pegae of the Turks. We stayed the winter there. In spring, it was found that most of our men, quartered on the townsfolk, had incurred larger debts than they could pay. Duke Roger sought to get the needful monies from the Emperor, but failed."

And so the townsfolk went unpaid, thought Lucas.

En Jaime moistened his throat with wine before he resumed:

"There were also riots with the Alan cavalrymen serving the Emperor, as well as the civil populace. The son of their chief was killed. In the end, that was not a lucky happening for us. . . . Well. Finally we marched forth. Philadelphia, the largest city in Anatolia, lay under siege. We routed the Turks and pursued them to the Iron Gates on the Lycian frontier. Meanwhile our fleet occupied Chios and other islands, gaining a good booty."

Which belonged to the Byzantines, Lucas thought.

"We wintered in Philadelphia, chiefly," said En Jaime. "At that time the *rich hom* En Berenguer de Rocafort arrived with reinforcements. It became ever more plain to us how little strength or honor the Imperial government had. In revenge for our disputes with the Greeks, our treasures, which we had stored in the city of Magnesia, were confiscated next year, and our people there were put to the sword. Duke Roger laid siege, but I confess we failed to take the city, for lack of engineers and war machinery. The Imperial armies demanded to be led against us, and our Alan auxilaries quit the standard and wandered about freely, living off the countryside. In the end, Andronicus' son, the co-Emperor Skyr Miqueli—Michael, they call him here—smoothed matters over. But as we had long been unpaid, and had lost our treasures, we levied contribution from the provinces.''

Lucas said nothing. He was thinking of certain men he had met one day in a Turkish camp: Greeks so embittered they had turned Moslem. They told of a land robbed bare. The only plentiful article was the bones of children who had starved to death.

"That autumn we crossed the Boca Daner," said En Jaime, meaning the strait which Gallipoli overlooked. "We took up quarters here and in various Thracian towns. Duke Roger visited Constantinople to demand our pay, but got only a small amount, and that in debased coinage. Wherefore our men taught the Greeks a sharp lesson by plundering all around. About this time, En Berenguer de Entenza arrived with reinforcements and—''

There was a deferential knock. A woman's impatient voice said, "Oh, be not a cur in your timidity, Asberto, as well as in your manners.''

She entered without waiting for En Jaime's leave. Behind her came the knight, Cornel. A stolen robe, on which he had wiped greasy fingers, draped his bow-legged horseman's body. His broken visage turned embarrassedly toward the *rich hom*. "Na Violante wanted—" he began shyly.

"Na Violante de Lebia Tari wanted to see this newcomer from Cathay, of whom so many rumors have been flying," interrupted the woman. As Lucas bowed, she gave him a slow, savoring smile. "And well worth seeing he is. Are they all so gallant in the East?"

Smooth habit answered for Lucas: "No, my lady, they are not. I'm long out of practice. Yet who would not try his best to be gallant in the presence of so much beauty?"

Asberto flushed. "See here!" he growled. "Let her alone, Greco, or it'll be the worse for you."

"Enough." En Jaime raised one hand. Asberto looked at his feet, gnawed his mustache, and said no more.

Violante continued to regard Lucas. He returned her gaze with frank pleasure. Tall, dark of eye and fair of complexion, she defied propriety by leaving uncovered the raven's-wing hair piled on her head, and by a gown of blue silk that fitted her richly curved body like a second skin and plunged low across the breasts. Her features were a little too strong in nose and chin, a little too wide in mouth; yet surely that mouth knew how to kiss. She had adorned herself with a barbaric overflow of gems: a diamond fillet above the low brow, a ruby smoldering in the cleft of her bosom, golden bracelets coiled on her arms. Her age, Lucas guessed, was a few years less than his own.

"You must forgive me, En Jaime," she said. "Asberto insisted you were entertaining privately.

Yet for just that reason I had to come. When else could I listen to this man, who has guested the Grand Cham in Cambaluc?"

"You are welcome," said the *rich hom* stiffly. Lucas thought he yielded more to a certain appeal in Asberto's eyes than to the woman.

"Oh, now," she murmured, touching his hand. He withdrew it. "Be not so stern. Why, you look like a flounder in Lent."

A reluctant smile twitched En Jaime's mouth. "Very well, my lady. You get your way, as usual. Pray be seated. If Maestre Lucas wishes to relate a few stories of his travels, we will all be grateful."

"Gladly," said Lucas. He felt Violante's presence like a tingle over scalp and spine. Evidently Asberto—best be sure to gratify that sullen dog with an "En Asberto"—no, curse it, "Nasberto," since the name began with a vowel—Nasberto Cornel was her lover. How had he gotten so desirable a creature?

To gain time for preparing witty phrases she could admire, Lucas said, "I should first hear out En Jaime's relation of the Grand Company. He left them here in Gallipoli, quarreling with the Imperium."

"Which tried, by conferring honors on En Berenguer de Entenza, to divide us against ourselves," said the nobleman indignantly. "But En Roger di Flor forestalled that by yielding his title of Grand Duke to de Entenza. Meanwhile the Turks again overran Anatolia and invested Philadelphia.

"This, as well as certain treaties being made in the West, which Rocafort feared might make us feudatories of Sicily—he is, in all confidence, Lucas, a man greedy of power—made both parties more willing to deal with each other. Or so it seemed. En Roger was created Caesar, which is just below the Emperor himself, and given many other honors and promises . . . but only four months' pay in debased coins, which we therefore compelled the Greeks to take at face value. We then agreed to march against the Turks.''

En Jaime fell silent. He held his goblet up to the light, twirled it, and dashed it against the wall. Glass tinkled to the floor, a red wine stain spattered the mosaic.

"They murdered our lord," said the Catalan thickly. "God will punish them. I say to you, we are the scourge of God upon this brood of snakes!"

Asberto growled an obscene agreement. Na Violante's cheeks flamed. Lucas sat very still.

"Have you heard the tale?" said En Jaime after a while. "Before departing to war, our commander, the Caesar, went to Adrianople to pay his respects to Skyr Miqueli. And there he was murdered. George, the chief of the Alans, whose son had been killed in the riots at Cyzicus—George wielded the knife. Oh, but the Alans shall mourn for that day! And the Greeks! Three hundred good Catalans who had been with En Roger were butchered in the streets. Only three men escaped to bring us the news. By then, the Alans were already at our throats. They slew all of us they could find dwelling in Thrace, and camped before Gallipoli to besiege us.

"So we sent a deputation to Andronicus, under safe conduct, to defy him and impeach him and offer trial of combat. On their way back to us . . .

they were slain and quartered in the shambles of Rhedestos town. Meanwhile our admiral and all Catalans in the captial were massacred by the people.

"Nonetheless the Grand Duke, En Berenguer de Entenza, took our ships to Perinthos. He stormed that city, avenged us upon its inhabitants, and filled his holds with plunder. But on his way back, he was taken by a Genoese fleet.

"When we heard this, certain faint hearts argued we should flee to a safer place, such as the island of Mitylene. But good St. George strengthened us in our resolve. We scuttled our remaining boats to end such talk. And we made banners to carry into battle, and elected En Berenguer de Rocafort to be our commander. And we sallied forth against the Alans and drove them away with great slaughter and won an immense booty.

"But it is only the beginning, Lucas. Only the beginning."

En Jaime rose, a little unsteadily. His voice had gone harsh with so much talk. He took another Venetian goblet from the sideboard. Asberto Cornel hastened to fill it for him. He drank deep.

Lucas kept silent.

After all, he thought, if the Empire is so far decayed that it does not even give its people protection for their unfreedom and the taxes wrung out of them, then the time is past due for a storm to lash Byzantium off the earth. A bold new people can erect something better on the ruins. I only wish I could forget how that peasant screamed as the lancer pursued him.

A gurgling called his attention back. Violante had

poured his own glass full.

"I thank my lady," he said, "but scarce deserve so fair a maidservant."

She sat down on a footstool before him. As she leaned forward, a goblet in her own hand, the blue gown shimmered along each curve of hip and leg, and his eyes were teased with glimpses of almost her whole bosom. But not quite, worse luck. His pulse jumped.

"Oh, I shall demand my wage," she said, smiling at him as if they shared a secret. "The whole tale of your adventures, Maestre. You may make the first payment to me at once."

He leaned back. Why should he flee from this: to sit drinking good wine and spinning out his own exploits before such a beautiful woman? A cultivated one, too, who showed exact appreciation of each polished sentence. After so much strife, this was like coming home.

Other conquerers had doubtless been as brutal as the Grand Catalan Company. When they had carved out their domain, if they did, one could expect them to settle down and rule justly. Or if not, well, this was a hard world. The maltreated would have their reward in Heaven. Would it not be presumptuous of Lucas Greco to ask more than that he and those he cared for should not be victims?

CHAPTER VI

The Catalan Officers did not take long to drill the Turks in their signals. About that time, Greek spies brought word that Michael Paleologus himself had left Adrianople with a vastly superior force and was on his way against them.

Some captains urged that they remain in Gallipoli, where their treasures were and which was readily defensible. But "In the end," wrote En Ramon Muntaner afterward, "the council said that God and the blessed monsenyer St. Peter and St. Paul and St. George, who had given us this victory, would also give us victory over that wicked man who had so treacherously killed the Caesar; and so, that we should on no account tarry in Gallipoli; that Gallipoli was a strong place and we had made so much gain that our courage might weaken, and so that we should, on no account, allow ourselves to be besieged. And again, that the son of the Emperor would not be able to come with the whole host assembled, rather it suit him to form a van, and that we should meet the van and should attack it, and if we defeated it, all would be defeated. And as we could not mount to Heaven nor go down to the depths, nor go away by sea or land, therefore it followed that we had to pass through their hands, and so it was well that our courage should not be weakened by what we had gained nor by the force we saw before us."

Leaving their women and a hundred men to guard their stronghold, the Company marched up the peninsula and over the Thracian hills. After three days, they came to the foot of a mountain and made camp. When darkness had fallen, a red glow was seen in the sky above the ridge. Scouts were sent forth, who came back to report that the enemy lay on the plain beyond, close to the town of Imeri and the castle of Apros.

Though he had been working daily with En Jaime de Caza, as amanuensis and Turkish interpreter, Lucas did not pretend to be a heavy cavalryman. Nor did he feel at home with the *jinetes*. En Jaime outfitted him from Alan booty, gave him a good horse, and put him with a section of Almúgavares.

This night he had trouble getting to sleep. Word had flown quickly through the bivouac; all knew the battle would stand tomorrow. Finally he swore, left his bedroll, and went over to sit by the nearest watchfire.

It was the frugal kindling of experienced soldiers. A bed of coals glowed white; tiny blue flames wavered above, occasionally spitting up in red and yellow. At such times Lucas could see a few infantrymen, lying fully clad beside their weapons. The upland chill had hoarfrosted their blankets, but they slept with animal ease. Then the fire sank down again, darkness came in like a tide, nothing was to be seen but other twinkling sparks, far-strewn beneath enormous constellations. Lucas pulled his cloak tighter around his shoulders and held palms toward the heat.

A sentry came by, pausing to throw on a few more twigs. He was typical of the Almúgavares, who had begun as Christian outlaws, savage in the mountains, when the Moors swept across Spain, and whom the crown of Aragon had later made into a formidable military institution. Pedro was a rangy man, barbarically clad in loose coat and breeches of hide, sandals, a pouch for flint and steel. He had never shaved; the beard poured down his chest, the long hair was done up with a steel comb. His only special protection was a pair of leather half-gaiters. A dagger was at his waist, a javelin in his hand. Across his back, above the knapsack, were three other darts. Their iron heads shimmered in the gloom.

"Why is the Maestre so late awake?" he asked. "I'll be glad when *I* go off duty."

Lucas gave him a wry smile. He had come to like these warriors, as one might grow fond of a pet wolf. They were simple, superstitious, thinking him half wizard and half saint because he was a Maestre, a learned man; but they were also utterly loyal, quite without fear, and possessed of a certain rough gaiety.

"There'll be time enough to sleep tomorrow, after the battle," he said. "For some, a very long sleep."

"The more plunder for the rest of us, then," said Pedro, his cheerfulness undiminished.

"If we win."

"If not, we'll be enrolled in good St. George's host. I daresay fine booty can be had from a raid on Hell, Maestre, seeing how many bishops and moneylenders dwell there."

"I wish I could be so sure we are fighting in God's cause."

"Why, of course we are. Priest says so. Priest knows about these things. A mercy of Heaven, that common folk like me needn't bother our heads. Your trouble is, you think too much, if I may say so."

"You're quite right," admitted Lucas.

"And it's not needful," Pedro insisted. "Our good commander, En Berenguer de Rocafort, he has all the plans made. He has everything in his head, he does."

"Everything? Our own dispositions, the host of the Greeks, the countryside?"

"Just so, Maestre."

"Why, then, En Berenguer's head is bigger than it looks," said Lucas innocently.

Pedro frowned, trying to understand. When the idea dawned on him, he slapped his thigh. "Haw, haw, haw! That's a rare one! Bigger than it looks. Yes, I take your meaning. Ah, you're a clever man. I must remember the jest, and try it on my relief. The commander must needs have a big head to hold all those troops. Yes, so. Haw, haw, haw!" He lifted his spear in salute and continued on his rounds.

Lucas bent closer to the fire.

Would God I were that easily satisfied, he thought.

After a while he heard footsteps and saw a lanthorn move toward him. It was held by Asberto Cornel, who lighted a way for En Jaime de Caza. Both knights wore hauberk and mail breeches; their esquires would put the plate on them at the last moment.

Lucas started to rise. En Jaime waved him back and sat down, too. "So you're also wakeful," said the Catalan. "I have been in search of someone to converse with."

Asberto grunted and joined them. By now Lucas knew he headed one section of cavalry in En Jaime's division, and that his family had been vassals of the de Cazas for generations. Between him and Lucas was a stiff politeness. They exchanged as few words as possible, for he took badly the flirtations of his mistress with the newcomer.

"A long night," he said. "Will Micer not go lie down, at least?"

"Not yet," said En Jaime. "But I told you before, there's no reason for you to follow me about if you're weary."

"There is, Micer." Asberto jerked a thumb at the glow from the enemy fires.

"Bah! No doubt they're aware of us, but you think not they've the spirit to attempt anything before sunrise, do you?"

Asberto spat into the fire. It sizzled. "Not those gutless Greeks," he said. "But they have mercenaries too. Alans and Vlachs and others. Night raids aren't unknown."

"I have heard they total over a hundred thousand," said En Jaime. "That may be an exaggeration. Still, many. Yes, I suppose among so many

95

there must be a few brave souls."

And we, thought Lucas, are perhaps ten thousand in all.

The fire burned upward as it caught the new fuel. En Jaime's face stood forth in red highlights along brow and cheekbones and long curved nose. Otherwise he was nearly lost in the shadows.

"I have a weakness, Lucas," he said. "I am always sleepless the night before a battle."

Lucas said, with some puzzlement, "I was at first . . . as a boy, unused to the idea I might be dead in a few hours. Then I learned to rest at every chance, though Doomsday were to be announced for the hour of matins. Tonight that habit has failed me, I know not why."

"Frightened?" gibed Asberto.

En Jaime grew stiff. "Never ask that of a comrade in arms!" His bark turned to bleak precision. "Ask the forgiveness of Maestre Lucas or go to your rest."

"My lord!" Dismay sprang out on Asberto's scarred countenance.

"Go." The noble spoke quietly. Asberto jumped up, threw Lucas one glare of hatred, and reached for the lanthorn. Then, with a glance at En Jaime, he left it there and shambled away.

"My thanks, Micer," said Lucas, ill at ease. "But I'm harder to insult than you. The man who says evil of me is either speaking the truth, in which case I couldn't justly take his life, or he's a liar and his words don't touch me."

"I have observed a certain flexibility in you," agreed En Jaime dryly. "Asberto needed a lesson, though. He's too blunt-brained to distinguish between pride and arrogance."

"In fact, if I may say it, he merely exemplifies his countrymen."

"True." For minutes, En Jaime brooded unspeaking. Somewhere in the night a horse neighed. The calls of watchmen went long-drawn, lonely, from post to post.

Abruptly, the Catalan said: "You must not believe I am that crude. God makes a grim jest, that all high purposes must be accomplished by mortal men. Ignorant, ill-smelling, selfish, quarrelsome, flea-bitten, fornicating swine! I myself don't think this chivvying of peasants is proper work for a knight, Lucas. It were far more valiant to settle the issue by trial of combat between champions."

"But supposing your champion lost, would you go home?"

En Jaime bridled. "Without a fight? Never!" The humor struck him. He laughed. "You rogue! I think I want you with me as much for your sauciness as for your clerk skill. More, I suppose. Sour-faced priests are easy enough to come by. . . . No, I would not go home."

After another pause, grave again: "I have no home save this, the Grand Company."

"Micer spoke of a wife and son, an estate, in Catalonia."

"Yes. I have been briefly there, now and again. When last I departed the place, I had been married a few months. That was . . . dear saints, ten years ago! No, nearer eleven."

"You have never seen your son?"

En Jaime shifted his position and scowled at the fire. "Oh, I will in time. In good time," he muttered. "I hear from my bailiff that all goes as well as can be expected. But how can the estate be maintained as befits my name, if I don't win enough treasure in the wars?"

"Many other men brought their families along."

"Yes. Some wives. Chiefly lemans, however. Sluts!" En Jaime raised his lip so the teeth gleamed. "That's what I meant when I said God's purposes— like this vengeance on the Greek betrayal, and extension of the Holy Catholic Faith—God's purposes must be accomplished by swine."

Lucas grinned. "I've observed you too, Micer, give way to Na Violante."

"Oh, her? She's a witch, first wheedling, then threatening, till it's easier to yield than assert oneself. And her husband was a gallant man. For his sake—still more so, for Asberto's, who has ever been faithful to me—ah, she punishes him enough for his sins. I'd pity any man caught in so foul a trap."

"I wouldn't."

"Be careful. Lechery is a mortal sin."

"There are worse ones," said Lucas, thinking of a servant in Gallipoli who was given twenty lashes for spilling hot soup on an officer.

En Jaime's tone grew gentle. "I am also a sinful man, Lucas. I dare not think how deeply I have blackened my soul. But by God's grace I have remained true, as a knight should be, to one God, one king, and one lady."

The fire sank low again.

"Not the lady that I wed," said En Jaime. "Mine is among the saints. These twenty years or more."

He got to his feet. "It were best if we both tried to sleep," he said roughly. He snatched up the lanthorn and strode into darkness.

When the first lightening came in the east, the army bestirred itself. Trumpets blew, a cold-sounding summons under the stars; men grumbled awake, jumped about on the ground, slapped arms over backs to work out the night's stiffness.

Lucas found himself at the head of a line of Almúgavares, before a booth in which a priest stood to hear confession. Every man was to receive Holy Communion before the battle. He had made a perfunctory account of sins in Gallipoli, for in this band no one but the allied Turks dared incur clerical disapproval. Now, with spears awaiting him beyond the mountain, he felt a sudden wish to be more genuinely at peace with God. But many must be shriven in the scant time available; and he was less troubled by guilt than by doubts, a sense of lostness, for which no absolution existed. With an inward shrug, he knelt and rattled off a few incidents of anger or envy. The priest gave him twenty Paternosters to say and dismissed him.

When the Host was elevated against a dawning sky, and a murmur of awe went through the weapon-clad thousands, Lucas felt himself altogether alone.

Then there was no chance to think. A snatched bite of bread and salt fish, a gulp of water. Trumpets resounded and kettledrums rolled. The three battle banners of the Lord King of Aragon, the King of Sicily, and St. George were lifted high. The wind caught them; the first sunbeams shouted in their colors. Lucas swung to the saddle. "Forward!" he said, needlessly, for the Almúgavares were already a-tramp.

Up the plowed mountainside the Grand Company went. On its height they stopped and looked down at the Imperial force.

Lucas rose in his stirrups to get a better view. Hauberk and helmet weighed on him; he carried a leather buckler on his left arm and a saber at his hip.

"One trouble with charging Greeks," Pedro said. "When they see you coming, they wet their pants so hard it turns the ground all muddy." Laughter barked down the hairy ranks.

The Company was drawn up in four divisions: Almúgavares, mounted and afoot, for the main body and the reserve; Turks on the wings; the chivalry at the center. Lucas was a little forward of his own battalion. To his left, he could see the Asiatics holding their restless mounts in check. Ahead and to his right, somewhat downhill of him, gleamed the knights. Their surcoats splashed brown earth and wan sky with color, their pennons snapped in the breeze. Many had donned full heaumes, turning themselves into faceless, slit-eyed monsters grotesquely crested.

Below the mountain and across the plain, still hazed, Lucas discerned town and fortress. The Byzantine army was drawn up on the plains. At this distance it appeared as a single mass, glittering at points where metal flung the light back into his eyes. He suppressed a whistle. That army spread across the valley floor; its camp, off to one side, was a city of tents and wagons.

For several minutes En Berenguer de Rocafort sat pondering. Finally he clapped his visor down. One gauntlet made a chopping motion. His standard bearer raised the gonfanon. His bugler sounded the advance. The other trumpets took it up till the mountaintop shrieked.

They moved forward slowly, keeping time. The knightly lanceheads rose and fell with a ripple, as if they were a grainfield in the wind. Except for a steady drum-thump, the deep ground vibration of feet and hoofs, everything became death silent. Far, far overhead, Lucas heard a skylark; he felt sweat tickle his ribs; there was an itch beneath his mail that could not be scratched.

This may be heroic—but I'd rather lie abed with Djansha, he thought. He tried to conjure up her image, while more pious warriors were rapt-faced envisioning the holy saints. Instead, he kept seeing Violante. She was laughing.

The advance lasted a century, but when it was over, a bare instant had gone by. Suddenly Lucas made out the Byzantine ranks as separate men, gaudy banners and horse trappings, an officer's plumes blowing about his gilt helmet. Was he here already?

Trumpets wailed, faint across the valley. The Imperial left wing, Alans and Turcopols, charged.

"Aragon and St. George!" The Catalan cry broke free like thunder.

Lucas kept his place. The gelding pranced under him. He stroked its neck. "Not yet," he soothed. "Not until we're told, my pretty. We will be, soon enough, never fear."

101

His tension slackened somewhat. He recalled that a battlefield was actually not too unsafe a place to be, except when the front of combat passed by. Even that was better than prolonged sitting in camp, where disease forever stalked.

Trumpets blasted closer by. The Catalan chivalry lowered lances and attacked.

They started at a walk. It became a trot, a canter, a full earthquake gallop. Lucas watched the standard of his own division. It began to move. He clucked to his mount. The Almúgavares jogged behind him.

Then their war shout filled the bowl of heaven. *"Desperta ferres!"* Awake the iron! As they neared the dust cloud boiling ahead of them, they struck their spearheads against the stones. The iron clanged and grated. Sparks showered upward.

The knights of Aragon smote the Byzantine hirelings with a noise that roared from horizon to horizon. Lucas heard lances splinter and horses scream. He had glimpses through the dust and flying clods—an Alan's spear glided off the poitrail of a Catalan horse, the Catalan sword smote, the Alan toppled from his saddle; another man lay with a crossbow quarrel in his throat; a steed bolted, dragging its rider behind from one stirrup.

The enemy charge broke. They surged back upon their own rear guard. The array of Catalonia and Aragon blazed onward, through squadron after Byzantine squadron.

Lucas did not see them. He was fighting with the infantry.

The well-dressed Greek lines stood firm before him, a wall of shields, helmets above and greaves below, pikes thrusting between, all brilliant in the strengthening sunlight. But even as he approached them, Lucas thought how his own men must look, long-haired, skin-clad, sparks whirling at their feet, yelping now the *"Aur! Aur!"* they had learned from the Saracens. A legion out of Hell!

Crossbows snapped. Their bolts whistled from the Catalan flanks. Lucas' own troopers threw their javelins. The clatter against Greek mail came dry and dreadful. Many stuck in flesh.

He spied one man down, tugging at the barbed steel in his thigh. He drew his saber and galloped for the breach.

Reining in, he hewed at a mouth which cursed him. The soldier ducked in time; Lucas' edge bounced off the helmet. An ax struck his greave. He cut at the arm that wielded it. There was the heavy bite of steel going into meat. The Byzantine yammered and dropped his ax. Lucas saw a pike jab from his left. He caught the point on his buckler. The impact jarred him. With spurs and knees he urged his horse forward, slowly, into the seething men. The pike-bearer heard the saber whine above him. He melted backward into the crumpling ranks.

Iron banged on hardened leather. The Almúgavares had closed in with daggers. Pedro sidestepped a thrust, got his belly next to an enemy shield, pulled that down with his left hand and stabbed with his right. His opponent threw a frantic arm around him. They rolled to the ground together. Pedro scrambled on top, struck, raised his dripping knife and struck again. There was no need for another stab. *"Aur! Aur!"* he howled.

Lucas' horse reared, whinnying, and a spearman charged, ready to skewer it. He leaned far over, as Mongols did, and cut at the man's arms. The Byzantine scrambled clear. No use trying to fight from horseback in this press of bodies. Lucas jumped to the ground, slapped his steed on the rump and let it escape.

His saber clanged on an enemy shield. For a moment he looked into the man's eyes. A sense of freedom leaped within him. This was no time for doubts or dreads. It was good honest war!

He smote, shouting.

All at once nobody stood in front of him. He spied a few scattered Greeks who were fleeing. Their main body had vanished into the dust cloud, routed. Corpses were stark on the ground; the wounded, most of whom would also die, groaned for water; flies settled on clotting blood.

Lucas looked toward the standard of his division. It stood high. Trumpets called for the lines to re-form. Panting, grinning, but quick to obey, the Almúgavares made ranks and moved onward.

They broke the next opposing battalion. And the next. And the next.

The Imperial army buckled.

Afterward En Jaime, who had witnessed it, told Lucas how Michael Paleologus tried to stop the retreat. The co-Emperor did not lack courage. He brought up the reserves; himself at their head, he couched lance and charged the middle of his foes. They held fast, but the combat was hard. Michael encountered a man in splendid armor on a fine horse, who seemed an officer of importance though

104

he lacked a shield. But he was only a mariner from Barcelona who had won his trappings at Gallipoli and had left off the shield because he did not know how to use it. Michael's sword wounded him on the left arm. The sailor urged his horse forward, closed with the prince and thrust with a dagger. One of those blows cut Michael in the face, so that he lowered his shield and fell from the saddle. Still he fought bravely, wounding the sailor again. That gave the Imperial guards a chance to rally around him and bear him off the field.

His men streamed after, division by division, the best of them fighting stubbornly, the worst of them stampeding. Toward sunset, the last skirmish was over. The Byzantines had taken refuge in Apros castle. *Te Deum laudamus* lifted triumphant from the throats of the Grand Company.

CHAPTER VII

"We could not take the castle," Lucas admitted, "though we were there full eight days. But then, most of that time we were plundering their camp and the neighborhood. We loaded ten carts with treasure, so high that each cart needed four oxen to draw it. The cattle we drove off covered the land as far as a man might see."

Djansha hugged her knees and regarded him with awe. Her coppery tresses streamed over the bare young breasts. "So you are made a wealthy *uork*, my lord."

"The booty has yet to be divided." He stretched luxuriously. Hardihood be damned, after two weeks in the field it was good to lie abed. They had entered Gallipoli at dusk, and En Jaime had invited Lucas to share dinner. Afterward, they drank wine together till late, speaking of far countries and of what great things might be done here. En Jaime had even shown courteous interest for an hour or more while Lucas discoursed of stars and planetary motions and the nature of comets, the first such conversation he had had for years. So he came late to his chamber and fell instantly asleep.

This dawn he had awakened to a fire blown up in a brazier, Djansha waiting to serve him his food. He ignored the piece of fat she threw in the coals, with a muttered invocation to Tleps, the fire god. Instead, he pulled her down beside him. . . . But that was two hours past. Now he felt a restless desire for he knew not what. So he talked, telling her about the expedition.

"My share in the proceeds will not be so little," he said. "Of course, the stuff is mostly war gear. But I'll trade with others who already possess jewels. Would you like a gold necklace?"

The tousled head bent. "It is enough that my lord lives."

He scowled. Now that the Company could take up a somewhat more assured residence, he wanted to shine as an officer. Djansha would excite admiration, envy, prestige—if she were a Christian of good birth who spoke Catalonian. Otherwise, she was a mere slave whom he might casually be asked to lend, like a whetstone or a horse. (No; one did not borrow a knight's personal steed.)

It seemed almost pointless, then, to dress her well.

She looked back at him with a return of fear. "Must you go out fighting again soon?"

"I don't expect any real battles for a long time," he said. "We broke the Byzantines; their losses were high and their resolution is gone. When we quit Apros, they were hastening toward Adrianople. I doubt Michael will be mad enough to take the field against us a second time."

"Shible shall have the worth of an ox for that!"

107

she exclaimed radiantly.

"Hold!" he said in alarm. "How often must I warn you, heathen sacrifices are forbidden here?"

"Then your god, Keristi, is that his name? Keristi I will thank, with an offering of—"

"No need! I *must* see to your education before—" he broke off. Damned be these endless nuisances, anyhow! If Father Pere baptized her, that prune-lipped old busybody would expect a substantial donation. And in order to establish himself in the respect of the great officers, Lucas had a thousand other expenses. Also, if she then relapsed, she was liable to ecclesiastical punishment, even to burning. It seemed best to wait a while.

He said quickly: "Of course, the war continues. We must force an indemnity from the Emperor, if he does not cede us this province. But as yet, we can't hope to take Constantinople or Adrianople. So En Jaime de Caza thinks we'll confine ourselves to raiding. That should be a frolic!"

"Oh."

"What's the matter?"

"Nothing. My lord must do as he thinks best."

"You need not fear for my life."

"No . . ."

"Well, then?" he asked, snappish in his impatience. Though uncertain of what he had expected of her, he felt disappointment. She had been sweet in his arms; but that was not the whole of life. Yet was he just in demanding a simple barbarian girl should appreciate his account of a military campaign and of future policy?

"Nothing." She slipped one long leg from the

bedclothes to the floor. Her voice was small. "If my lord allows, I will bathe and dress myself."

He seized her wrist. "What ails you?" As she remained silent: "I command you to tell me."

"I do fear you will be slain," she mumbled. She sat on the edge of the bed, her back to him and her face turned downward.

"God's mercy! I can't stay at home when my comrades are fighting! I thought you wanted a warrior."

"Forgive me, my lord. It is stupid of me. And—"

"Yes? Out with it!"

She gulped. "I am so lonely here."

He let her go. She stood up and walked toward the tub of water standing beneath a peacock mosaic.

"Well," he grumbled, "I can do little about that. I can't afford another . . . another slave. Not yet."

"I could not talk to her," Djansha stopped at the edge of the tub. A flush reddened face, throat, and bosom. "Nor would I want anyone else—No, forgive me. My lord must do as he pleases."

"I like not bread and milk," he barked. "Have you no pepper in you at all?"

She stared at him. Her accent worsened. "I not understand, pray pardon."

"Oh, no matter, no matter," he sighed. "I suppose you have found confinement to this house wearisome. But didn't I say you could walk in the city while the host was absent?"

"Empty." He saw the shudder go along her flesh. "So many houses empty, my lord. A few people ran away and hid when they saw me coming. In one house, no one had taken away the corpse. Her arm

109

was cut off, I saw. Rats had eaten half of her."

"Be still!"

"And walls. Everywhere walls! No trees, no children, only walls."

"Be still, you whimpering bitch!" He sprang from the bed. She went to her knees. The long hair fell past her cheeks, hiding her countenance.

"There was much evil committed here," he agreed, unwillingly, his words so blurred in his haste to be done with them that she most likely did not follow. "The Company had just gotten the news their chief was murdered. Their own allies had attacked without warning. A few of their comrades quartered outside the city fled here, telling how all the rest had been slaughtered. They're fiery men. They avenged themselves on the nearest Greeks to hand. It's done now. It will not be done again."

She huddled where she was.

He spat an oath, went to the tub himself, sponged his body and dressed. By all foul devils, he thought, she took satisfaction in spoiling his victory for him!

He walked stiff-legged from the chamber.

Of course, he thought as he went down the hallway beyond, she had good reason to fear his death. Into whose hands would she pass? He should make some provision—Later, later. Why did these women never leave a man in peace? And why could she not have spoken her fear honestly, instead of pretending it was *his* life which mattered to her? He was nothing but a master more easy-going than she had expected. Too easy-going, no doubt. What else *could* he be?

Why did it make any difference what she felt, a slave?

He wished he had some work to occupy him, but the main body of the Company was still on the road with their plunder. The leading knights had exercised privilege of rank to ride ahead of the oxcarts, thus gaining an idle day or two in Gallipoli. Their immediate attendants had accompanied them.

Djansha was right, Lucas admitted, about those graveyard streets. He himself had no wish to enter them. New inhabitants must be recruited, he thought. This could become a great port—crowded, busy, happy, given a wiser government than the Emperor's. A hundred years hence, Gallipoli would be thankful the Catalans had taken her. Nonetheless, he did not want to leave the house.

He came out on a portico and went down the steps. The house surrounded three sides of a garden, with an ivy-covered wall to close the fourth. The flowerbeds had been ruined by soldiers going in and out the gate; horses had been stabled in one wing, outside which the grooms squatted, dicing and speaking obscenely. But a row of willows blocked them from view. The weeds that had sprung up were a brave green under heaven. Though dry, the stone fountain in the center was graceful to look at. Lucas paused to soothe himself with the sculpture of the basin, young Perseus unchaining Andromeda.

"Good morning, Maestre."

He wheeled around with a jerkiness that told him how on edge he still was. Na Violante de Lebia Tari smiled at him.

He bowed. "Good morning, my lady. Your servant."

"Would that were true," she said. "You would be

111

an admirable servant: quick, clever, and amusing. But—" she cocked her head—"a better master, I think."

Bewildered, for this carried their flirtation well beyond the bounds proper to a lady addressing a man, he felt his skin go hot. He looked around. No one else was to be seen. "You are up early," he said clumsily.

"Like yourself. The rest are still snoring." Her fan fluttered along the low crimson bodice, which seemed delightfully in peril of bursting asunder. One ankle peeped from beneath sweeping skirts. As usual, she ignored decorum and covered her blue-black hair with no more than a mantilla. "I had nothing to do except walk in the garden. My maidservants dressed me. I told them to stay behind, though. An hour alone is too precious a thing."

"I beg your pardon, Na Violante. I'll depart at once."

"No, no!" She caught his hand, then let it go, her fingers slipping across his knuckles. "You didn't let me finish, Maestre. True, I often wish to be alone with my thoughts. But good company is the rarest pleasure of all. I shall be very angry if you leave."

His tongue began to find its accustomed glibness. "Then, since my lady's anger would also provoke that of great Jove and any other god with eyes in his head, I must stay."

"La! Are you French, Maestre Lucas? They say the Provencals are the world's most shameless flatterers."

"No, my lady. I am—" Lucas stopped. What was he, indeed, he wondered with a returning emptiness.

"Oh, yes, Venetian. I know. So I have met at least one Venetian who can outflatter any minstrel from Provence. You know not how refreshing that is, after a lifetime of dour Hispanics, cringing Sicilians, and Easterners who can hardly talk at all."

"I do not flatter, bella Donna," said Lucas. "In the presence of such splendor I am stricken nearly dumb. At best, any words are a poor, pale tribute."

She sat down on a stone bench. "Come, join me," she said, and drew her skirt aside. After a moment, he did so. There were still some inches between them, but he had a sense of being enveloped, as if in the odor of jasmine. Since it drowned out that certain desolation in him, he prolonged things with chatter.

"Is not that fountain a beautiful work? Ancient Grecian, beyond doubt. The pagans could make stone come almost alive. And yet, if Na Violante had posed for a Venus, I think the sculptor would never have dared pick up his chisel. On the one hand, his finest efforts would still have done you the grossest injustice. On the other, he might fear a divine power would suffuse him and make him actually reveal the truth, actually portray my lady—in which case, envious Queen Venus would strike him blind."

They had jested like this before, from time to time over the wine cups. Half the amusement for Lucas had been to make Asberto Cornel glower; for he could never forget the peasant who fled. But today, suddenly, she laid a hand on his knee. He stopped talking and looked at her, stupefied.

"My thanks," she said, low and hurried. "But I've somewhat else to ask of you."

"Why . . . anything." His Adam's apple seemed large enough to stumble on.

"Tell me about the battle, and its aftermath, and what we can await in the future."

Words abandoned him utterly. She withdrew her hand and said in rising anger: "No one else will do so. The *richs homens* are far too grand to speak reasonably with a mere woman. They're shocked enough that I won't stay in my mousehole and creep forth only when called. As for Asberto, I might as well ask his horse for information. It would understand more, and explain better. At least it would show more courtesy!"

"But—"

The red faded in her skin, leaving it again like ivory, finely blue-veined at the temples. Her nostrils still flared a little, and the eyes glowed. But she smiled, however strained it was, leaned back and said straight to his face: "You are God's gift to my solitude, Maestre Lucas. The few people I've met in my life who had any learning, any skill with words, any concept of a world beyond their own snotty noses—ah, forgive my vulgarity, I am a soldier's daughter—the few such have been clerics or sycophants or otherwise hardly men. You, though, you have wrought like ancient Hercules, and pondered what you saw and did, and found words to clothe your thoughts as if for a festival. Will you not stop this meaningless sugaring of me, and speak to me in such a way that for a while I can cease cursing the fate that made me a woman?"

He prepared a deft answer. Then, watching her, he decided against it. If nothing else, impersonal talk was safest when both of them were so taut. "Na Violante's wish is mine," he said. "But I pray you, stop me when I grow tedious. Well, you know we marched up the peninsula—"

As his narrative progressed, he lost the feeling of imminent explosion. Instead, he found himself almost back in the war, so vividly did it come back to him. This was not like the few blunt sentences he could offer Djansha, who did not know a mangonel from a supply train and to whom a map was a sorcerer's tool. Violante was transformed, scarcely female at all, blood-eager and vengeful but not the termagant she often was. Rather, she could have been a high-born Catalan boy who had never seen war and was wild to do so. She interrupted with many questions, but they were keen ones, asking knowledgeably why this was done and that was omitted. He was often embarrassed at being unable to tell her. In such cases, she became the woman again, briefly and with quicksilver ease, leading him on toward things he had witnessed himself. She made him describe his own part in the battle, blow by blow. There his tale became a romance. A man in combat seldom knew what he did. He struck out at strange faces, uncertain most times if he even bit flesh; afterward he remembered only a huge confusion. Before such an audience, however, Lucas felt obliged to paint the truth in brighter colors.

"Ah," she said at last, "royal, royal! Would my father had been there!"

"He was a knight?"

She nodded. Her gaze went beyond him. As she spoke, the fierceness drained from body and voice, until nothing remained except love.

"Yes. A captain among men. Do you know, my earliest memory is of him about to ride forth? He was all in armor, it shone like the sun. His helmet was on his saddlebow. The plumes tickled my legs as my mother handed me up to him. He raised me high, laughing. . . . I remember too when he came back. That was between sext and nones. He had not stopped for siesta. I heard the clatter at the gates, through the courtyard. I left my bed and drew the curtains from the window. And there was my father. That time he wore a pourpoint merely, but he had thrown a gallant cloak over it, all blue and gold. He saw me in the upper window, and waved his bonnet and cried, 'Hallo, there, my darling, I've brought you home a victory!' "

She fell silent. Lucas heard the stablehands guffaw behind the willows, and was angry at them. Na Violante did not appear to notice. She regarded the hands folded in her lap. They grew tense again. One tear, caught in her lashes, flung back a tiny point of sunlight.

"After he died," she whispered, "the castle was so empty."

"I have gathered my lady was wedded young," ventured Lucas, hoping to turn her from so disconcertingly swift a sorrow.

"Anything to escape!" she burst out. "You know not what it is to be a well-born girl in Aragon . . . not unless you've spent a few years in an oubliette."

After a while, she drew a long breath and said calmly—coldly, almost, and looking straight ahead—"En Riambaldo Tari was not a bad man. He was brave. Dull, perhaps, but who could match my father? Since God has not seen fit to give me children, I persuaded my husband to take me with him when he went off to the Sicilian War. Thence we came to Constantinople with the Grand Company."

"A pity he was slain," said Lucas.

"Last year." Her tone was flat. She did not stir. "Late last year. A Greek who drew a knife. Asberto Cornel was there, too. He avenged my husband at once. He had long been a good friend to us. Do you understand that? I want you to understand it. I know I've shocked many, by putting myself under his—his protection. So soon after Riambaldo's death, too. But Riambaldo—Asberto was his friend, his avenger. Now he is my protector. We cannot wed. Asberto has a wife in Aragon. But together we've bought masses for Riambaldo's repose, burned candles, said prayers. What more can we do? He's dead. He's with God. I am not wanton, Lucas. I call my father in St. Michael's host to witness I am not wanton!"

"I never believed that, my lady," said Lucas.

He lied. It was common knowledge that she had had several lovers, including Asberto, while her husband still lived. And yet he saw how white she had gone. Her nails dug deep into her palms. She was not speaking of light matters.

She rose. "I thank you for your courtesy, Maestre," she said, a little unevenly. "I must go now. Asberto will be awakening."

She hurried back into the house.

CHAPTER VIII

After their second victory, the Catalans were in full
control of the Thracian shore of the Propontis. The
Imperial armies garrisoned Adrianople and the
capital, but did not venture beyond sight of those
walls. The invaders harried elsewhere and up to the
very gates. One Almúgavare even entered Constantinople afoot, with no more following than his two
sons. They found a pair of Genoese merchants
shooting quail in a garden of the Emperor's, brought
them back to Gallipoli and got three thousand gold
hyperpera as ransom. When that exploit was announced to the Grand Company, the chortlings
reached heaven.

"I must go out myself, before all the booty has
been taken," declared En Jaime.

"I've been thinking about that," Lucas answered.
"You said a few days ago you'd not put burning
splints under the nails of peasants to learn where
they've hidden a few coins."

En Jaime's features darkened. "True," he said.

Both of them skirted the fact this was happening
daily. Lucas hastened on: "I've inquired among
prisoners, and even more among Greeks disgusted

118

with their own government and thus willing to help us. I believe a few bold men might carry out a deed worthy of themselves, and win a reward in proportion." He smiled. "Also, it would make a merry tale afterward."

"Let me hear." En Jaime tugged his beard. At first he said, "You've gone mad!" Lucas talked further. Then he said, "A good idea in principle, but the odds are so much against us—" Lucas resorted to oratory. At last he said, "Yes, by the sword of St. George!"

Lucas went down to the harbor. There were still only a few craft at the docks, but he found a good-sized boat, a leny whose lugsail could drive it at a fair clip. He had no trouble recruiting some mariners to help, even though he proposed to go up the whole Sea of Marmora with a skeletal force. They would not embark until the wind favored them, he promised, and would thus not have to row very much.

On the day chosen, En Jaime led a small band of horsemen out of Gallipoli toward Constantinople. Lucas was so favored by the weather that he reached the rendezvous agreed on in little more than two days and a night. It was a fishing hamlet some miles from New Rome. He cast anchor. A boat rowed out to see what he was. He waved his sword. "Franks!" he shouted. The fisherman backed water and fled. Presently the whole population of the settlement streamed inland.

"Will they not bring the Emperor's men down on us?" worried a sailor.

"They would in any honorable country," snorted Lucas. "But Andronicus and his soldiers aren't about to risk their precious hides fighting on behalf of mere subjects. Come, we may as well make ourselves comfortable under a roof.''

When the knights arrived, they found the crew taking their ease in the fisher cottages. "Well," laughed Lucas, "you dawdled enough, my friends. Did you find a tavern on the way?"

Asberto Cornel bridled. "I've had enough of your insolence!''

"Be calm," said En Jaime. "He's only jesting." To Lucas: "Ah, this was as easy a ride as I've ever had. Good roads, and no sooner were we spied than all ran away from us. Saints have mercy, we were so few that two score peasants with flails could have destroyed us. And yet they ran, even those who bore weapons. Are they men at all?''

"The word has gotten about," said Lucas, "that Catalans are ten feet high, with iron skins and fiery breath, and that they eat soldiers for dinner.'' Earnestness descended momentarily on him. "I think they lack leadership here, En Jaime, and a reason to fight, rather than true manhood. What is this Empire that anyone should die for it? Should even live for it? How can there be courage without devotion, or loyalty to masters who offer nothing but oppression?''

Asberto looked still more disgusted. Before he could complain at such maundering, the headiness of the scheme took Lucas back. He pointed at the beached leny and said, "Well, gentles, do you want supper now, or shall we take refreshment in Pera?''

They did not tarry long. Leaving four disconsolate men—chosen by lot—to guard the horses, the rest floated the leny and scrambled aboard. Lucas had cheap mantles ready, to hide armor. Theirs might have been any boat, rowing up the Bosporus on a casual errand. There was considerable water traffic at this end of the sea.

Constantinople rose clifflike in the sunset, but Lucas continued on to the suburb of Pera—a wealthy place, where many foreign merchants dwelt and where the Byzantine overlords owned much property. Just about eventide, the boat docked. Lucas' line of Greek banter and swearing had given the harbor guard no reason to mistrust this late arrival.

The Catalans crossed the gangplank and threw off their disguise. For one horrible instant, the watch saw mailed men confront them, grinning faces, long Frankish swords. Then the cry rang out: *"Aragon! Aragon!"* The watch dropped their weapons and bolted.

Up into Pera, Lucas led his troop. The intelligence from the Greeks he had questioned was good. He almost could have made his way blind through this town, though he had never been here before. In a few minutes, they stood in front of an uncommonly sumptuous house. A sailor threw a grapnel over the garden wall, swarmed up the rope and released the portals from within. By that time, the gatekeeper had fled to warn the dinner party within the mansion. But he was too late. The Catalans entered behind him.

Lucas looked over the throng with a calculating eye. Everyone here was rich; he wanted the richest for himself. Quickly he decided that the fat middle-aged Byzantine in green silk was a high noble. He

121

thrust through the crowd and clapped hands on the man.

"You belong to me," he said cheerfully. "Come."

"You wretch!" stormed the other. "This will cost you your—" Lucas prodded him delicately in the stomach with a sword point. He subsided into red-faced gobbling.

Lucas gave him a sack. "Now come," he repeated. "You're old enough to labor for your keep, Kyrios. I want this, and this, and this." His blade flicked around to point out articles of gold and silver. "You, there, give me those rings you're wearing. Ah, and I'll have your purse, my friend over yonder behind the couch. Toss it here, then you may play hide-and-seek as much as your heart desires. . . . Let's look in the next room. Forward march!"

The raiders needed but little time to fill the sacks their prisoners carried. En Jaime took a lamp from its chains and led the way out. Night had fallen. The empty roads echoed to their boots. Faintly, through the twisted streets, they heard a trumpet and the shouts of men.

"The garrison's gotten the news," said Asberto. "They'll be on our necks in two Aves. I told you we should have cut down everyone in that house."

"It would have taken longer to play the butcher, and made more noise, than simply helping ourselves," said Lucas. His exultation was wearing a trifle thin, his mouth felt dry and his pulse hammered. He didn't want that. He wanted adventure. When he saw light seep from the cracks in a door and heard voices, he stopped. "Hold! I'm as thirsty as a German herring. And here's a tavern."

"What?" choked En Jaime. "Have your senses departed?"

"That's what you asked me when first I broached this plan." Lucas opened the door and stepped through, prodding his captive along. Silence took hold of the smoky room. Men gaped at the armed newcomers. One cup crashed to the floor, but nobody stirred.

Lucas swung his sword so it whistled, thumping the flat of it on a table. "Landlord!" he shouted. "What sort of place is this? Wine!"

Shaking, the boniface came forth with leather bottles. Lucas stuck his sword in a bench and raised the skin. "Wine for everyone!" he ordered. "Each man a bottle! Throw 'em out—on the table there—so! Now, valiant friends, I trust you'll drink with me?"

Still they regarded him with stunned expressions. A few moved, mouse cautious. Lucas waved his wineskin. "What sort of courtesy do they teach you here? Hoist bottles, I say! Open your mouths— squeeze—squirt the juice down your gullets! A toast with me: to the Lord King of Aragon!"

They drank. Lucas flung some coins on the floor. "There, innkeeper, the score and a bit over. Take the money without fear. I came by it as honestly as the former owner. Now, my friends, goodnight. Sweet angels guard your dreams." He drew his sword from the bench and strode back to the door, waving the steel in salute. "Until we meet again!"

The childish demonstration had returned his gaiety to him. The watch could now be heard very close, but none of the Catalans protested further. A reproach to Lucas would have been an admission that they feared those Greeks.

The boat waited untouched. They clattered aboard, tripping over the thwarts and cursing the gloom. Lucas called for help, emptied three barrels of oil over the side, and pitched a lamp when the leny was clear. Fire sprang up among the docked ships. The light painted his companions' faces Hell color.

"That'll delay them awhile. They can sit down to warm their feet and roast chestnuts while they brag how they repulsed us."

"We've a long way home yet," warned someone.

"Oh, but we have En Berenguer de Entenza's mistake to guide us. We'll not go far by water. Row, lads!"

They went swiftly, driven by the knowledge that warcraft would soon be out in search of them. Well before midnight, they were back at the hamlet. They loaded treasure and prisoners onto the extra horses and started home—overland.

That was a joyful trip. Lucas spent much of the time bargaining with his aristocrat prisoner. They settled on the ransom and despatched a messenger. Suddenly Lucas was wealthy.

He determined to give a feast. By now, the efforts of such conscientious officers as En Ramon Muntaner had restored some order. Word of the situation had gone abroad and merchants were beginning to arrive at Gallipoli harbor with grain and other supplies. The Catalans had good means of payment—Greek slaves for the Turkish traders, inanimate loot for the Christians. They expected business to grow brisk in the next several weeks. They felt able to live lavishly.

Djansha still maintained Lucas' apartment, but he set about finding a house of his own, and native servants. Meanwhile, he used En Jaime's dining chamber for his banquet. A delicate parade of courses awaited the knights, nobles, and their ladies; musicians had been hired to play as the feast progressed; there was no limit to wines of good vintage. Looking about the colorfully clad assemblage, listening to spirited conversation and to compliments both fulsome and blunt, Lucas thought how fortunate he was. This was something else than being astray in the windy world.

"A few more such exploits, Maestre, and we'll have no choice but to make you a knight," said Muntaner.

"If he's not made himself a duke first," said En Jaime, somewhat drunkenly. "This youngster has verve, I tell you. I knew it the first hour we met."

"Ah, yes, be a duke," purred the high-born Byzantine mistress of one officer. "You'd keep a cheerful court, I'll wager. No vinegar decorum where you are."

A hand touched his shoulder. He looked up into Na Violante's flushed countenance. She leaned against his chair, smiled down at him, and ran her fingers through his locks. "He'll not be a nobleman," she said. "What, and grow roots like any tree? No, our friend here is too good for that."

Her words were a little blurred with the wine that had also brightened her eyes and moistened the full red mouth. He stopped himself just short of throwing an arm around her waist and dragging her down on his lap. "I'd ask you to spare my modesty," he said, "but hearing such words from such a vision is far too great a pleasure to let any puling virtue get in the way."

"Indeed?" she murmured, and leaned forward. He smelt her breath, musky with the grape. When he turned his head sideways, her lips were near his and the deep white cleft of her bosom was before him. "Pray, what other virtues would Maestre Lucas consider mere obstacles in the path of what other pleasures?"

He didn't think it would be wise to answer, though the drink buzzed in his own brain. She regarded him through drooping lashes. Her smile was not quite like the ones of their past teasing.

"Yes," she said, "you are too good to become a *rich hom*. Would that have suited Lancelot, Amadis, Ogier? Though I believe, myself, you are Huon of Bordeaux, he who became a lord in France." She felt his tunic. "If I looked closely, I might see a little dust of Faerie clinging to this. Like tiny stars."

Asberto Cornel had gone out a few minutes ago. Now, beyond Violante's bare plump shoulder, Lucas saw him reenter. He froze in the doorway. Even by candlelight, Lucas discerned the redness and the fury which mounted in him.

Swiftly, he covered the length of the room. The others paid no heed until he stood looking down on his host. His fists were jammed against his hips, doubled so tightly the knuckles stood bloodless.

Violante straightened. The color left her cheeks. In the silence which began to fall, flute and harp shrilled idiotically.

"Before God," said Asberto. The sound exploded against the farther wall. "Were I not a guest here, you would be dead this moment."

En Jaime half rose from his chair. "Nasberto," he warned.

"Yes. Yes." The lesser knight continued to stare at Lucas. He swayed a little on his feet. He had been drinking heavily and joylessly all evening. "Peace among us," he said. "For now. Oh, yes. Come, Violante, bid these people goodnight. We must leave."

Her lips made the word of denial, but no voice came out.

"Come, you filthy harlot!" screamed Asberto.

Lucas got to his feet. "Micer, that's not the way to address a lady."

"I should kill you, Asberto," said Violante, syllable by syllable. "I should have killed you long ago."

The Catalan snatched her wrist. She raked the nails of her free hand across his arm. Blood oozed in the scratches. He didn't seem to notice. The noise of his breathing filled the room.

"Nasberto, are you possessed?" demanded Muntaner. "I beg you, no, I order you—"

"She's mine!" Cornel shouted at them all. "My concern alone! Is she not? Who'll deny it? Who'll claim rights over her? Is she not my whore?"

Violante struck him across the mouth. Her rings cut. His grip on her wrist tightened. She cursed in a whisper. He let her go and cracked his palm against her face so she staggered.

"Well?" he rasped. The blood coursing into his beard was somehow less meaningful than the sweat which stained his doublet and ran down his countenance. "There she is. She's no slave, I admit. She may appeal to any of you gentles if she wishes."

Rarely had Lucas heard so much pain.

Violante touched the bruises already beginning to show on arm and cheek. The light glittered off half-shed tears, turning her eyes blank. As if guiding itself, Lucas' hand reached toward her.

Asberto's tone became merely a snarl again. "There they are, slut," he said to the woman. "Choose any of them. Go with him. You're free to do so. If you come with me, you'll taste my cane on your back once more."

"Signora—" began Lucas.

She didn't seem to hear. Asberto spat on the floor, whistled for her, and went out. She followed him.

CHAPTER IX

Lucas might have hazarded action, for Violante's image kept him sleepless all that night. But the next morning, heat in his skin and an evil flavor on his tongue showed that more than wine had attacked him. By afternoon he lay abed, and that evening he passed into delirium.

It stretched on, endless as damnation. Now and then he was aware of Djansha holding him in her arms and wiping the greasy moisture off him. Twice he glimpsed En Jaime's lean anxious visage. But they were dim, unreal visions, seen through a waterfall that roared. He lost them quickly among skewed pagodas, where his mother fled singing from a fat man who hurled his teeth at her. The sky was red. When it began to press inward, he saw that it was made of iron and the red was its fiery glow as St. God hammered on it with a hammer as heavy as the world. The sky closed around his skull and he shrieked.

An eon after Judgment Day, the first morning light grayed the windows. Lucas opened his eyes. With thin clarity he saw Djansha thrust a Catalan chirurgeon out the door. She had a dagger in her hand and was wild enough to frighten any man; could this be his little Circassian? "No!" she yelled. "You will not bleed him! I know what he needs! Go before I kill you!" She slammed and bolted the door. Lucas watched her stoke the brazier, cut the throat of a white cock, and begin some heathen chant. He smiled with a tender kind of exhaustion and drifted asleep.

Whether or not her witchcraft saved him, he never knew. He told the saints he was not responsible, having been helpless at the time, but would nonetheless light many candles when he recovered. That, however, took a weary pair of weeks. Even after the last fever was gone, he seemed bonelessly feeble.

En Jaime was often in to visit him, which greatly relieved the tedium. Others came too, but they sat about, uncomfortable, and groped for words. "By Heaven, Maestre, you're looking better. Indeed you are. The rest of us, we're all fine so far, God willing. If I had a mistress as handsome as yours to tend me, I think I might get sick, too. Haw. Well, you're looking better. Take care of yourself. I, ah, I'd best be going. Work to do. Take care of yourself."

En Jaime crossed one long, black-hosed shank over the other, leaned back, and asked how the astrologic learning of the Saracens in Asia differed from that he had encountered in Spain.

Toward the end of Lucas' convalescence, the *rich hom* said, almost diffidently, "I fear I must desert you for a space. But you should be hale again when we return."

"We?" Lucas sat upright. His joints felt stiff and

painful from long motionless. "The whole Company?"

"The major part, anyhow. Do you know the cities Rhedestos and Panidos? They lie on the shore, close to each other, halfway between Gallipoli and Constantinople. Well, the Council has decided to seize them. A much overdue task, but our folks were too occupied with gathering the first fruits of victory at Apros. Now at last we'll march on those towns. The day after tomorrow."

"Oh, by all the stinking imps in Hell!" groaned Lucas. "Here I lie!"

"You'll not miss any glory, I assure you. Neither place is well defended at all. What soldiers they have will likely escape by sea when first we arrive. As for the booty, I've arranged that you shall be considered assigned to the garrison here and thus entitled to a share."

Djansha entered, dropping on one knee to offer a tray with wine and fresh cakes. The Catalan waved her aside. "No, thank you, my dear. I must be gone." As Lucas gave him a look of disappointed inquiry: "There's always plaguey much to do, preparing for even as short and easy an expedition as this. The chief reason we go at all, besides plunder, is that Rhedestos is far better located for foraging than Gallipoli. Rocafort wishes to move our headquarters thither." His brows drew downward. For a heartbeat, his expression was so grim that the girl shrank from him. "Also Rhedestos is the city where our envoys to Andronicus were murdered. Hung up in the shambles like beeves! That abomination has yet to be cleansed. . . . Well, Lucas, good day. I'll look in

131

again tomorrow. God heal you quickly."

When he was gone, Djansha adjusted Lucas' pillows, gave him the tray, and sat on the edge of the bed combing his hair. "You grow stronger each hour, my lord," she consoled him. "No matter if you cannot be on this campaign. En Jaime himself said it will be too easy to add honor to your name. Did he not? And you know these Franks by now. When they say a task is easy, believe them! Most days, they cannot swat a mosquito without boasting of its ancient Saracen lineage and the desperate battle it gave them."

She spoke so demurely that he needed a little time to be startled. Then he remembered how she had driven the chirurgeon hence, and wondered if any human being ever really knew another. He mumbled asininely, "These are good cakes. Have you made them yourself?"

She blushed with pleasure. "Yes, my lord. They are very much like those baked among the Adygei for big feasts. I had to make some changes. Some herbs I could not find, no matter how I searched the fields outside this town. And the price of honey would freeze a bonfire. I haggled for I know not how long with a Turk trader, down near the ships, but—Well, at least when I had the honey I was free to call him a bleary old pig." She giggled. "If only you could have seen him go Emperor purple! It would have refreshed you so much. But my lord is not interested in woman-doings. I have learned a new song. New for myself, I mean. Would you like to hear?"

She danced across the room, which she had filled

with blossoms and fragrant leaves. Lucas decided she must have made a special effort, day after day in the hours while he slept, to improve her Venetian. Today she wore a plain white smock, sashed at the waist, her legs bare beneath and her hair flowing free above: a liberty of dress possible only to wantons and secluded concubines. But she had not been very secluded of late, he thought. She had braved the city again and again, even gone beyond the walls, to fetch what she believed he needed.

And yet—

"I've never seen you so happy before," he said.

She threw him a shy glance across the one-stringed Asiatic harp she played. "I am helping my lord recover. And also, I am beginning to think—" She stopped, coloring still more deeply. "No. Best I speak no more of that until I am sure." Her voice trilled forth in a ballad he had once remarked he liked.

Restless and irritable, he paid scant heed. His attention went out the window, toward sunlight and birdsong. Distantly he heard a trumpet blown. Merciful Lord Jesus, how time dragged!

A couple of days afterward, he heard the Catalan Company depart: drums, horns, boots, hoofs, metal and leather. By then he could totter about, a few more hours each attempt. He blasphemed his fate in every language he recalled. Had they waited a week, he could have gone along!

Suddenly he broke off.

"My lord appears to have had a happier thought," said Djansha.

"Well . . . yes," he replied, but told her nothing else.

The next morning he had her summon a barber to shave him and trim his hair. Then he ordered a good suit of garments laid out. "I'll walk about today," he explained. "I feel strong enough."

"Best you lean on me," she said anxiously.

"No! You are to stay here! I'm well able to get about alone. Do you understand?" As her mouth quivered, he realized he had shouted. Contrite, he said, "Forgive me. I'll take a stick if you wish. But I must try my own unaided legs sometime, must I not?"

She glowed at him like a small sun.

Actually, he felt no need of the cane. The idea in him lent unexpected strength. He studied himself in a mirror. He had lost flesh, the bones of his face stood out clearly, but they were good bones, he reassured himself. Flinging a forest-green cloak across one shoulder of his cloth-of-gold tunic, he waved Djansha a cherry farewell and sauntered down the corridor.

The house seemed bare with En Jaime and his men gone. A few servants scuttered about. Lucas halted one. "Ah . . . tell me," he said with a poor attempt at casualness, "is Nasberto Cornel about?"

"No, the noble knight Cornel is gone with the great Lord de Caza. I thank the good saints that Despotes Greco has won back his health."

"The devil you do," said Lucas, but tossed his informant a coin and hummed a tune as he continued.

At the door of Asberto's suite he paused. Was this honorable when the man was gone to war—? He

134

recollected Violante leaning across his chair. His pulse grew loud. Satan might have all these niggling Catalonian niceties! In no case did an animal like Cornel merit them. Nor did he mean to force the woman. He was paying her a social call, and if something else came of that, she had free will to choose her actions.

He knocked for a good five minutes.

"Belly of Bachus!" he said at last, disgusted, and hobbled out into the garden. There he found a maidservant who told him what he suspected. Despoina Violante had accompanied her noble protector to Rhedestos. A number of ladies had done so, in fact, for the journey was short and the attack would afford an entertaining spectacle, at a discreet distance. . . . Once, beside this fountain, Violante had wished, through her teeth, that she were a man. Of course she had gone to Rhedestos.

Lucas slept badly that night. He woke with a decision. "I'm going after the army," he said.

"No!" gasped Djansha.

"Be still." His coldness shut her mouth. "Prepare food and clothes for me. Fetch my groom that I may give him orders."

After an hour she dared ask, "Is there anything my lord must do there, that could not wait until he is quite himself again?"

"I'm strong enough now, God smite it!"

"Well . . . may I come, too? I will be no trouble, I swear; and if anything should go wrong—"

"No. Stay here." Presently Lucas comprehended her hurt enough to say, rather impatiently: "I'm sorry. I can't tell you my business. You're very good to be so concerned. But after all, I am old enough to look out for myself, eh? I'll be back in a few days. You need a rest, girl. Be glad of this chance."

Her farewell kiss the next day was so tremblingly amorous that he was tempted to stay. However, that would make him appear a fool.

Especially since he had no good reason, even in his own mind, to go. He could think of nothing he might accomplish in Rhedestos. He simply could not keep away.

Leave for the jaunt had easily been cajoled out of the garrison captain. Accompanied by a pair of mounted Almúgavares, Lucas rode forth at noon. By dusk he was worn out, but slept all the better and woke up ready to fight elephants. The following day's ride, at a leisured pace under sunny breezes, was pure, healing joy. Early the third afternoon, they went by Panidos. A forlorn Imperial standard on the battlements showed that the Catalans had not yet found time to capture it. They pushed on to Rhedestos.

Tents and wagons formed an extensive camp some distance from the latter town. Pennants fluttered jauntily through wind-whipped smoke and dust; folk swarmed about. The city gates stood open, with the Latin flag of St. George above. Carts trundled forth, toward the camp. So this place had fallen, evidently with little or no resistance, and was now being ransacked. . . . The hills ran green with grass and orchard, yellow with ripening grain, down to a sea which glittered and danced.

"Well, Maestre, where shall we report?" asked an Almúgavare.

Lucas reined in his horse. It curvetted, restless as himself. "To En Jaime, I suppose," he said absently, "In the camp yonder."

"Your pardon, Maestre, but he's more like to be in the town till nightfall."

"Um-m-m . . . yes . . . so he is, isn't he? Let's seek him there, then."

Time enough, Lucas told himself through a thick pounding, time enough to find Violante when less important affairs had been set in order. He might even pick up some gem today, keep it illicitly for himself, and give it to her with a suitable flourish when—"Hoy! Gee-up, there!"

They galloped to the portal, passed a cart loaded with the contents of some Orthodox church, avoided a party of drunken men-at-arms, and clattered into Rhedestos.

The first thing Lucas noticed was the smell. It hung heavy, sickeningly sweet, with gangrenous undertones, denser for each yard he advanced. The houses stood blind along streets where the only traffic was the looting squads. When had he ever seen so many flies in such fat black clouds?

"Look there," pointed one of his Almúgavares. "I hope the lads got some use out of 'em first."

Lucas looked in the direction indicated. Half a dozen women lay sprawled in an alley mouth. They had been dead for two or three days. He thought lances had killed them, but he couldn't be sure.

Not far beyond were some dead infants. Their skulls had been dashed against a wall.

The old, sick, helpless anger rose within Lucas. "Have the Mongols come?" he asked.

"I see the promise to avenge our envoys was not idle," said his other attendant with satisfaction.

"Would I could have helped," said the companion. He guided his horse directly over a beheaded man. Bones crunched.

A gang of Almúgavares came around a corner, with one *jinete* leading. They were quite drunk, and were herding along some threescore children. The children were in rags; dirt matted in their hair, running sores covered their legs, thirst had crusted their lips. Some could still cry, most stumbled ahead as if blind. The oldest was perhaps thirteen.

Lucas reined to a halt so hard that his mount reared. "What're you doing?" he snapped.

The *jinete* waved his sword. "Found these little vermin here and there, hiding, after the executions were finished," he answered cheerily. "We'll save 'em for the Turkish market. We're off now to make eunuchs of the boys. Come along if you'd like some sport."

Lucas struck spurs into his horse.

Afterward, he never remembered very well what else he saw. But when he entered the marketplace, he heard thunder in his head.

The rest of the ride was forever a blur to him. He knew in a far-off way that he fled from the town, vomiting as he went. Later he was in camp, afoot. He had discarded his soiled upper garments someplace, and wore merely breeches and hose. And sword. He clutched the hilt of his sword as if to keep it from jumping out of the scabbard.

He must have asked his way, though he could not recall having done so. He staggered weeping among tents, carts, cookfires, soldiers who tended armor and horses, who sat about laughing and drinking. He saw their women and older children, their Byzantine she-captives bruised and stunned and passed from hand to hand, cattle, dogs, priests who had lately said a mass of thanksgiving. . . . In all that roil, no one troubled to question him. His half-nakedness shocked the Easterners but not the Latins; as for his distress, maybe the poor devil had lost a brother to some lousy Greek.

And so in the end Lucas found Asberto's tent.

Violante stepped forth when he called her name. She wore a robe of white silk, loose about her hips, open in the front; her hair was tumbled, and she blinked sleep from her eyes. They must have begun their siesta early today in this tent. "What in the blessed world—?" she said.

Lucas sank to his knees and embraced her. "O God, God, God!" he rattled. "Has *my* army done this?"

She swayed back, alarmed. His grip was too strong for her to break. He buried his face against her and shuddered.

"Help me, Violante!"

Slowly, then, her hands moved forward until they lay on his head. "Are you ill?" she breathed. "They told me you had a fever. Have you come here in its ravings?"

"I thought I was a hardy man," he whimpered. "I've killed. I've seen folk die and rot. I've witnessed torture. I've watched slaves driven to market. Often. . . . Violante, my lady, my lady, have I fallen among fiends out of Hell?"

139

Awkwardly, frightened of the fit upon him, she rumpled his hair. The tent immediately before this one, and the side flaps of the entrance, screened off all but passing glimpses of the camp. Talk, footfalls, fire-crackle, wagon-creak, clang and clash and thud, seemed remote. "Lucas, let me go," she said urgently. "Asberto's asleep in there. You'll wake him—"

Lucas clasped her so hard that she bit her lip with pain. "They were hanging in the marketplace!" he sobbed. "Everywhere flies and crows. The smell! Does God Himself dare count how many there were?"

"Let me go!"

"Men and women and children! Quartered! Hung up on hooks in the marketplace! A whole townful of them! Why has the sun not turned black?"

"For all the saints' sake, be not such a weak-livered woman!" she rebuked. "Have you never heard what was done to our own ambassadors in this city?"

"But the small children—"

"Let me go, you wretch! Let me go or—Asberto! No, Asberto! He's sick! He knows not what he's doing!"

The knight's boot smashed against Lucas' ribs.

He fell at Violante's feet, in a jaggedness of pain. His tears blurred her, so that she towered above him like some pagan idol, the Great Mother worshipped among remote Asiatic tribes . . . yes, he had been seeking his mother, as if once again he were a little boy who had put a bare foot into something sticky on the beach, and looked down to see a rotten corpse washed ashore. . . . "Get up!" grated

Asberto. "Get you hence!"

Lucas focused on the pocked, broken countenance. Asberto had been napping in his clothes. A sword was in his hand. As he rose, a black peace descended upon Lucas.

"I daresay you aided that butchery," he said without tone.

"Go, I say! Or Satan eat me if I don't run you through!" A fury beyond all reason shook the Catalan's voice.

Lucas spat in his face.

Asberto roared. His steel whipped in a long slanting cut toward Lucas' neck. Violante backed against the tent.

Lucas had already drawn. He parried the blow. Metal belled. He hardly felt the shock. Bouncing aside, he released his opponent's weapon. Asberto lurched foward, off balance. Lucas cut him in the leg.

Asberto recovered himself with trained speed. The swords whirred, clashed, leaped and thrust and struck. A sweep of the Catalan's edge sheared down one tent flap. Lucas lunged. Asberto reacted fast enough to save his breast from the point, but his left shoulder was gashed open.

He counterattacked with a hail of blows. It was as if he had three swords in his hand. Lucas gave ground, warding himself, coldly alert for a chance to kill. As they emerged in the open, he saw Violante again. She had gotten back her color and stood with fists clenched, lips parted, eyes ashine.

Now that the fight was visible to all the camp,

141

men shouted and hurried to intervene. But only a suicide would have gone between those two. Steel bounded, shrieked and rang. The crowd became spectators. Soon they were cheering.

Asberto's flail tactics drove Lucas backward. *Whsssh, clang!* At the edge of vision, the latter discerned a solid wall of soldiers and camp followers. He could retreat no farther.

Well, then . . . God send the right!

His blade blazed. It smote Asberto's so that the knight's grip trembled. Reckless of cuts, Lucas slid his weapon along the other until he saw a steel x centered on his enemy's heart. At once, he withdrew his own pressure and fell to one knee. The Catalan glaive flashed an inch above his head. He thrust upward and felt a somehow bulky impact.

The maneuver was not quite successful. Asberto was not skewered under the breastbone and up through the lungs. The steel pierced him higher, and a rib deflected the point. Even so, blood spurted forth as Lucas withdrew.

Asberto dropped his sword. He turned gray. "Holy Mother of God . . . pray for me," he choked, and went on all fours.

Lucas stood aside, panting.

Chaos broke loose. A dozen men engulfed Asberto, each with his own idea of helpfulness. A dozen others moved in upon Lucas. He swung his reddened sword and they milled back. He heard some of their words, through all the babble. "In the name of mercy, Micer. . . . Send for an officer . . . a priest. . . . Brawl. . . . Affray between gentlemen. . . ."

Violante was at his side. Her face burned. She breathed as if she had run a long way. But never had Lucas heard greater haughtiness than hers:

"Take Cornel away. Take him to what help he can use, priest or leech. Don't stand there! Go! This was an honest duel and no affair of you peasants!"

"But my lady—" bleated an *adalid* of Almúgavares.

"Silence!" she commanded. "Nasberto nor I will thank you for meddling in his quarrels. We'll see the proper authorities about this in our own good time. I know you well, Perico. And I say, woe betide you if any oafs come interfering!"

"But my lady—" The wild man rolled his eyes as if seeking an escape.

"Perico, I make you responsible for keeping everyone away from here. You'll rue it if you fail. Enough!"

She took Lucas' arm.

Mindlessly, he followed her back into the tent. It was large, well supplied with camp furniture. A hot yellow light filtered through its canvas. She dropped the remaining flap across its entrace, plucked the sword from his unresisting fingers, laid it next to the pallet and seized him at the waist. Her nearness rushed over him.

"Oh, Lucas," she said, "know what you did?"

Out of the crazy satisfaction in him (crazy, for how had he avenged those people whom he never saw alive?) he answered, "Yes. I've done what was needful. Nag me not about trouble I may have caused myself."

"Enough of that," she said with a flick of scorn.

"You have En Jaime's favor. My own influence is not so slight, either. And the laws of honor—well, they must either agree you are of gentle standing, and therefore right to challenge a man who kicked you; or admit that someone base-born defeated a Catalan knight. Which they never would do." The gladness leaped forth: "He was among the most famous warriors in the Company. I didn't think another man alive could best him. And then, that it should be you—oh, all my sins must be atoned for, if this can happen!"

She threw her arms around his neck and pulled him down onto the pallet.

Chapter X

En Jaime looked stern, but when Lucas remained impenitent, standing with folded arms and a one-sided smile, the *rich hom* became merely serious.

"Well," he said, "let's talk no more, then, of rights and wrongs in the matter. I suppose it is indeed to your credit as a Christian man, if what you saw in the marketplace unhinged your reason for a time. An ugly business. I hope you know it began without clear orders. A few knights and priests, including myself, tried to halt the massacre, but the troops were out for blood. We could do nothing which would not have provoked a mutiny. And should we have done that for the sake of some worthless schismatical Greeks?"

My mother was a Candian Greek, Lucas thought, and her uncle who led me into Homer's world was an Orthodox monk.

But that was not a very good retort. He said instead: "Could they not even spare the children?"

"God's wrath is terrible, Lucas."

"I fear I've forgotten most Holy Writ, but—" With calculated malice: "Is there not a text which

145

says, *Whoso shall offend one of these little ones which believe in me, it were better for him that a millstone were hanged about his neck and that he were drowned in the depth of the sea—?"*

Lucas had not expected En Jaime to recoil so violently. "Have done, you devil!" the Catalan shouted.

He quickly composed himself. "There are so many texts," he said. "Who but the saints have read them aright? You know not how often I've asked to know God's will, and been unanswered. We sinners have no other guidance vouchsafed us than Church and King. Have we? Is not our duty as soldiers the best service we, who are not saints, can render to God?"

Lucas' virulence was lost in embarrassment. He was not truly pious, and he winced at such blundering earnestness in others. Once, when he was En Jaime's servant, he had found a scourge clotted with old blood at the bottom of his master's trunk. It took him a long time to realize that the knight kept it for himself.

The return to worldly matters was a relief. "If you were clearly of gentle rank," said En Jaime, "there'd be no question but that there were faults on both sides, leading to an affair of honor. In all events, you're no simple commoner who must be punished for assaulting a cavalier. Confound it, Lucas, you aren't anything! Neither in birth nor nation nor way of thinking. Does anyone alive understand you? Do you understand yourself?" He shrugged. "Enough. I've worked like a hero this day and night on your behalf, since Na Violante first informed me of the duel. I would not speak to you before I could say that something clear-cut had been achieved, that you would hang or go free. And where were you in all that time? Not on your knees in the chapel tent, I know!''

Lucas' grin became shamelessly wide. It was hard to believe that yesterday he had been on the point of quitting the Grand Company. Violante had ways to change a man's decisions. He was, at least, no longer in a hurry to go.

(Down under the surface was darkness, and shapes not of earth flitted quietly from cavern to reef to ancient wreck. For one instant, awareness rose toward sunlight. *I am in no hurry to go. But I no longer think of these as my newly won countrymen.* Frightened, the shape dove down out of sight before its strangeness was fully seen.)

''I know he's a trusty man of yours, En Jaime,'' said Lucas, ''but except for whatever trouble this has caused you, I don't think the injuring of Cornel requires any penance.''

''Oh, there was trouble in surfeit.'' En Jaime tugged his beard nervously. ''Lucas, a lord must stand by his men. Had Asberto died, I could not, in honor, have striven to protect you from the consequences. By God's mercy, though, he'll evidently recover. Come, we must see him now.''

Lucas grimaced, but followed him out of the tent and across the camp to another.

En Jaime went inside. Lucas heard an oath as first answer to the nobleman's words; but little by little Asberto was soothed, until En Jaime could summon Lucas within.

The wounded knight sat up on a pallet, leaning

against a plank. He was very pale, which heightened his uncomeliness, but the clean bandages on his hairy breast showed that bleeding had stopped. The surgeon had told En Jaime that it did not look as if there would be much inflammation. Since that killed more men than outright wounds ever did, Nasberto Cornel could already give thanks for his deliverance. He seemed in no such mood, however.

"Well, Greek," he said, "my master persuaded me to spare your life both by sword and by the law, since you crawl back offering restitution. But I'll want you to own your fault before all the Company, d'you understand?"

Since that would end his chance of rising to more than a sort of scribe cum man-at-arms, Lucas bristled. "You twist En Jaime's meaning, Micer," he stated flatly. "My offer was to let the affair pass. But if you wish to invoke the law, I stand ready to tell the world what shame you brought on yourself. As for the sword, Micer, mine is always prepared to resume our dispute."

"Be still, both of you!" snapped the *rich hom*. "Isn't there enough battle to wage?" He stood erect, dominating that narrow space, his dark, gray-tinged head brushing the canvas top. "I've worked to conciliate all the officers who wished to make an example of both you brawlers. Now, by the Host, you'll do as I say! Both of you! I command you to swear peace!"

Asberto picked at his coverlet. His breathing came loud and painful. "My lord," he asked finally, forcing the words out, "will the Greek remain in your service?"

"Yes."

"My lord would not consider . . . sending him elsewhere? Even to some post of honor, so it be not with my lord?"

En Jaime shook his head. "I've need of his wit, Asberto, as I have of your strength."

The remark that Asberto's strength had not shown so well, either, was on Lucas' tongue. But he checked himself less from fear of En Jaime than because, looking at the man hunched on the pallet, he lost all wish to jeer.

"So. I could plead with you to decide otherwise. But no Cornel was ever a beggar." Asberto lifted unhappy eyes to his chief. "I swore I'd obey you in all things, Micer, and I will in this, too. Only ask me not to withstand more temptation than poor Cain. If the Greek must abide with you, send me away."

En Jaime's composure was a trifle shaken. "What?"

"The army is about to divide itself, Micer, as you know," said Asberto feverishly. "A part will remain at Gallipoli, the rest will leave. Whichever town my lord chooses to dwell in, let him find a place for me in the other. Until the Greek goes away."

"But I've need of your sword arm, Asberto."

"Lord, if I see the Greek every day, the time must come when I forget any peace-oath sworn and kill the dirty little beast. Sword arms are plentiful enough. . . . I can serve Micer's interests well elsewhere . . . until I may come back to serve Micer's banner—" Exhausted, Asberto lay down. "May that be soon."

Lucas shifted from foot to foot while En Jaime

pondered. At last the *rich hom* sighed. "As you wish, Asberto."

"So you do choose him—" The wounded man closed his eyes. En Jaime led Lucas from the tent.

Later, the disputants vowed separately, but formally, not to pursue their grudge. For his part, Lucas was sincere. He had never liked Cornel; at the time of the fight, he had wanted nothing in the world except to kill the man, who happened to be the closest at hand of the murderers in the marketplace. Cooled off, Lucas was not self-righteous enough to believe he must punish anyone: especially since he also remained with the army. Asberto Cornel became simply a man who had lost his lady, his self-esteem, and his chieftain: an object of rather distant pity.

The Catalans took several days to complete their work. Panidos surrendered on demand, its few craven guardians having already departed, and while thoroughly plundered, was spared massacre. The Company had had its fill of blood for a while. Furthermore, if the new headquarters was to be established hereabouts, some native population was required to maintain the towns. It sufficed as revenge that any Almúgavare could enter any house at any hour, line up all the women, and take his pleasure of whichever he fancied.

Lucas kept apart from such doings. Even had he not felt disgust at the idea, Violante's demands took all his returning strength. When desire had been spent, she would still not let him alone. Sitting up among tangled bedclothes, she asked so eagerly about his past adventures that En Jaime himself was

150

not a more entertaining companion. Now and again—increasingly often, as time passed—she would debate philosophy with him. It usually began when she made some statement so ignorant that he must pause to remember she had been brought up aristocratically. He would point out her error, she would dispute. At last she would understand his point . . . and throw herself into his embrace. In that fashion, he took better than a month to convince her the ancients were right about the earth being round.

"Ah, Lucas my beloved," she breathed in the dark, "you must teach me to read. To think I once believed it an unmanly art! There's so much you must teach me. Can you understand what this means, having a man I can truly talk with—for the first time since my father died?"

Not that she was always so mild. When she had a whim for something, which was often, and was not gratified at once, her language would make a mule blush. If Lucas seemed at fault, she would turn on him, with harpy screams that often led to attacks with fingernails or hurled crockery. Loathing such fights, he was apt to give in, or else to walk out of the tent. Afterward, she would again be so pleasurable that he abandoned the thought of discarding her. But she never admitted herself to have been wrong. He needed weeks to realize the full measure of her strangeness.

By then, he was back in Gallipoli. Though the Company was to establish itself in Rhedestos and Panidos, the city commanding the Boca Daner must also be retained. Rocafort moved the standard from

Gallipoli and took nearly all the soldiers, with wives, mistresses, children, servants, and slaves. En Ramon stayed behind with the seamen, a hundred Almúgavares, and fifty horsemen. These had charge of the treasures, magazines, and arsenals.

Though he did not say so, it was a fair guess that En Jaime de Caza chose to stay with Muntaner because the latter was an honorable and kindly knight who had openly condemned the excesses at Rhedestos. Gallipoli under his governorship would no longer be a base from which to ravage a helpless countryside; leave that to Rocafort. It would instead be a trade center (if most of the trade was in slaves and loot, that could not be helped) and a first line of defense against the outside world.

Lucas was relieved. But certain questions did arise. As they rode side by side down the westward highway, with the Propontis asparkle on their left and a lushness of green growth on the right, En Jaime said to him: "Do you remember that pretty little estate a few miles down the coast from Gallipoli? You came with some other attendants of mine to dinner there one day, when Nalfonso Boxadors invited me. It sits atop a steep cliff overlooking the water, with a large garden and some ancient sculptures— Yes, that one. Well, now that he's moving to Panidos, I've gotten the place off Nalfonso for a small sum. I mean to spend as much time there as I can."

"A sweet spot," agreed Lucas. "But an hour's ride from town."

"So much the better. Have I work to do in town, a brisk ride will start my blood coursing. I like not yon city, my friend. I'll like it even less when a mere few hundred of our people are left to rattle between the walls."

"There should soon be some life there again. Merchants from abroad; Greek artisans and laborers coming to live, if only for lack of other domicile."

"What have I to do with such rabble?"

"I think, all told, I've found more pleasure in the company of rabble—peasant, carpenter, smith, sailor, barbarian herdsman or hunter, from Italy to Cathay—honest folk, not afraid of laughter—more pleasure with them than with any other sort, save perhaps a few scholars. These stiff-necked, stiff-brained lords and ladies—" Lucas saw himself headed into offensiveness and swerved smoothly—"such as you are not, but as far too many are: they weary me."

"Each to his own taste," said En Jaime with a touch of hauteur.

They rode on in the muted music of the troop; plop of hoofs, squeak of leather, jingle of metal, rumble of wheels, played for a mile along the seashore. When Lucas decided the Catalan's geniality had returned, he cautioned, "Bear in mind, Micer, an isolated estate is prey to attack."

"It's inconspicuous from the sea," En Jaime answered; "the upward path is readily defensible; to landward, someone approaching can be seen in ample time either to close the gates or to retreat by water. Or overland: the hills are wide and free, and he'd be a poor horseman who could not stay ahead of pursuit the whole way to Gallipoli. In all events, Lucas, what foe would stop to search for nooks like

153

mine? He'd go straight against the city.''

"True.''

"It's so peaceful there." En Jaime spoke almost too low to be heard. Under the plumed bonnet, his gaze lost itself westward across the sea. "Like the house where my lady dwelt—ah, blessed Virgin, was it that many years ago? A man might find God in such quietness.''

He straightened in the saddle. "The estate has a few cottages," he said, more himself. "I'll use them for the families of such guards as I do keep out there. Would you like one, or a room in the villa?''

"My thanks, but—" Lucas shifted position, not quite at ease. "I've, ah, already discussed the question of living accommodations with Na Violante—"

"I did not invite her, Maestre.''

"Oh. Indeed. Um-m-m . . . just as well. She hates open countryside. She spoke of our taking a house in town, and some more servants.''

"You could ride in to see her when you must," said En Jaime sourly.

Lucas chuckled. "Micer, I'd wear out too many horses.''

"Have you no shame whatsoever?''

Lucas didn't answer. "Well, as you wish," said En Jaime.

"My actual work, as Micer's adjutant, would all be done in the city, anyhow.''

"True. Though you might be more useful attached directly to En Ramon Muntaner's staff. The management of our stores and trade will require learned men." Sensing Lucas' hurt, the knight laughed and clapped his shoulder. "Why, you chat-

154

tering rogue, I do believe you think I've turned enemy to you. God forbid! Who'd be left for me to drink with and not have to watch my tongue every moment? No, no, I thought of nothing but your own good, and the Company's. We'll see how matters stand once everyone is settled down again."

Looking into the gray Catalonian eyes, Lucas felt an odd thawing in his breast. He wondered if it felt like this to have an elder brother.

"There's one kindness I might beg of you," he said.

"I'll grant it gladly, Lucas, if I can."

"Simple enough. My slave girl, Djansha the Circassian—"

"A charming lass, that. I cannot understand why you would choose to— Well. What of her?"

"Violante . . . um . . . likes not the idea of having her about. She told me. And Djansha herself abhors the city. Since you plan to dwell out in the countryside, En Jaime, would you accept her from me? As a gift?"

"No!" Presently: "You mean well. At least you've heart enough to care about her fate. But I am a chaste man."

"Oh, she's an excellent cook and housekeeper. And I'm sure she's not lied in claiming skill with a garden. Her duties need be no more than these, if you prefer."

En Jaime frowned at his saddlebow before he said, "I'll take her as a servant, then! But I will not own a woman. You must retain title."

Lucas agreed happily.

Entering Gallipoli land gate, he spied Djansha on

155

the edge of the Catalan assembly who welcomed the troopers back. She was a small figure, muffled in robe and cloak but wildly waving to him. She must have returned home at once, though, for he saw her no more as he went about the day's business. At dusk, he crossed the threshold of the house En Jaime was leaving. He turned toward Asberto's former apartments—he and Violante would use them until they found a satisfactory dwelling of their own—but paused, remembering the slave.

"Oh, damnation," he muttered. "She must be awaiting me. I'd best tell her before she worries."

Reluctant, for no good reason, he walked to his old door and opened it. The odor within was overwhelming, like all springtimes that ever had been. The chamber was heaped with roses, violets, tulips, wildflowers, ferns and green branches. Candles burned in silver holders polished dazzling bright. A table stood crowded with wines and dainties.

Djansha went to her knees, kissed his boots, and rose again. She wore a thin robe of white silk, through which her flesh seemed to glow, a gold-worked girdle, tiny red slippers, jewelry on hands and arms and bosom. The auburn hair was drawn back in the latest Catalan mode. But, chiefly, he noticed the heart-shaped face. He had not often seen such gladness.

"W-w-w—" She gulped. "Welcome home, my lord."

"But you are crying!" he said, astonished.

"Only because I am so glad." She reached up fingers that trembled very faintly, to stroke his cheek. "Shible—I mean Keristi be thanked and fed,

156

my lord has his health back. You are still too thin, but we can soon set that right. I hope you have not supped. See, I've spent days preparing a feast.''

"No," said Lucas, "I haven't eaten."

"Will my lord n-n-not be seated, then? Here, I've new slippers for you. Let me draw off your boots—"

Lucas remained where he was. "You are very good," he said. "I wish I had known. I'm expected elsewhere to dine."

"Oh." She stood mute for a few seconds. Then, tossing her head: "So be it. I can always make another meal." Softly, she added, "I hope my lord will not be out too late this night?"

"Well—"

"No!" She seized his hands. Her words bubbled forth. "I can *not* wait any longer to tell you. My lord, I am with child."

"What?"

"Yes. I was not certain when you left. Now I am. Your son!"

Lucas looked away. The silence grew.

Finally she whispered, "Are you not pleased?"

"Yes. Of course. Fear not, I'll make provision for you. And the child." Lucas drew a long breath so he could tell her swiftly: "In fact, I've planned this beforehand. I know you don't like the city. En Jaime will take you to his new estate. Far beyond the walls. Grass, trees, hills. You'll be kindly treated. Now I must go. You need not wait up for me. Goodnight.''

He went from the room, slamming the door so it would block off the sight of her.

Chapter XI

The next several weeks roared.

The fame of the Grand Company went through all Europe and near Asia. In the West, King Fadrique of Sicily found himself suddenly deferred to because of those mercenaries he had been so anxious to be rid of, and pondered means to get them back under direct leadership of his princely house. Encouraged by Pope Clement, the Venetian Republic arrived at a convention with Charles of Valois for the joint conquest of Byzantium, as if this were the Fourth Crusade all over again. Fortunately for the rotten stump of the Roman Empire, nothing came of that, the allies being too jealous of each other.

In the East, Seljuk and Ottoman Turks rapidly reconquered those parts of Anatolia from which the Catalans had driven them. The Moslems held no grudge; rather, they admired the Catholic warriors and were eager to help them exploit Orthodox Christendom. Two thousand men from the tribes under Alaeddin of Roum crossed over to enlist with Rocafort. Afterward another eight hundred cavalry and two thousand infantry came. Many of them were Greek-born, who had renounced their religion on discovering that the emirs were rulers more wise and lenient than the Emperor. In all the later adventures of the Grand Company, these allies kept faith.

Westerners, too, began to flock thither. En Ferran Ximeno de Arenos had quarreled with Roger di Flor the first winter and gone to the Duke of Athens; now he returned with eighty men and was made welcome. Taking a band of some five hundred, he harried as far as Constantinople, bringing back a crowd of cattle and newly caught slaves. The Imperialists met him in a pass with sixteen hundred men, horse and foot; he overbore them and got a huge booty.

Rocafort, himself, raided the main enemy shipyard and naval base, burning all the craft he found. That destroyed Byzantine opposition by water and Gallipoli became freely accessible to visitors. The Greeks still held the castle of Maditos farther down the peninsula, but it was now a mere heap of stones which occasionally made a futile catapult shot at passing vessels.

Galloping out of Rhedestos, the Catalans daily pillaged Thrace and Macedonia. One such expedition, within sight of Constantinople, massacred five thousand cultivators of the soil. Town after town was sacked and burned; orchards were cut down, vineyards destroyed, inhabitants brought to the slave mart at Gallipoli. Quarrels over the loot destroyed more men than the Greeks had. But the moment there was fighting to be done, the whole snarling, rutting, flea-bitten Company closed ranks and worked with grim discipline.

A baron of the Kingdom of Salonica, Sir George

de Cristopol, came with eighty horsemen to visit the Emperor. Seeing the chaos all about them, they determined to practice a little banditry on the Catalans and attacked a wagon train sent out from Gallipoli to bring in wood. The mules were worth money. The train was guarded by four foot soldiers and a crossbowman named Marcho. When Cristopol swept down upon them, the soldiers retreated to a nearby tower and defended themselves with stones, while Marcho ran to Gallipoli for help. Muntaner had let almost all his horse go in a foray with Rocafort; he had only six full-armed knights and eight *jinetes*. With these, and as many foot as he could assemble in a few minutes, he hastened forth against the Salonicans, attacked on sight, and took thirty-seven dead or prisoner. The rest he pursued as far as the tower, which the four soldiers were still holding; "And we recovered these four men," he wrote afterward; "then we let the enemy go and returned to Gallipoli. And next day we had an auction of the horses and of the prisoners and of what we had taken, and we had, of the booty, twenty-eight gold hyperpera for each armed horse and fourteen for each light horse and seven for each foot soldier, so that everyone had his share.

"And I have told you this fine adventure in order that you should all understand that it was due to nothing but the power of God, and that this was not done through our worth but by the virtue and grace of God."

That was the only warlike action Lucas saw during this time. It cheered him greatly—not so much his part in the gold as his part in the deed. When En

Ramon clashed down visor, lowered lance, and charged, the noise seemed to drown out the remembered sound of peasants shuffling along a dusty road to the slave block.

Muntaner had one failure, when in August the Genoese who held de Entenza returned homeward. He tried to obtain his friend's release, but they would accept no ransom offer. Muntaner was only able to give de Entenza a thousand hyperpera out of his own purse, to lighten the captivity a little.

Emperor Andronicus was bargaining too, but more frantically. His bad faith and the corruption which had gutted his treasury found their punishment as he tried to negotiate the withdrawal of the Catalans. They insisted that all prisoners be set free without ransom, that their arrears of pay be made up in honest currency, and that the ships captured with de Entenza be given back. Certain of their power, they added a demand that he pay them for all booty they would be unable to carry away! The Emperor groaned. Peacock-feather fans cooled the royal brow as he sipped a restoring beaker of lemonade. Could Genoa, the century-old ally of his dynasty, offer any hope?

Genoese traffic was indeed moving through the Boca Daner. So was that of other nations. The military republic of the Catalans was shrewder than to antagonize foreign powers by attempting an impossible blockade of Constantinople. Rather, they—Muntaner especially—wished to attract ships to their own port. And ships came, drawn like flies to the wealth now stuffed in Gallipoli. Many men aboard those vessels stayed, not only adventurers to join the army but merchants to establish factories. These were chiefly Catalans; but Castilian, Frenchman, Venetian, German, Jew, Moor and Turk also saw their opportunity. As had been foreseen, a number of Greeks even dared return, to form an oppressed class of servitors. Life flowed anew in Gallipoli, a hectic, lawless, many-colored life in which Lucas and Violante often sought amusement. This trade created a need for his skills, both with languages and with accounts. The grandeur of the Company was founded on the unspectacular organizing toil of men like Muntaner and himself.

Thus the summer wore away.

In September, a new full-scale expedition was mounted. Greedy for gold, fanatic in their faith, the Catalans still kept one desire that overpowered all others, to get revenge for Roger di Flor. It had pleased them greatly to hear that the Alans had quit the ill-paid, incompetently led Imperial service and had begun plundering on their own account. But the Company did not therefore forget that George, the Alan chief, had wielded the knife which struck down the Caesar. Now word came that his tribe, nine thousand horse and foot with their families in tow, were trekking northward to serve the King of Bulgaria. If they could not be overtaken, they would soon pass out of reach.

The Catalans moved all their own women and children and treasures back to Gallipoli, which was more defensible by a small garrison than Rhedestos. That garrison was assigned almost at spearpoint, so reluctant were they to stay. Muntaner, their commander, insisted on a third share of booty for them, and said it was little enough compensation. Nonetheless, the night after the army marched forth, a part of his men decided to follow. Muntaner avoided mutiny only by giving them leave to go, on condition they pay half their gains to the seven knights who remained with him. Besides these, who stayed chiefly from personal loyalty, Gallipoli was now in the care of a hundred and thirty-two foot, some being seamen and some Almúgavares.

"And so I remained," he wrote, "badly provided with men and well provided with women, for, altogether, there remained with me over two thousand women, one with another."

That news was quick to reach Constantinople.

Lucas entered his house. Two doormen bowed to the tiles. Two footmen removed his flame-colored cloak and bonnet. "Do the master and his lady wish to dine at the usual hour?" asked the major-domo, as if his salvation depended on the answer.

"No," said Lucas. "I've had a hard day's work. The devil with eating in state."

"But Despotes, my noble lady said—"

"I'll change my noble lady's mind. Prepare food, but I may want it brought to the boudoir. Fetch a flagon of red Cyprian wine, with two goblets. Jump! I'm thirsty, I tell you!" Lucas made a pretense of drawing his sword. The major-domo turned white and scuttled backward. Lucas was instantly sorry. He didn't want to abuse his Greeks. A man often forgot how a rough jest affected those who had lived through horror.

Well, there were other things to think about. He

strode over Persian carpets to a marble staircase, and thence along a second-floor hallway whose windows overlooked a garden of nearly Arabian intricacy. The sky was purple overhead, the first stars twinkling forth in the east. A slave went by, lighting bracketed lamps. Too big a house, he thought for the hundredth time; too silent; we creep about in all this stolen wealth like mice. But if she wants to dwell thus, let her.

It was easier to give way to Violante than to suffer curses and blows and glassware thrown at his head—though surrender often left her cold toward him. But then he would grow angry in his turn, and suddenly she offered him a purring, teasing, endlessly inventive body. He could seldom predict her; sometimes her darker moods frightened him. Her lighter ones, though— He increased his pace.

A boy was on hand with the wine when he reached the bedroom door. They went through together. Violante was lying back among cushions on a couch, while one slave girl brushed her hair and two others trimmed her nails. The boy's eyes popped, for she had just come from the bath and was not yet dressed. She paid him no more heed than any other domestic animal. A reddening went up her skin, however, as she saw Lucas. "You know I am not to be disturbed when preparing for dinner," she said coldly.

"But you aren't." He began to unlace his doublet. "We'll not trouble with dining like *richs homens* this evening."

She sat up straight. "What do you mean, you son of a merchant?" The movement caught one girl by

164

surprise, so that her manicure scissors scratched milady's hand. Violante twisted about with an obscene oath, caught the girl's hand, took the scissors and raised them to stab. Before they had pierced the slave's skin—she was only about twelve years old—Lucas was across the room and had grabbed them. He threw them aside.

"Go," he said. "All of you." The attendants scampered out.

Violants damned him, struggling to rise. He held her down by one shoulder. "See here," he declared, "we've had this trouble before. My patience is at an end. The servants are to be treated as human beings. D'you hear me?"

"You dung-clod—!"

"Be still! If you want to dine in the banquet hall, you'll dine alone. God's teeth, I'm tired and worried and I want to take my rest!" Violante broke free and rose, hissing in her fury. He put a foot behind her ankles and flipped her down on the couch again without effort. "Remember," he said, "I'm quite able to kill you."

It was spoken heedlessly, and at once he wished it unsaid. But before he could beg forgiveness, the tensed muscles seemed to melt. A smile as warm as any he had ever had from her quivered forth upon the full, softening lips. She sat up, but slowly and meaningfully, throwing back her loosened hair with a motion that lifted her breasts toward him.

"Your pardon," she breathed. "I didn't understand. I, too, was on edge. Of course we'll do as you wish."

Confused, about himself as much as about her,

and trying to cover the fact, he turned his back and poured out the wine.

"I simply want to drop stiff garments and courtly manners for once," he explained: "have a long drink and be nothing except myself."

"I hope you aren't *too* weary," she insinuated.

He slipped off his doublet and shoes. When he brought back the goblets, Violante had thrown a robe over her nakedness, but it was loosely sashed. She accepted a glass, regarded him above the edge, and lowered it untasted. She was not without perception.

"You are in a fret," she said. "Sit down. Tell me. Has there been trouble with those Genoese?"

"More than trouble." He let himself into a chair and drank deep of his own wine. Violante came around behind him and brushed his chestnut hair with her hands.

"I fear there's going to be a hard battle," he said.

"Again? Are any left who dare stand against the Grand Company?"

"But the Company isn't here."

Her sleeking fingers paused, then resumed. "Tell me the whole story," she said in a man's brisk tone. "From the beginning. I knew En Ramon was treating with some insolent Genoese, but paid no heed."

"That's all I told you, for it seemed unimportant at first. Yesterday's talking revealed what an ominous turn this is, but I stayed so late at the conference of our captains—I being the record keeper—that you were asleep when I returned. Today—"

Violante began massaging his neck. He took another large draught, leaned back a trifle more at ease, and said:

"Now we've learned that full eighteen Genoese galleys under Ser Antonio Spinola reached Constantinople on a mission of state not long ago. Great ships, each holding over a hundred fighting men. Hearing that our force is not in Gallipoli, Spinola got splendid terms from the Emperor if he can take this city. You realize what a blow?

"So he came here in two ships and defied us." Lucas grinned. Wine and the woman's hands were soothing him, restoring his humor. "I must say his challenge was a resounding one. He commanded us and told us, in the name of the Commune of Genoa, to get out of their garden, meaning the Empire of Constantinople, which was the garden of the Commune of Genoa; otherwise if we did not get out, that he defied us in the name of the Commune of Genoa and of all the Genoese in the world. Our answer was a soft one, but he repeated his demand and we repeated our refusal, and so it went back and forth, with all the formalities, public letters being delivered of each challenge and each reply.

"Well, Spinola had our final word today. Old Muntaner told him—ah, you Hispanics!—we had come here in the name of God, and to exalt the Holy Catholic Faith; and required him in the name of the Holy Father, and in the names of the King of Aragon and the King of Sicily, to join us against that treacherous schismatic, the Emperor. If he would not help us, he must not hinder, or God would see that we were innocent of any bloodshed that might ensue, for we were only defending ourselves."

"Why are you laughing?" asked Violante, startled.

"I could never explain to a Catalan," said Lucas.

"Spinola is now bound back," he continued after a while. "He vowed to return with his full complement. They can get here well before Rocafort learns of our plight and sends help."

Her grasp tightened on him. "The more glory for us!"

As if that arrogance were a magic formula, Lucas felt the wine take hold of him. His forebodings vanished. There were still a few days before anything happened. By all the demons of Tartary, he wouldn't waste them in fear! The Grand Company was invincible! He emptied his glass, set it on the floor, and reached around to pull Violante down on his lap.

"Lucas! What are you doing?"

"Haven't you noticed?"

She frowned and resisted him. Her fond mood of a few minutes past was gone, overwhelmed by an ardor for war. "Not yet," she muttered. "I want you to tell me about our battle plans, and—"

He slipped a hand inside her robe. "Later. After the more important matters are off my mind."

"How dare you say such a thing?" He saw her temper kindling and said:

"I dare say much. For instance, a sonnet in the Italian form."

"What?" Completely taken aback, she stopped resisting him.

"For you, my lady. A poor tribute, but the best I could."

"Me? But . . . but no one ever—" Her blush could have been a maiden's. "Oh, Lucas!"

"In other times I played the troubadour,
Or thought I did, like any lovesick youth,
And for my lady's sake let fancy soar
On flashing-feathered wings above dull truth.
By foam-born Venus foamily I swore
That in my love of her was naught uncouth,
But 'twas her heart and soul I did adore,
Those beauties which we know defy time's tooth.

"The devil now may have such dreary bliss!
Your mortal self is what has made me blest.
Your shining eyes, deep riches of your hair,
The springtime drunkenness within your kiss,
The lovely upward surging of your breast,
Soft skin, round hip, slim leg—these things are fair."

"Oh, my darling! You . . . you'll have me weeping for joy— How can I please you? What would you have me do? Anything you desire!"
The Catalan version made the eighth language in which he had rendered his poem. All translations had been equally successful.

Chapter XII

On a Saturday, about the hour of vespers, Lucas
looked down at the Genoese fleet. He whistled.
"Twenty-five of them, Micer! The Emperor must
have added seven of his own to Spinola's
command."

"Seven or seven hundred, it's as nothing in the
sight of God," said En Ramon Muntaner. But he
squinted toward them with a soldier's eye, observing
and calculating.

At this point, the seaward walls of Gallipoli rose
above rugged slopes. Some distance off, the
Catalans had followed their custom of erecting a
barbacana, a lower wall, to serve as first line of
defense and help cover any retreat. This was a
wooden stockade, but strong and well designed, its
top breast-high above a scaffolding where the
defenders would stand. Beyond, the earth rolled on
down to the beaches. The strait lay like burnished
steel against brown Asiatic hills. The galleys came
rowing to their selected anchorage: long, full-bellied
craft, high in bow and stern, sails furled but pennons
vivid at the mastheads. Their decks swarmed with
men.

"Might we send out fireships?" wondered an esquire.

"My goose is talking," snorted Lucas. "What wind have we? Let's pray they don't come in and burn our ships at dock."

"If they wish to do so, why, that's where we'll fight them," said Muntaner. "But they'd scarcely be such fools. Our catapults and ballistae cover the harbor." He slapped his hard horseman's thigh. "Come, we've work to do."

The Genoese promptly began assembling ladders and siege engines for an assault. All that night they could be heard at work. Lanthorns hung in the rigging made their ships a faerie spectacle, firefly hosts on blackly glimmering waters, but Lucas was too busy to grow homesick for the festivals of Cambaluc. He must follow the governor from point to point, readying all defenses.

Casks of wine and bowls of bread were set out in the streets, and whoever wished could eat from them, for the garrison could not spare men to keep a mess. Not only must extra weapons be stocked where they would be needed; physicians must also be put in readiness to aid the wounded, so these could return to battle at once. The Genoese habit was to shoot ceaselessly with the crossbow, so every Catalan was ordered to wear a good cuirass. It was not proof against a quarrel fired close by, but would protect from bolts nearly spent. Of armor the city had no lack.

Muntaner ordered the women into armor, each division in charge of a Catalan merchant, that they might guard the walls.

Lucas snatched a little sleep before dawn. He was up in time to hear mass; there would not be much more religion on this Sabbath. Afterward he waited for Violante, who was to seek her own post atop a *barbacana*. The sky overhead was still dark and full of stars, but eastward it had paled and a dim sourceless light filled the streets. Violante's tread rang loud on the cobblestones. She saw Lucas and ran to embrace him.

"Behold me, my dearest!"

Her hair was in tight black braids under a morion helmet. Cuirass, tasses, and greaves enclosed her, but the breeches showed what fullness lay within. She had a dagger at her belt, spear in one hand and light leather targe on the other arm. With flared nostrils, teeth gleaming between red wet lips, eyes afire, she could have been some heathen goddess of war.

She crushed herself against him. He had not heard her voice so joyful, even at the heights of love. "Oh, Lucas, my father looks down from Heaven and sees me like this!"

Then she hastened onward.

In mail and pourpoint, Lucas mounted his best horse and went out the gates with En Ramon's men. The animals whinnied and danced, sensing battle. Their riders sat calmly; but their eyes smoldered beneath the plumed helmets. The Almúgavares shook their lances and set up a yell that the hills flung back. They looked no less savage with breastplates above their leather garments. The mariners tramped more stolidly, pikes rising and falling, bordon swords slapping booted legs. A breeze

172

unfurled the banner of Aragon at the army's head and the banner of St. Peter above the city.

Trumpets blared, kettledrums banged, the Catalans marched forth.

A Genoese galley was already being drawn into the shallows by two boats filled with armed sailors. When those were beached, the men would haul the ship inward till it grounded. *"Desperta ferres! Aur! Aur!"* The defenders rushed to stop them.

Lucas saw an arbalestier stand up in the foresheets and take aim. From the corner of an eye, he saw Muntaner's standard advance, streaming from the pole. He lowered his spear and urged his own horse into the water, which sheeted over his knees. For a ridiculous moment he was chiefly conscious of the water in his boots . . . the live rippling of muscle between his legs, the cropped mane and the ears that rose and fell in gallop, odors of horse and oiled metal. . . . Crossbow quarrels whizzed past on either side of him. The man at whom he aimed wore a leather doublet but an iron helmet. His face was fleshy, sunburnt, with a big nose, several days' growth of beard . . . an Italian face. . . . His mouth fell open, he screamed and tumbled backward. The lance caught him in the armpit.

Lucas pulled the shaft free and wielded it against the oarsmen like a pike. Confusion churned around the boats. The sailors sprang overboard, weapons in hand. The water was chest high. They struggled shoreward, assailed by the horsemen. As they reached shallower water the Catalan foot attacked. Metal and wood rattled. Men splashed about, cursed, howled, moaned, and gurgled.

Those Genoese who could swim retreated to the galley, which had cut loose and was hurriedly backing water. The rest were hewn down. The first full sunlight struck on corpses awash in red-streaked ripples. The Catalans cheered like wolves yelping.

Several further attempts were made, each halted by Muntaner's patrols. But about the hour of tierce, as he had known must happen, superior numbers overcame the advantage of ground. Two separate melees near the city occupied his entire band. Meanwhile, a few miles off, ten galleys snatched the opportunity.

From the saddle, where he smote with a saber at men who stood in a wildly rocking shallop and hit back with oars, Lucas glimpsed the enemy landing. A ship grated on sand, anchors were dropped, a gangplank was lowered. Knights guided restive horses to the water and up onto the beach. Toylike under the cliffs, their surcoats and shields colorful splotches, they moved about planning their battle.

A yell slashed through Lucas' attention. He waded his horse back toward shore and tried to see what had happened. Muntaner's standard had swayed above a turmoil on the strand. Now it was gone, the armored tower was gone, hostile mariners raged where Muntaner had been fighting.

"The commander is killed!" Lucas heard the gleeful Genoese roar. They had also seen. "The commander is killed! At them!"

He spurred up to the affray. Others were also converging on it. He saw a knight spit two sailors on a lance, break off the shaft, lay about with the stump as a club, and when it was in splinters draw a sword.

174

He, himself, engaged a pikeman; they sparred until an Almúgavare came from behind and stabbed the fellow. By that time the foe had been cleared from around En Ramon. He stood red-splashed, gasping, beside his mortally wounded charger. Blood ran from his own cuts; his left shoe squelched with blood.

An esquire sprang to earth. "Take my horse, Micer!"

Muntaner ignored them all and knelt by his fallen animal. Bewildered agony looked back at him. "Ah," he breathed, "so, Orlando, my pet, so, so, my lad. Goodnight, and thanks." His misericord flashed. The horse gave one jerk and lay still. Muntaner climbed painfully up on the other mount, took the esquire behind him, and rode off to have his hurts dressed.

Lucas joined the re-forming Almúgavares. They sat down on the beach and panted. Water bottles went from mouth to crack-lipped mouth. They could do nothing more to halt the Genoese landings. They could only resist the attack when it came.

Spinola's arrangements were complete. He made skillful use of his overwhelmingly greater numbers. One banner with half the crew issued from each galley. If any man in combat got tired or hungry or wounded, he returned and a counterpart—pikeman or crossbowman—took his place. Thus the assault was continuous, which rarely happened in war.

The air grew dark with Genoese quarrels. Lucas' ears were so full of their buzz that he ceased hearing them. Now and again, one would strike near him, otherwise he paid no heed. In all that shooting, however, no man outside was struck. When the Catalans had been driven back close to their fortress, they saw that some of the women on the *barbacana* had been hit, and a bolt had gone down a chimney, injuring a cook preparing fowls for the wounded. On the whole, though, the arbalestiers were useless: which somewhat lightened the odds against Aragon.

But it was still a deadly strife. Pike thrust at shield and cuirass, seeking flesh. Sword smote until the edge was so dulled the weapon became a mere club. The long Almúgavare knives leaped and probed. As the day progressed, men grew too weary and thirsty for battle cries. A strange stillness descended on the beach. The only noises were clatter and thud, grunt and gasp, a whimper of pain.

Lucas fought with the light horse until his own steed was hamstrung. Then he was glad enough to get down among the mariners and wield his blade afoot. He had only acted as a *jinete* because cavalrymen were so few.

The retreat was a foretaste of Hell. Long before it ended, he was stumbling, his lungs a dry fire, the sweat baked out of him. Yet the Catalan lines held firm. They entered their gates about nones in good order.

That maneuver was covered by the women on the stockades. When their javelins and quarrels were expended, they fought with stones piled ready for them. Again and again, the Genoese outflanked the Catalans and raised ladders against the *barbacana*. They were met by shrieking female devils, who stabbed, hurled stones, poured kettles of scalding water, and overthrew the ladders.

When the enemy withdrew to reorganize itself, Muntaner abandoned the outer defense. It had served its purpose. His folk took places atop Gallipoli's own walls. Men and women intermingled; they fought beyond sundown. The Genoese made bonfires to illuminate the night, and continued to attack at widely scattered points until morning. Their hope was to break through the thin Catalan force, but each attempt failed.

Once past the gates, Lucas had a lengthy rest, for none of those assaults were made near his assigned post. Standing on a battlement in the dark, he took off his helmet and the quilted cap beneath, to let the breeze cool his head. The city was a mountainous gloom behind him, around him, below him, down toward the beach where watchfires picked out galleys like stranded whales. Other fires made red stars over the hills. Far off along the wall he saw torches bobbing, even thought he glimpsed steel as it whirred and hammered. But his ears were his chief source of information. Shouts, clangor, drum and trumpets, made a stirring music—at this distance.

The half-seen woman beside him came closer. Her voice was triumphant: "Before God, this day has been worth all the rest of my life!"

"A day to be proud of," he agreed. He wondered if the fight was at Violante's post. He tried to imagine her, wild among the spears. But the image which rose before him was of a tall, spare, limping man, whose countenance meshed in fine lines as he drawled some jest. Now why should I be lonely for Brother Hugh the Hospitaller? Lucas wondered, almost irritated. I hardly knew him.

An answer came: Because this is an honorable combat, not waged for plunder or revenge. Unused to such inward whisperings, half-afraid it might have been a demon—or still more terrifying, an angel—Lucas crossed himself and sought diversion. He traced out the constellations, watched the morning star rise, counted the meteoric streaks criss-crossing in utter silence. But he found no comfort. A sense of the stars' remoteness filtered into his breast. He shivered and prayed for dawn.

When it came, the night grew unreal in his memory, as if everything had been a dream.

Soon afterward, Spinola recalled his exhausted mariners. From their walls the garrison saw a turmoil among the galleys, until a freshly formed host moved up toward the iron gate. The multiplicity of shields with armorial bearings showed that some four hundred men of the best Genoese families were in the van. Sunlight winked on their metal and burned in their five banners.

An esquire of Muntaner mounted to Lucas' parapet. "Maestre, En Ramon summons you." Running down into a courtyard, Lucas discovered that he was to be one of a hundred picked men. The seven knights were there on fully caparisoned horses, but lightly protected themselves. Muntaner addressed them calmly. They were to discard all armor, keeping only a shield; each man would receive spear, sword, and dagger. Then let them take their ease.

Lucas was glad enough to sit in the shade, for already the air quivered with unseasonal heat. A servant proffered bread and beer; an Almúgavare and a sailor joined him in lazily rolling dice. The noise of

Spinola's assault on the gates, and the inflexible Catalan resistance, rolled like summer thunder.

"I mislike being in shirt and breeches only, with quarrels flying every which way," said the mariner.

"Why, you snotnose fool, haven't you seen they're firing no more?" replied the Almúgavare in an amiable tone. "They spent 'em all yesterday. Me, I'd fear melting down, did I wear iron in this warmth."

"As the Genoese are doing, while we sit cool and refreshed," Lucas laughed. "En Ramon's a leader of my own stripe. . . . Ah, seven."

The fight at the gate was hot in every sense. Muntaner waited patiently. At last a messenger came to say the Genoese looked almost ready to withdraw. The governor swung into the saddle. Having crossed himself and said an Ave, he reached for his helmet. Banners lifted; the troop moved out of the courtyard; the gates creaked wide.

Knowing this meant a sally, the Genoese pulled back a trifle to dress their disordered lines. Out came Muntaner and his pets.

Lucas felt sick of bloodshed, but his muscles were rested. As the Catalans broke into a trot, he heard "*Desperta ferres!*" roared so loud it shivered his skull. In a vague astonishment, he realized that he had given the challenge.

The enemies shocked against each other. A face glared at Lucas over a shield rim. He saw that the man was gray with dust and thirst had made his lips scummy. He jammed his spear forward. Something yielded. He stabbed deeply.

Now, in among the pikes! Lucas hardly felt the

blows that pounded on his buckler. Beyond the gap in the Genoese line loomed a horseman. A standard bearer! Lucas flung his shaft. Struck, the horse reared and screamed. The rider fought to control it. With a Catalan on either hand, Lucas forced his way up to the flag. Their swords flickered and bit. The rider sank to the earth. The standard was trampled underfoot.

Four of the five Genoese banners were cut down in that first blow. Panic broke loose. Spinola's men threw away their weapons and fled, but he stood his own ground with a number of noblemen. And then the Catalan wave broke over him. A sword piped in the air. Antonio Spinola's head leaped from his shoulders.

The combat grew fierce again on the beach, where the Genoese rallied. Despite hideous losses suffered while they fled, they still far outnumbered their opponents. Their rear guard covered the launching of the galleys until it was annihilated. Then the Catalans splashed out among the sailors, who were still going up the rope ladders, and boarded. Once more Lucas found himself on a deck. His sword whistled and hewed. He chased two men into the rigging and fought them crawling along the yardarm. One after the other, into the sea! That ship was captured, and three more. The rest escaped, simply because there were not enough Catalans to take them.

Lucas helped bring in the prize. A last struggle continued on a hill. He went there and observed some forty Genoese under a big man they called Antonio Bocanegra. One by one, they were slain, until their captain alone was left, making such thrusts with his sword that none dared approach. Muntaner rode up. Lucas heard the governor order his men back and beg Bocanegra many times to surrender. The Genoese spat refusal. Muntaner gave reluctant orders to an esquire on an armored horse. The esquire rushed in, the poitrail struck Bocanegra and knocked him down. The soldiers cut him into a red unrecognizable heap.

Up and down the beach, from hills and battlements and towers, a hoarse chant of thanksgiving lifted heavenward. Lucas bared his head but did not join the singing. He trudged along a patch to the city wall. Now, he thought wearily, I can sleep. Mary, grant me one boon, that I do not see Bocanegra in my dreams.

And yet it had been an honest encounter between honest warriors. Muntaner had offered the man peace. Surely so brave a death was better than rotting with pox or leprosy.

Surely, whatever he might say about other deeds, Brother Hugh could only praise this day of knights.

Nonetheless—

Was the possession of certain bricks and roofs worth so much death?

What is it, thought Lucas, that forever dulls the color of my finest moments and draws gargoyles among all my lions?

The path ended at a sally port which someone had opened, now danger was past. Beyond lay a small plaza. The houses enclosing it stood shuttered, unpeopled, their walls flimmering in white noontide. The praise of God and the clamor of trumpets were everywhere, but no person was to be seen.

Until Violante appeared.

Her corselet seemed afire, so brightly did it shine under the hard sky. As she neared him, Lucas saw that it was scratched and dented. Her face was sooty, with paler streaks traced by sweat. The blue-black hair was rudely chopped off, hardly longer than his own. Her left hand was painted with dried blood. Yet she came to him more eagerly even than in yesterday's dawn.

"What brings you here?" he exclaimed.

"I saw you from the wall." She slurred out the reply and forgot it as insignificant. "Oh, Lucas, we are victorious!"

"So I'm told."

She pressed close to him. "And I fought them," she stammered. "I stood on the *barbacana* and threw stones. One of mine hit a man. I saw it happen! I swear so! But more, much more than that, Lucas. Last night my post was assaulted. They nearly took us. A few men got onto the battlement before we killed them. We! I had a spear and helped! Carlet struck him with a sword, but I put my lance in his belly!"

"What have you done with your hair?"

She tossed her head. "It was in my way. My helmet wouldn't sit properly. I cut it off myself. If only it could have been made into bowstrings. . . . But Lucas, my darling, my darling, I stood face to face with that mariner on the wall. I stabbed him myself! Look here. When he was fallen I dipped my hand in his blood. Blood that I had called forth.

"I *felt* my lance go into him!"

"Well . . . well," he mumbled, ill at ease, "you fought bravely. Now I think we may go home."

She seized his arms so her nails bit through sleeves and skin. "You don't understand," she said. "You shall. I want you to. Riambaldo's ghost is gone from me. I know not why. I only know, when I stood before that palomer and killed him—though he could have killed me—I ceased being a murderess. My father smiled on me again."

"What?" He stepped back.

"Oh, yes, yes, yes," she gibbered. "Not that I killed Riambaldo, myself. No. But I'd grown so weary of him, and of all the pretense . . . both before him and before Asberto . . . I know not what happened within me that night when they drank together. I told Riambaldo to his face, to both their faces, Asberto was my lover. He may have suspected that—I think he did—but now I gave him no choice. They fought there in the house, up and down the room, into the hall. Asberto killed him under one of those saints' images. Ugh, how that horrible Eastern saint stared out of his big eyes! Afterward Asberto killed a Greek servant who had witnessed the fight. Together we arranged things so it seemed the slave had stabbed Riambaldo and been hunted down by Asberto. What else could we do? What would it benefit Riambaldo, to have Asberto disgraced or . . . or even beheaded? We bought many masses for his soul. But I could never forget what had happened—until now. Now I have also looked in the eyes of a man who wanted to kill me. It set me free."

She dragged Lucas forward by the wrist. "This

way," she said. "In yonder alley. I want to be in armor when it happens."

"When what?" he asked, stunned.

"Need I tell you? How often can you take me? I want it to be many times. Lucas, hurry!"

"Merciful angels!" He pulled free. She reached for him again. He backed up. One hand fell to his sword.

She stopped and stared at him. Finally she laughed aloud. "So you are too tired? Asberto would not be. You should have seen him after the revenge at Rhedestos."

"Go seek Asberto, then!" He swallowed. "No. Forgive me. The battle, and now this heat, they were too much for you. You're in a fever. You know not what you say."

"For the first time, Lucas, I do know."

"Then your case needs a priest, not a physician."

She shrugged. "That's for me to decide; I know you'd never denounce me to the Holy Office." The scorn dropped from her. As if seeing a vision, she murmured, "But I think I must have been absolved last night, by my father among the saints. For I am no longer guilty. I can feel I am not. Oh, I'm free and I want you!"

Like a morning glory before him, there arose the cool image of Djansha. He had not known he was brave enough to dismiss it and tell Violante: "I shall believe this is only a fever talking. Come home with me and I'll summon a leech."

Her gaze ran up and down him, from tangled hair and broad snub nose to the feet which neared her with a cat's gait. "Lucas," she said, "if you won't take me now I'll find a hundred Almúgavares who will. But I'd rather it was you.''

He caught her. For a moment such lust sprang up in her expression that he almost yielded. He mastered himself and began marching her forward. When she realized he was only taking her home to be cared for, she struggled. His cheek was raked by nails and his shins bloody from kicks before he lost his temper and clouted her. Thereafter she obeyed him as meekly as a little girl.

CHAPTER XIII

The next day word reached the Company, homeward bound from the north, that Muntaner was besieged. Eighty of the best-mounted men went more than three journeys in a day and a night. The following afternoon they entered Gallipoli.

"Aye, we made a great conquest of the Alans," said En Jaime. "When their chief George was killed, En Roger avenged, God smote them with terror and they broke. Not three hundred horse and foot escaped."

His gaunt, hooked face looked exultantly ahead: into the sky. The land stretched big and rough, wind murmurous in long grass, clouds piled in the east but heaven still bright above. At the road's edge, a cliff tumbled down to waters gay with whitecaps. Asia lay hazed beyond them, only half-real.

"We had many wounded," he continued, "but a mere forty-four killed. The Alans outnumbered us, and are accounted the best soldiers in the East. Yet we heaped their dead on that plain. For who can stand against the wrath of God?"

"Well," said Lucas dryly, "the heathen Tartars

are still very much alive."

"Their punishment will come."

Lucas shook his head. "I cannot believe that He Who gave His only begotten son to die, unavenged, would deliver the wives and children of those Alans into our slavers' hands."

Though sometimes I think God has turned His back on this world, his mind went on, because where is there left a happy people?

En Jaime looked hurt. Not wishing to annoy his friend—the only Catalan whose faith was not simple, blind fanaticism—Lucas said quickly, "Between Alans and Genoese, we seem to have defeated our last foes."

"Just so," nodded En Jaime, with evident relief at the diversion. "I hope now to enjoy my villa for a while, in peace. I am glad that you're coming to stay with me. The first time since I bought the place. Why would you never come before?"

"There was always something to be done," said Lucas. Such as carousing in waterfront taverns with outland merchants, he thought, or gaming with the sailors, or making love and prating learnedly to Violante. In short, anything which might blur the remembrance of how all that wealth was gotten.

"Eventually you'll face an enemy you can't conquer," he warned. "Famine, when you've finished turning this country into a desert."

"Then we'll march elsewhere."

Lucas made a face and fell silent. The procession of the knight, his guest, and his servants wound on across the cliffs. After an hour, they turned off the highroad and went down a graveled path. Screened by oaks and elms, a line of cottages stood near a walled enclosure. Inside was a colonaded house, not large for a nobleman's country retreat, but gracefully proportioned. At its rear, beyond the stables, an extensive garden—hedges and trees artificially clipped, flowerbeds now little colorful in autumn, lichened statues of nymph and faun—dropped in such steep terraces that from the upper ones a man could look across the top of the seaward wall, down the cliffs to a boat landing.

Lucas filled his lungs. "Yes," he said, "you've chosen a pleasant site. Would it were mine."

"Use it as yours, whensoever you desire." As they dismounted in the flagged court surrounding the house, En Jaime rested his hand briefly on the younger man's shoulder and smiled into his eyes. "My son," he added.

He clapped down formality like a protective visor. "This is the hour of siesta. We both need rest, after so much war. Demetrios, show Maestre Lucas to his room."

He was led to a chamber hung with silks and tapestries. Wine, water, oranges and cakes, stood on a table. Several books lay next to the bed. Lucas examined them with interest. Sophocles and Aristotle from antiquity, Procopius and Psellus of Byzantine days, and most especially the Almagest, promised him happy hours. Unable to read, En Jaime must have gone to much trouble with some literate Greek prisoner, weeding out of a captured library what he thought Lucas might enjoy. The picture of the Catalan warrior, turning a volume over in sword-calloused fingers and barking questions at a terrified

188

scholar, was both comical and touching.

The draperies rippled. Outside, a noisy wind chased clouds across the sun and away again. The heat of a few days past was dissipated, true autumn had come overnight. Lucas felt no desire for sleep, or even for study. He put his cloak back on and went outside.

House and grounds looked deserted, the staff taking an opportunity to rest while the master did. A man or two was surely on sentry-go, but beyond the walls. Lucas wandered among trees that tossed and soughed in the great streaming wind. Light and shadow fled across the world. In all that restlessness, even a marble nymph seemed to dance. A pergola roof lifted above a hedge, its copper ablaze. High overhead passed a spearpoint of geese, southward bound from Flanders. Dazzling white against a clear cold blue, clouds scudded in their path.

O God, thought Lucas, to have wings and be up there—a mile above this swamp of blood!

"My lord."

Afterward he was surprised that he heard so timid a voice through the gusty air. At the moment, it was the quick tightening of his gullet and galloping of his pulse which seemed unreasonable.

He turned about with an effort. Djansha stood in front of a rose bower. A few faded petals remained, fluttering off one by one as the wind snatched them loose. She wore the gown and wimple of decorum, so he could only see face and hands. The face was huge-eyed, lips parted, red and white chasing like the cloud shadows. Her hands strained against each other.

Well, he thought, I knew I'd see her again. She was always one reason I cared not to visit this place . . . though why I should fear her is hard to understand.

"Good day," he said, after clearing his throat.

She curtsied. As yet, he saw, the life within her had filled her breasts more than her belly. The cloth was drawn tight over her bosom. Skirts flapped in the wind, revealing ankles whose trimness had always been a delight to watch.

"I trust you are well," he said.

"Oh, yes, thank you, my lord," she gulped.

"En Jaime assured me you were well treated."

She nodded, never looking away from him.

"That's good," he said. "Have you friends here?"

"They are kind to me, my lord. I can talk a little Greek, now."

"That's good. Er . . . yes." Lucas regarded his shoe, which dug in the earth. "En Jaime said also he'd have you instructed in the Faith."

"I learned a little," she faltered. "A priest sometimes came out here. But he was angry when I asked so many questions. I have not seen him since."

"Oh. Well, of course he went off with the army. Or, well, he and the others, even En Jaime, forgot about the matter. I'll see to it myself, then . . . that you are taught the truth and baptized. Then I can manumit you and, um, make provision. For you and the child."

"My lord is very kind."

He looked away, beyond terraces and wall, down

to the strait. A flock of dead leaves whirled and rattled at his feet, like a tiny yellow Tartar horde going hell-for-leather to conquer the lilybed. A shadow rushed along the Boca Daner, surrounded by sunglitter. It was as if all the world were migrating today, it knew not whither, only desirous of escaping this land given over to rain and black nights. Somewhere westward, southward, there must lie a new horizon.

Lucas' fingers twisted and untwisted behind his back. "I'll do what I can for you," he said. "You know I will. I rescued you from whoredom, and protected you, and, um, I'm concerned about your salvation and bodily welfare." He had thought the list impressive, but as he recited it, the wind yanked the words from him and scattered them out to sea. In haste: "I wanted you to know I'll find you a good steady husband after you're christened. A mariner or sergeant, perhaps. Or a merchant's journeyman. I know some good steady bachelors. Of course I'll provide your dowry."

The gale alone answered him.

He stared at Asia until he thought she must have gone. No, when he looked back she still stood there, but she had turned away from him. The wind pressed her clothes against the curves of waist and thigh. How beautiful she was!

"Well?" he snapped, annoyed at his own awkwardness. "Have you no reply at all?"

"Y-y-you are kind—" She raised a sleeve to the eyes he could not see. "So kind, my lord. But—"

"Yes?" His heartbeat outshouted the wind. As if his legs belonged to another man, he took a step and one more step in her direction.

"You need not—need not marry me off." Her voice came thin and wobbly.

"But I must get a protector for you."

"I think En Jaime . . . would let me remain. As his servant."

"But—"

"And you could more easily see your child."

Lucas halted. "I may not remain here much longer," he said.

"What?" She whirled about. Sunlight gleamed on tears. "You go away? Forever?"

"I know not," he sighed, hardly noticing that he told her what he had confessed to none other. "Had I some country to return to— As matters stand, if I leave the Catalans I must become a soldier of fortune again. Here I have wealth and safety. Anywhere else, my gains would simply make me the prey of every freebooter and greedly lordling. . . . I know not what to do. But I'll at least see to your welfare."

"My only welfare is with you!"

Appalled at her own boldness, she shrank from him. One small fist was clenched to her mouth.

His grin twisted sadly upward. "You speak without understanding, Djansha. These are not your green Caucasian glens. A camp follower's life is filthy, dangerous, and short."

"Would that matter?" She broke off. Slowly, her gaze went down to the burden under her heart.

"Yes," he said. "There's always sickness in the army. Few children outlive their first year."

She caught her lip between her teeth.

"I know not what to do," he repeated dully. "I've

seen enough charnel sights here to fill all Hell, and I'm sick of them down to the marrow. Yet the Catalans only do with more vigor what every overlord and every army, from Spain to Cipangu, does as a matter of right." Lucas beat his fist on the arbor trellis. "In Christ's name, can a man who wants mercifulness do nothing but become a monk?"

"If my lord wishes that—" She laid a hand on his arm.

His laughter barked. "I know myself too well. They'd cast me out in half a year, and I'd thank them for it. . . . No, I can't think what I want, or where to find it, or how to get there. I may not even have the will any longer, in this blood-guilty soul, to go off searching. But if I do, it had best be alone."

She let him go. "Yes," she said.

He looked at the ground again. "But before I go I'll first get a good husband for you, Djansha."

"No," she said. "I beg of you, no. En Jaime will stand godfather to me if you ask him. He'll protect me. He—can raise your son to be a knight."

"Why, so he can," said Lucas, startled. "I'd not thought of that." Then, roughly: "My son, a member of the Grand Company?"

"I do not wish a husband, my lord."

"Why not?"

"It was enough to know you."

She fled.

Lucas gaped after after. "Djansha!" he called. "Come back!"

She vanished among the hedges. With an oath, he started in pursuit. Stumbling like a blind woman, she was soon overtaken. He reached out, caught an edge of her wimple, and pulled her to a stop. The cloth tore. Suddenly her hair burned under the sky.

He snatched her around to face him. They stared at each other. She fell into his arms.

Gallipoli boiled. The rest of the Company had arrived. Though disgruntled at finding no battle, but rather a victory more glorious than their own, they were soon rejoicing. There were to be solemn processions of thanksgiving throughout the week. On this first day, however, all made merry. Drunken gangs of men, arms linked, bawling the wild songs of Catalonia, filled the streets as they lurched from tavern to bawdyhouse and back again. The merchants gave wines, delicacies, clothes, ornaments, and trinkets in exchange for booty, at a pace whose briskness was hindered only by the need to use this rich chance of cheating. Cockfights, dogfights, boxing and wrestling matches, were varied by baiting any Greek unwise enough to show himself . . . down the street at sword point, toss him in a blanket, roll him in the mud, make him dance, throw him off the dock and see if he can swim or not! A few picked squads tramped about on guard, less anxious to prevent stabbings than fire.

Lucas guided his horse uphill toward his mansion. The headiness of yesterday was worn off by this re-entering the city. He felt as if caught in an invisible net. For how could he, indeed, travel elsewhere with Djansha, except in the sordid way of all adventurers who carried women around . . . mud, dung, flies, coughs and runny noses and a flux in the bowels, the eternal likelihood of rape, and each year a tiny grave to dig—? Of course, he might conceivably get the patronage of some important man and settle down. But which was worse, being one of the tyrants now or one of the oppressed then? Would he not do best, for Djansha and their children if not himself, to swallow his conscience and remain here?

He squared his shoulders and clucked to the horse. Hell could have all such problems! His plans for the next several months were clear enough. Follow En Jaime's urging. Move out to the villa, where Djansha awaited his return (she had bid him farewell this morning and skipped off to prepare the feast that would welcome him back at sunset; he could not keep his gloom in the presence of so much bubbling, singing, laughing, caressing happiness). Spend as quiet a winter as possible. Come spring, he might have discovered what he truly desired, or even have reconciled himself to the Grand Company.

After all, he thought, the Catalans are brave. Most of them have treated me well. Some few possess wit and learning. Need I ask more?

Yes, said the devil which Violante had awakened on the plaza.

He entered the courtyard of his house, summoned the major-domo, issued orders. The servants broke into a whirl of activity.

And now—This would be unpleasant. Directed by a retainer, Lucas walked down the halls to the solarium.

Violante sat listening to a girl sing. As Lucas came in, she dismissed her and watched him with unwinking dark eyes. Sunlight poured through the glazed windows, evoking sensuous colors in her garments of satin. Since the regretted impulse which shortened her hair, she had ceased defying propriety; her face was framed in its own wimple and a peaked head-dress trailed gauzy veils.

"Well," she said. "I didn't expect you home so soon."

"I had affairs to tend to," he replied.

"So I hear. What a scurry throughout the house!" She did not humble herself to show curiosity.

He folded his arms and studied her. That part of him which asked justice reminded him how much pleasure she had given. They had fought, but oftener they had kissed, and he would always miss the quick intelligence and the voluptuousness unhindered by any shyness which he had found in her more than in any other woman. Seated there, sun and shadow rounded across the deep curves of her, she was beautiful.

This much his mind admitted. The rest of him felt horror.

"I hope you're well now," he made himself say.

"I was never ill. It was only your whim to pretend I was fevered, to have me bled and seek a separate chamber each night." The stiff pride departed. She rose and held out her hands. Her smile came forth, as if stretching itself after sleep. "But you may have been right, my darling," she said. "If so, believe me when I say I am well again."

He did not accept the offered embrace. She stopped, puzzled, a ghost of fear in her aspect. "I am well," she reiterated.

"God be thanked," he said tonelessly.

"I suppose I did shock you." Her lashes fluttered downward. "What I told you . . . after the battle . . . must have seemed unwomanly. I hoped you would understand. You understand so many things."

He could not think of a response.

"Well," she sighed, "I was raving, then. Delirium. The sickness is past."

"That's good news."

She looked up again. "I'm so glad you're back early. You know not how I've missed you."

"My lady is too gracious."

She caught his arm with the sliding, stroking motion he well knew. The arching of her mouth invited him. "Come," she said, "whatever your business, surely you can spare an hour or two."

"I fear not."

She rubbed against him. "Lucas," she murmured. "I love you."

He held himself unmoving, regarded the wall beyond her shoulder and said: "Na Violante, the servants are packing my gear. They'll bring it out to En Jaime's estate. This day."

She blinked at him, as if she had not comprehended.

"The mansion here you may keep, and of course all the female things," he told her. "As for the cost of maintenance—"

She sucked in a sharp breath. "What are you saying?"

"That I am leaving this place." With an attempted friendliness: "We've had a pleasant time together. But all things must end, must they not?"

197

She shook her fantastically attired head. The veils swirled. "You are leaving me," she said in a flat, small voice. "Without even a warning."

"I'll make provision for you," he said, becoming irritated, wishing only to be done with this.

"As you would for an old horse." She stared at nothingness.

"Na Violante is too unkind to herself." Weirdly reminded of yesterday, he said, "You needn't fear loneliness. Anyone as fair and well born as yourself can choose a husband from—"

"No doubt you'll go back to that whey-skinned savage." She had not heard him.

She picked up a porcelain vase. For a while she turned it over and over in her hands, staring at the colors. Lucas eased a trifle. He had expected fireworks. But evidently the infatuation was as dead in her as in him.

She took the vase by the neck and smashed it across his face.

He flung up an arm barely in time to save his eyes. The thing shattered, cut sleeve and flesh, raked his jaw, and exploded on the floor. Violante snarled one foul sentence and ran from the room.

Lucas stood swaying and shaking until he recovered enough to call for his Greek valet. The little round man brought water and towels, and treated him.

"The hurts aren't serious, Despotes," he said. "Give thanks to all the kind saints."

"I will, Alexios." Lucas grinned lopsidedly. "From this day, I'll heed their omen and steer clear of Xantippes."

"Despoina Violante left the grounds. Afoot."

"She'll come back, but I trust we'll be away before then. How goes the packing?"

"Well, Despotes."

Alexios looked so distressed that Lucas said, "What's wrong? Speak what you will. I'm no servant beater."

"No, Despotes, you are not. You have been merciful. You have even cared about us, helped us, as if we were your own people. I will remember how you made Zoe, the scrubwoman, stay abed for a week when she fell sick. And, what would have become of me, had some mild saint not guided you to notice me? . . . Despotes, in Christ's name, don't leave us!"

"That's a flattering wish, Alexios," said Lucas, more moved than he dared show. "Of course, I'll bring you along to the villa."

"But the others! Left alone with the Despoina!"

It was like scratching a half-healed ulcer. "God's death!" Lucas yelled. "Am I St. Christopher, to carry the world on my back? I've my own life to live. Get out! Get to work!"

Solitary again, he fumed up and down the chamber until he spied a carafe of wine. Having tilted that directly to his mouth, he was a little soothed. Presently he went out to speed the labor of packing.

Alexios whispered that Violante had returned, in a black temper. She had carried some bundles into the bedroom Lucas had lately been using, and bolted the door behind her. He gave little thought to the information, but a shiver went through him. These

Catalans were all as proud as Lucifer. He had offended her greviously; one did not discard Na Violante de Lebia Tari like any trull. That much he could understand, and he felt a detached compassion for her. What made her gruesome to him was the lunacy he had seen revealed under a furnace noon. Thinking back, he could now recognize it in episode after episode. His skin crawled. He had no desire to see what she was doing, alone in that room.

Well, the Christ who cast out devils might yet have mercy on her. Meanwhile, Gallipoli was strangling Lucas. He wanted clean air again, and Djansha.

Toward evening, all was ready. A train of horses carried his monies and what seemed a fair share of plate from the house. En Jaime's vaults could safeguard it for him, as they already did the loot of the *rich hom* and his men out there—for Muntaner was to be trusted, but not Rocafort, and thus the Company coffers in town did not seem to offer completely safe storage. Accompanied by Alexios and two grooms to drive the horses, Lucas rode forth. A serving maid wept, loudly and hopelessly, as he passed by. He tightened his heart.

An hour's ride through lively air and evening light cheered him. When steel flashed far behind and a dust cloud bespoke several men a-gallop, he thought no evil. Armed messengers, perhaps. Or marauders, who just had word of some juicy target as a supply caravan going to Maditos. It was no concern of his. He turned onto the path toward the estate.

The gates were being opened for him when the squad drew up behind. The gatekeeper's mouth fell wide at sight of the men in armor and the black-robed Dominican friar who accompanied them. Others came swarming to see, until the courtyard was full of menials and soldiers. Lucas glimpsed En Jaime's lean form on the steps of the house—and yes, yes, there was Djansha, waving to him from the fringe of the crowd—

"Lucas Greco!"

The summons brought him twisting around in the saddle. The officer of the squad shied back. Then his dusty, sweaty form straightened. "Are you Lucas, called Greco?" he queried.

"Yes. What do you want of me?"

"In the name of the Lord King of Aragon, and on behalf of the Holy Inquisition, I arrest you on the charge of witchcraft."

CHAPTER XIV

En Jaime returned, bleak of aspect, with the Dominican. "It's true," he said. "She has means of sorcery hidden in the bedchamber I gave her. Peeled willow sticks, chips marked with heathenish symbols, a bag full of herbs and feathers."

Djansha moved backward until the wall stopped her. They stood in the atrium of the house—she and Lucas and the soldiers. No one had thought to light candles, and as the sun went down, darkness thickened under the ceiling. The girl's face made a white blur. Bright above her gleamed the cruel shape of a halberd.

"That is nothing," she pleaded. "No harm. I would never harm anyone, lord. I do not know how! They were only charms I made. To keep off evil. To guard my lord and my child. I meant no harm!"

Her Catalonian was almost too thick to understand. The friar looked at her as he might look at an impaled frog. "Did your lover know anything of this?" he asked.

Speechless, she shook her head.

"Are you certain? He was only with you last night. Has he never seen you raising devils? Has he never helped you?"

Lucas strained forward. The men gripping either arm anchored him. "Of course not!" he yelled. "I own that she did a bit of magic when first I knew her. How could the poor child know it was wrong? I told her not to, but—" He broke off.

"But what, my son?" asked the black-hooded man gently.

Lucas wet his lips. The drumming in his head made thought nearly impossible. All he could think of was a man he had once seen being racked and the noise Djansha's bones would make as they left their sockets.

"You must not conceal your knowledge, my son," reproved the Dominican. "Your soul can only be cleansed by reparation."

"She's not yet christened," Lucas got out. "En Jaime will tell you I wanted her instructed and baptized, but with all the interruptions—raids, battles, the Company's work—"

"Her salvation was neglected. You showed scant zeal." The monk's fingers darted out in accusation. His words grew sharp. "Your own mistress in Gallipoli brought the charges. She showed me pentagrams she had discovered, drawn in blood under the carpet of your private chamber, and obscene waxen images hidden in a jar. She took oath she had often heard you muttering in an unknown language at night, and even seen you make passes when you believed yourself unobserved. By your own admission, you have spent years among Tartars and

203

Saracens; you consort with schismatical Greeks; you practice astrology; you read profane books; you came here with a heathen slave who is now revealed as a witch. You must agree the Holy Office is duty bound to investigate a matter so grave, supported by so much proof."

"Proof trumped up by a perjuring madwoman!"

"Be careful of accusing noble persons unjustly. It will not redound to your credit." The friar addressed the *rich hom*. "With your permission, En Jaime, we had best stay here overnight. The powers of evil are exalted after dark." He crossed himself. A stirring and whispering went through that murky room, from man to man. Djansha covered her eyes. "Tomorrow we will bring them back to Gallipoli for interrogation."

The knight stood near enough that Lucas could see how thin his mouth was drawn. "Just so, Frey Arnaldo." His tone was quite steady, and one fist hung clenched. "I myself will accomany you. I cannot believe Lucas truly at fault."

"Perhaps not. There are tests. First, his witch yonder—"

"No!" Lucas burst free of the hands upon him. A soldier grabbed at him as he ran forward. Lucas caught the man on his hip, helped him along with his own motion, as they taught in Cathay. The fellow sailed through the air and crashed against the wall.

"Sorcery!" screamed a voice in the shadows. "I saw, Frey Arnaldo! I saw him make Juan fly!"

In this bad light, with a headful of supernatural terror, a man might see anything, Lucas thought. But no time to argue now. He swept Djansha to him and whispered fiercely, "Do whatever they tell you. Can you understand me? Confess to anything they ask. Admit I wrought black magic."

"No!" she cried.

He slapped the dear face. "Do as I say! I command you! Your silence won't help me. You'll only be tortured till you lose the child. D'you hear me? Till you lose the child!"

They closed in and dragged him away. Djansha tried to follow, but others held her fast. She called his name, once, before they put a gag on her spell-casting mouth.

"What did you tell her?" snapped the monk.

"Lucas, Lucas," said En Jaime, "don't you know how much worse you're making this for yourself?"

Lucas drew a long breath. And another. There was no peace in him, not yet, but the calm of Cathay descended. "I told her to admit the truth," he said.

"What?" The wrinkled mouth pursed in disbelief.

"Question her tomorrow and see. But only with words, you devil!" Lucas turned to En Jaime. "Friend—"

Some of the men looked askance at the *rich hom*, as the sorcerer addressed him thus. But he answered firmly, "Yes, what would you?"

"I'd remind you, Jaime, that Djansha is still a pagan," said Lucas. "Therefore she does not come under the authority of the Holy Office, which exists to stamp out heresy. They have no right to try or condemn her. If she did wrong, it was in ignorance, and she must be taught rather than punished. I've ordered her to admit freely what the brothers seem determined to find out. What more can they want?"

"Your own confession," said En Jaime. "And then you will burn."

He reached out, not quite able to touch Lucas. "You know not what you do!" He begged. "Violante's testimony, by itself, might well be upset. But thus corroborated—Lucas, hold fast, in God's name!"

"You seem anxious to help a man arrested for witchcraft, En Jaime," said Frey Arnaldo.

The knight looked from man to man. Every face, half visible in the twilight, had become hostile to him.

"If you are my friend, Jaime," said Lucas, "protect my lady and my child for me."

The knight studied him for an entire minute. At last: "I shall."

He turned back to the monk. Suddenly he looked old. "There's an unused shed outside," he said. "It will do to confine the prisoner overnight."

"As for her?" Frey Arnaldo pointed to Djansha's huddled figure.

"She is a woman, and to be respected as such. Let her be kept in a bedroom, under guard. Goodnight."

"Goodnight," said Lucas.

They led him from the house. Outside was a cold greenish dusk with yellow smears lingering in the west. The courtyard flags rang underfoot as the squad went toward the long low building that held stables and mews. Several household servants and troopers of En Jaime's personal entourage stood watching, motionless, except to cross themselves.

Lucas felt oddly light-headed. They were going to

question him. It would be under torture. He did not know if he should resist confession. It would only prolong the racking and thumbscrewing. Perhaps En Jaime could find proof of his innocence. Though that search would be a friendless one. Every man's hand was against those whom the Church had accused.

It might be simplest, after all, to admit consorting with Belial. Surely En Jaime's influence could then win for him, from the secular arm which carried out the execution, a fire of the humane sort. One that produced fumes the victim might breathe and pass into unconsciousness before he seared.

But you could be as brave as you wished, as smug as you wished about saving an innocent girl from torture and death; the prospect for yourself remained just as vile. Lucas struggled for self-mastery.

A short plump man burst from the spectators. "I heard!" he screamed in broken Catalonian. "I heard! You a sorcerer! A devil man!"

"Get back, Greek," ordered a sailor.

Alexios danced about, shaking his fists. "Listen-a me! I his retainer. I live in his house. I know he a sorcerer! Trouble, all he make is trouble. I hate-a dirty sorcerer!"

He evaded the guards, ran up to Lucas, and pummeled him. "Traitor to God!"

"That will do," said Frey Arnaldo. "We shall take your evidence tomorrow."

Alexios ripped at Lucas' tunic and spat in his face. "One side, you!" A pike butt thumped into the valet's round stomach. He fell over backward, retching. The Catalan laughter barked loud and uneasy.

The shed was built at the end of the stables. Some-one brought a forkful of straw for the dirt floor. Lucas' hands were tied behind his back, his ankles lashed together. He was shoved inside. The door slammed shut, the bolt was fastened. Lying in pit blackness, he heard voices and hammerings as a crucifix was nailed above the entrance.

He rolled over prone and wriggled until he worked out the thing Alexios had slipped inside his tunic. His tongue confirmed its nature. A sheathed knife.

He began to tremble.

When that fit had passed, the resurgence of strength and clarity was like a rebirth. Laboriously, with his bound hands, he drew the knife and caught the haft between his heels. God be praised for his litheness—and for no one's having thought to bring real manacles. Even so, sawing the bonds on his wrists across the edge of the blade was slow work. Often the knife slipped loose, and he had to wedge it back in place. But when his hands were free (after several hundred years, it seemed) he slashed the rope on his ankles with three vicious motions.

Rising, he took stock of his situation. The shed was sturdily constructed. Only a few chinks under the roof showed starlight. Feet tramped back and forth in front of the door. Now and then the two guards spoke, comforting each other. One of them swore he heard devils buzzing around the roof like mosquitoes. Both began loudly reciting Paternosters.

Lucas felt his way to the opposite wall. What would they think when they found him gone? *If* they did; escape would be precarious at best. Would they suppose the Old Serpent had come to rescue his own? No, hardly. They were not fools of that particular sort. They'd see plain enough, the prisoner had dug his way out with a very mundane tool. Someone would remember Alexios, but undoubtedly the little Greek was even now pattering through the night. With ordinary luck, he could lose himself among his anonymous countrymen and make his way to Constantinople. Well, God be with you, Alexios. I gave you a few kind words, and you gave me back my life.

Djansha? Oh, she was safer with Lucas absent. His flight would provide the final evidence of his guilt, leaving no reason to interrogate the girl—as En Jaime could be trusted to emphasize, with all his well-known piety and secular authority. No one cared if an unbaptized slave did a little magic. Even in Europe, every village had some old granny who mixed love potions and cast spells against cattle bloat. The Church was not concerned with such peccadillos of poverty and ignorance.

But an officer, an educated, widely traveled, wealthy man, who practiced the forbidden arts . . . that was something else again. He must have done so knowingly, for grandiose reasons. He must, in short, be leagued with Satan.

Violante's sick imagination could manufacture proof enough. If the mansion stood unwatched, as was likely (Lucas remembered how careful the police of Cambaluc were to guard the scene of a crime until everything had been studied; but this was Christendom)—she might well be planting more diabolisms at this moment.

Lucas dug his knife into the floor.

With so small a pick, hands for shovels, eyes blinded, the work went slowly. After a while, he lost all hold on time. Nothing existed but sweat, aches, soft heavy earth, the heart-stopping instants when silence outside brought a conviction that the sentries had heard something, renewed resolve and renewed labor. . . . When finally his blade grated on a flagstone, he needed many seconds to realize what that meant.

The vision of flames revived him. He undercut, toiling for air as he lay beneath the shed wall. Dirt collapsed over legs and hips. He wondered if it would fill his nostrils and bury him. With slow care, muscles shuddering from the effort, he eased the stone loose and let it down in the pit. Stars leaped amazingly into view.

He freed himself and crouched against the wall, listening through his own pulse beat. Back and forth on the other side, the sentries went. The house was a blur against lightlessness. But the east was pale. Dear Jesus, had he been working all night? They'd come for him in an hour.

He stuck his blunted knife back in the sheath, which he hung at his belt. On hands and knees, he glided from the shed. It was backed up almost against the estate wall. To reach the garden he must cross an open space, in full view of the guards.

Good saints, he thought, I am not a pious man. I own to doubting, even now, if you truly intervene in human affairs; for the philosophers of Cathay told me Heaven had more dignity than that. But if you do . . . watch over Djansha, you saints. And if you will hearten me in this my fear, I shall always be grateful.

Keeping close to the wall, he moved forward.

It seemed impossible that he should not be spied. The sleepiest men, in the worse light, with a bare few seconds to notice a shape black with dirt, must still do so. For all the stars flung their rays down to tinkle on his head and all the trees pointed their twigs at him, and the first awakening birds shouted, "Look! Look! Look!"

Yet somehow he was behind a hedge, down a path, gripping ivy at a part of the wall screened by trees. He crawled to the top, dropped on the farther side, and loped off westward.

The revelation came slowly, but in the end it stunned him. He was free.

He was not going to burn.

"Unless they catch me," he added between his teeth.

On the crest of a hill, he paused to consider his next move. The estate was already hidden; he saw only darkling copses and wet meadows. He wondered if he could double back to En Jaime's landing and steal the boat he knew was there. No. It was too big. He could never row it himself, and if he tried to step the mast he'd make enough noise that Emperor Andronicus in Constantinople would buy earplugs.

The idea brought a tired grin to his mouth. In a way, this was a happy moment. He had lost Djansha, but refused to admit he could never get her back. Meanwhile, he had broken out of the invisible net. No stolen treasure, no murderer friends, no helpless underlings, only his fugitive self. Who must, however, be kept alive.

And was trapped on a peninsula.

Though a man might hide a long time in this hill-scape. Or . . . hoy! . . . why not seek refuge among the Byzantines? The commandant of Maditos castle would gladly receive a turncoat, who could give information.

The boyish sense of freedom slumped in Lucas. He remembered all the Greeks driven by misgovernment to call themselves Turks. What would he gain, springing from Catalans to Byzantines, except his own shabby life?

"Of which I'm rather fond, though," he told himself, and started walking.

Full daylight found him in neglected plowland going back to weeds. He was faint with hunger and abominably thirsty. No help for that till darkness returned. He needed a hiding place. A thicket surrounded a tall elm, which still had most of its leaves. He climbed up to a crotch from where he could look widely over land and water. Some distance off lay a tiny stubblefield. A few people must still be left hereabouts, to do their cultivation in fear and trembling.

Weariness surged downward through Lucas. He did not fall truly asleep, but he dozed, two minutes nodding and one minute awake. Nightmarish visions harried him.

That ended about noon. Peering back toward hidden Gallipoli, he saw sunlight flash on corselets. The day was clear and chill, with a breeze from the northeast. Across miles he discerned the antlike riders. They moved straight overland as he had; yes, Catalans beyond a doubt, and what could they be searching for except him?

212

What were those dots crawling just ahead of the troop? The wind brought him an answer. At this distance it was the ghostliest murmur. He knew not if he heard it with his ears or with his soul. But the knowledge stabbed him.

Hounds!

The hunters had gone back to the city and obtained hounds.

Lucas was down from the tree, sprinting across the field, before he noticed how he had skinned hands and thighs. Only when he had broken through a hedge did he think how plain a trail he was leaving.

He forced himself toward coolness, eased his breath, pressed elbows against sides and slowed his dash to a long, swinging trot. His fear whetted his senses as he considered the lay of the land, hues of yellow and brown and faded green. A brook might run yonder . . . no? . . . well, this downslope afforded a quick way to the strait. If need be, he could swim—

Thirst crowded out all else. His tongue was a block of wood. If he did not drink soon, he would fall down unconscious.

A cleft in the hills opened before him. A single poor cottage lay at its near end, the remnant of a hamlet which otherwise was sooted wall stumps and sour ash heaps. The door stood closed and the single window shuttered, but smoke curled from the sod roof.

Lucas halted and knocked. There was no answer. "Hallo!" he croaked in Greek. "Where's your well?"

"At the rear," called a woman's frightened voice.

213

Lucas found it behind a plane tree which over-shadowed the earthen hovel.

"My thanks," he said, when he had drawn a bucketful and slaked himself as much as he dared.

"If . . . if you would thank me . . . then go," she stammered from within.

He tried the door. Bolted, of course. "Give me a loaf of bread and I'll ask God's blessing for you," he said. "The Franks are after me."

"Go!" she shrieked. "Isn't it enough they've burned the other houses and dragged my kin off to the slave marts? Would you bring them down on me and my baby too? Go!"

More loudly down the wind came the clamor of the hounds.

Lucas' eyes went from the well to the tree to the house, and on along the cleft. Its farther end opened on a zigzag path which must lead to the water. This had been a settlement of tenants, who worked the plowland and did some fishing. Evidently a few sur-vivors who had hidden from the first Catalan onrush had crept back to resume a furtive life. They dwelt widely apart, lest they draw a fresh raid by their numbers. This woman and her child were quite alone here, meeting the others only to till the soil. At night?

"I'll go," said Lucas.

"The saints be with you," she sobbed beyond the door. "If I let you in, the Franks will kill us all. I have a baby. They caught my husband—"

He bounded off, down the path to a landing slip and shed under the cliffs. The only other trace of life was a gull, wheeling above empty waters.

Lucas turned at the shoreline and retraced his steps upward. Now he must act swiftly. He need not climb the trunk of the plane tree, leaving his scent on the bark; a limb drooped low enough for him to catch. He chinned himself onto it, worked his way upward, and sprang across to the roof. At the vent's edge he hooked fingers in the sod and lowered himself into choking, stinging smoke. A tiny fire burned immediately beneath. He swung like a bell clapper, let go, thudded to a dirt floor, and whipped about with the knife in his hand.

The woman screamed. She was young, he saw, and must have been pretty in better days. Even gaunted by hunger, in a tattered black dress, she was not ill looking. The hut was single-roomed, gloomy, bare of all except the rudest furnishings. An infant lay in a cradle.

"Be still!" hissed Lucas. "No harm will come to you. Tell the Catalans I went on when you refused me admittance."

She snatched up the baby. Her wail gurgled to silence. "That's better," said Lucas. He found a heel of stale bread and began devouring it.

Horses clattered hoofs, metal rang, dogs bayed. A voice shouted, "Open up in there!"

"Ah, no," moaned the woman. "I dare not. I . . . I am alone—"

"Open or I'll beat your door in! We're trailing a sorcerer. He came to this threshold."

"Don't argue in that Greek pig-lingo, Simon," said another man, speaking Catalonian. "Break in and we'll see." Lasciviously: "The woman might be worth the trouble by herself."

215

"With a warlock abroad?" snorted Simon. "Are you mad?"

"S-s-s-someone came here," the woman chattered, "He asked me . . . for water . . . he said the F-f-franks were pursuing him. . . . I didn't let him in."

The hounds, which had been questing over the ground, broke into a full-throated belling. "This way!" called a soldier. "He went down yonder trail!"

Simon cursed. "No doubt the wretch has swum off, meaning to come ashore elsewhere. Now we must cast up and down the clifftops all day, trying to pick up his scent again. Come!"

The noise dwindled into silence.

Lucas sat down, leaning his back against the wall. "I don't think they'll return this way," he said. "Of course, now they know you're here, you'd best find another dwelling. I'm sorry about that, but need forced me."

Light seeped through the smokehole, down onto the woman. Her face was shiny with sweat. "When will you go?" she pleaded.

"After dark. No harm shall come to you meanwhile." He fumbled at his belt. "Oh, bah! I wanted to pay for my lodging and the trouble I've caused, but now I remember they took my purse as well as my sword." He attempted a smile. "You must be repaid, then, in thanks and prayers."

She watched him mutely, trembling. He found water in a jug and washed the worst filth off his exposed skin. "I'll not dismay your Eastern sensibilities by taking a real bath," he said. "Ahhh!" He lay down on the floor. "I'm going to sleep. Don't come near me. I might wake in a panic, stabbing with this knife in my hand. But otherwise, be not afraid. I'm much too weary to harm anything fiercer than a cockroach."

His eyelids drooped.

"Are you really a magician?" she asked.

"Eh?" He jittered awake. "What? A wizard? Oh, God, no. A canard invented by my enemies. If I had diabolic powers, I'd not be here!"

"I thought so," she said bitterly.

After a long while, rousing him again from the edge of sleep: "You must know how things are in the world. Do you expect the Turks will conquer this land? Each night since they took Nicholas away, a half a year ago, each night I've prayed the Turks will come."

"I suppose they will someday," he mumbled.

"I'd gladly be a Turk. We used to hear from men who'd been across the strait, in Anatolia, not all Turks are bad. They leave Christians in peace. Only taxing them, I hear. Less than than we pay to an Emperor who can't even protect us! But I would be a real Turk. I would raise my son to fight for Mohammed. How else will I ever get revenge on the Franks?"

"Yes, yes. Now, I beg you of your mercy, I'm three parts dead and one part sick. Let me sleep!"

He awoke much later. Dusk hung blue in the smokehole. The infant slumbered. The woman squatted over the fire, stirring a pot. Lucas' body was one lump of stiffness and pain. But after he had exercised and drunk half a gallon of water, he began

217

to feel a little like himself.

"That stew smells good," he said wistfully.

"You swore you wouldn't harm me," she said. "I can barely make milk for Doukas. Would you rob me of the means?"

"No." He sighed. "Give me another hour and I'll be on my way."

She looked at him closely. "Where will you go?"

"I'm not sure. Perhaps to Maditos."

"They take no one in. They want to keep their supplies against a siege. I tried."

He lacked heart to tell her he might have a special entree. "Have you any suggestions?"

"Where would you like to go?"

He thought about it. "West and south," he decided. "I have a friend on Cyprus who might give me some employment. But I fear that's too long a swim."

The dark head cocked, studying him. "My father once visited Cyprus. They have Latin kings, don't they? He said the Greeks there are oppressed. But surely no worse there than here, today. Do you know?"

"I don't suppose one is set upon and ravished, or killed, or sold as a slave. More than that I can't say."

"What is your name?" she asked abruptly.

"Lucas. And you?"

"Xenia." She stirred the pot with more energy than was needed. All at once, rising and handing him a bowl: "I know where a boat is hidden. Could you sail it alone, with me to help a little?"

Joy sprang in him, but he answered cautiously,

"The autumn storms will soon be upon us."

"If we sink," she said, "have we lost very much? I often thought of taking the boat myself, but I could never rig the mast. None of the people left hereabouts could handle a boat of that size. All our men and youths are gone. Only a few women and aged ones are left. So I kept the knowledge secret, always hoping—"

"Given your own food supplies to start with," he said, "I think we might catch enough fish to keep alive. I'm a fisher lad myself."

"Oh, blessed Mother Mary! That I should be granted this!"

Having slept so much already, he tossed wakeful after dark. Sometime toward midnight, he heard a rustling from Xenia's pallet. He sat up. By the last light of the banked fire, he saw her beckon him and crept across the floor.

The thin arms closed around his neck. "Lucas," she cried softly. "The world is such a terrible place. Help me forget."

CHAPTER XV

On the slopes of the Troödos Mountains, along a road which wound red and dusty among pines, now and again opening on a wide view of peaks, plains, hills whose vineyards and orchards were blurred by distance into shadings of autumn color, Lucas fell in with a band of muleteers. They were bringing wood down to Limasol, and glad of a stranger's company.

"What may your business be?" asked the leader, a burly black-haired man called Petros. "Who's your master?"

"None," said Lucas.

They looked so shocked that he hastened to add: "Oh, I'm no outlaw." Not on Cyprus, he thought, and then, wryly: Not yet. "I came here in search of work."

"Hm." Petros scratched his head. "You've not found so good a place, then. Some Frankish lord may well lay hands on you as a masterless man and make you a slave in all but name."

Lucas scowled. This was not the first time he had heard from Cypriotes of the harshness under which they lived. The island was rich, a crossroads of trade, mild of climate and beautiful to behold. But it was also the last remnant of the Crusader kingdoms. The French dynasty of Lusignan and their barons ruled with high-handedness, exacerbated by the fact that the serfs, peasants, and workmen under them were Greek-speaking Orthodox Christians. The native hierarchy had been made subject to a Roman archbishop; their churches were small and poor, deliberately made inconspicuous, and the life of the people followed the same pattern.

By contrast to their brethren under the Catalans, or even under the Empire, the Cypriotes were fortunate. But it was only the difference between slaughterhouse and shearing shed.

God of justice, thought Lucas, have You brought the Turk down on us because we forgot to honor our fellow Christian?

"Did you hear what I said?" asked Petros impatiently.

Lucas started out of reverie. He was glad to bring his mind back to the chilly sweet air under the pines. "Oh," he said. "Yes. I knew that danger. But I'm not afraid of their bailiffs. Not after eluding so many others."

"How so?" The nearer men edged closer, eager for any story that would break the tedium of their lives. Then, as the mules began lagging and straying, they returned to apply the whip. Oaths rolled richly through the forest shadows.

"I fled from Gallipoli peninsula," Lucas said. Those who could hear him looked rather blank. Only the dimmest rumors of the Grand Company had reached these folk, rooted like plants to their patches

221

of soil. Few of them even knew the geography beyond this island; it was a wide, vague world, filled with heathen, monsters, and Franks. Better stay safe at home! Lucas spent so much time explaining matters known to any Venetian sailor that he had little left for his own adventures.

That suited him. He had to leave out all the truth about himself anyhow, posing as a common Byzantine fisherman, lest he start gossip which would draw unwelcome attention. The simple fact of his Latin father might have cost him the friendship of these men.

What he could tell was picturesque enough in retrospect, though it had been miserable while it happened. Xenia's shallop was too big for him to row. Sculling, he could barely move it along. They were therefore dependent on sail, and the lateen rig made heavy labor for a single man who must also take the steering oar. The woman was too frail to help, and preoccupied with her infant, which sickened horribly at first.

The lack of a periplus added hundreds of miles. Once they had gotten through the narrows, at night, they had to pass among the Dodecanese, with no other guide than the Asiatic shore itself. Often they lost this, when weather or the sight of a ship (which in the Aegean Sea, where all government had failed, was likely a pirate and certainly not a friend) drove them west. Then Lucas beat back as well as he could, inquiring at dagger point of lonely islanders where he was. He took only as much food from them as he believed they could spare, and even so he cursed himself. But the thin crying of the child gave him no freedom in that matter. His trolling for fish had not proved very successful.

He did not even want to remember the gales they encountered.

Toward the end, though, luck turned. The last few days brought slow but steady airs, pushing them east under a mild sun and a big yellow moon. He had robbed a cask of salt pork and another of wine. An occasional pilchard on the hooks helped fill shrunken bellies. Doukas became less fretful, gained weight, crowed at the sea birds and went quietly to sleep on his mother's breast. Beyond the archipelago, this late in the year, they were not frightened by other vessels. At night, moonglow on the water, land hazy and unreal to larboard, a thousand stars, the lapping and swirling of wavelets under the bows . . . it had been sweet.

Perhaps the hardest task of the whole voyage had come on shore, when he made himself ignore the wistfulness in Xenia's eyes and left the convent which had given her shelter.

"Where was your landfall?" inquired Petros.

"On the north coast, near Kyrenia," said Lucas. "I sold my boat to a fisher for enough money to buy a clean outfit and get me to Limasol." He spat. "The vessel was worth a good deal more, but he could see I dared not offer it openly, less I attract the notice of the damned Frankish baron."

"What hope brought you walking all the way across the island, then?"

"I think I can find employment which would not be too onerous with the knightly Order."

"What? Great stinking horse apples!" Petros

gestured violently. "You've no idea what you speak of. Go to Famagusta. There's work on the docks, however ill-paid. But bind yourself not to those friars of Satan."

Lucas stopped in his tracks. Understanding came. "No, wait, what I meant was—"

Petros growled on, red-faced, too angry to have heard. "Listen. When the knights came here, the king gave 'em right to buy broad lands. They'd wealth enough, and they soon showed us Cypriotes how they got it. Usury, rack-renting, fines, taxes, extortion! Oh, they'll hire you with scant questioning, my friend, but you'll soon find why they only keep their serfs. Blows, curses, a pittance of wage—gouged back into their coffers on any pretext—wretched huts to live in, sour Romish rantings: that's all you'll get from the Knights Templar!"

"But I meant the Hospitallers. Everyone has told me they're honest."

Petros fell silent. Only the crunch of feet and hoofs, a breeze that made sunflecks dance on the brown forest floor, a starling far off across the dale which the path overlooked, were heard. Then the muleteer slapped an animal's rump with a shattering noise, and laughed.

"Name of a blue-bellied hog! I'll wager my mucking manhood against a clipped Venetian quattrino you've heard only good of them. But how could I tell you meant the Knights of St. John? No use hunting employment there. Too many others have grabbed the chance to work for such masters. They'll give you a doss and a meal, aye, without asking you to do more in return than chop some wood or hoe some furrows. If you're sick, they'll nurse you to health, and send you off with a Godspeed so hearty you'll forget it's Popish. They'll even try to get a decent master for you. But hire you themselves? Where'd they find the room?''

"No harm in asking.''

"Well—'' Petros gave Lucas a shrewd look. "Perhaps. I've begun to think there's more to you than you admit. No simple fisherman walks so swingingly, with head so high . . . yes, and your hands aren't misshapen from drudgery. So be it. I can keep a closed mouth. I've scars of the lash to remind me.''

He paused, hesitant. "If you should find favor, Lucas— if you should see a place for one more— would you tell them my name? I'd work my butt off!''

They trudged on. Recalling Hugh de Tourneville, Lucas had guessed the Hospitallers would be less odious than others. But when he started his leisured ramble and cautious inquiries, from Kyrenia across the mountains, down through the royal city, Nicosia, and on over the plain to the Troödos range, he had not expected the Cypriotes would with one voice praise the gentleness, open-handedness, justice, tolerance, and wisdom of these warrior friars of the hated Roman Church. The news was immensely cheering.

If only they were not mere tenants in a misruled kingdom—

If only Djansha were here!

Brother Hugh tugged his beard and limped up and

down the room for what seemed a long while. Finally he stopped, but his squinting gaze pinned Lucas before he spoke.

"What did you hope of me?" he asked.

The tone was no less friendly than that with which he had first welcomed his acquaintance, when, after endless arguing, the impoverished unknown was brought inside to see the Knight Companion of the Grand Master. But he had lost effusiveness. The calculations of a leader were again running through that narrow skull. And the most generous chieftain in the world, Lucas thought, must learn to make harsh decisions.

As if reading Lucas' thoughts, Hugh said with care: "I hope you realize I'm no longer in the position of an English noble. Once I could grant you anything within my means, simply because we spent a few hours in comradeship. Now I am an instrument of the Order."

Lucas leaned his elbow on the windowsill and looked past a thick mass of wall toward daylight. The Commandery stood outside Limasol, which raised its battlements in the east above an argent gleam of sea. Down below, a pair of brothers, mere sergeants, but bearing the same black mantle and white cross as his exalted friend, crossed a paved courtyard. A native workman bowed to them and was answered with a grave nod: neither servility on the one side nor haughtiness on the other. A horseman on patrol duty rode by. His armor was unadorned, but burnished to brilliance; the surcoat made a brave red splash. He was the only warlike token in all that landscape.

"I didn't come to beg," said Lucas, abashed. "I offer my services."

"Ah . . . judging from your narrative, I doubt if you have a call." Hugh's dryness removed the sting. "Do you really wish to vow poverty, chastity, and obedience?"

"Faith, no!" Lucas wheeled about. The plain whitewashed room echoed with his loudness. The two men regarded each other and broke out laughing.

"Well-a-day, that was nothing but a tease," said Hugh. "We do indeed have use for a variety of skills, and often hire them outside of the brotherhood." An enigmatic expression came over him, which Lucas remembered from Constantinople. "Within the next few years, God willing, there'll be places for many."

"What do you mean?" Lucas' heart thumped.

Hugh waved the question aside. "But then is not now." he said. "At that moment— Well. Look you." He began to pace again, hands behind his back, eyes to the floor.

"When Acre fell," he said, slowly and with a pain that grew as he spoke, "an age ended. You're too young to understand. No one who was not there can understand. Did you ever lose a much-beloved child? No? In all events, you've worked and failed. So it was with us. Those who were not blind knew that the end of the Christian dominion in the Holy Land was upon us . . . even before the last day had come. We knew it had been a cruel reign. The final assault on Acre was provoked by wanton Christian persecution of peaceful Moslem subjects. God took away from us what we had ceased to merit. And yet we fought. We fought like demons. Even after the final retreat, we strove to come back, by that grotesque alliance with Ghazan of Persia . . . and God in His mercy vouchsafed an instant more. But no matter. For us as men, a lifetime of losing struggle was brought to a close. For the Order, for our sister Order of the Temple, nearly two centuries of hope and prayer and bloody toil ended in failure. In my own heart I think it almost blasphemous that the King of Cyprus also claims the crown of Jerusalem. No Christian banner will fly above those walls, ever again. Unless, long after you and I are dust—

"Well." He cleared his throat. "I digress. I ask you only to imagine the weariness, more of soul than of body, which came to us when we had escaped to Cyprus. This is a strange land. 'The luxury of France, the softness of Syria, the subtlety and guile of Greece,' as has been written. We still had riches, not only brought with us from Acre but in broad estates throughout Europe. The care of them inevitably entangled us in worldly concerns. The Lusignan court made us welcome. Oh, very welcome, in a thousand brightly colored ways. Can you imagine the temptation? Can you forgive those brothers who strayed from their vows?"

Lucas grinned. "I find it harder to understand those who did not." Seriously: "That must be why the Templars are so abhorred."

"Peace!" commanded Hugh. "Speak no evil of others." But he shook his head. "They have surely provoked much hostility," he said unwillingly. "Now the Pope has summoned their Grand Master to reply

228

to certain grave charges—But no matter. I can say for the Hospitallers that we also fell into softness and luxury. Not entirely, I trust. *We* never forgot . . . ahem! We did maintain our prime purpose, to guard and care for Christian folk. From this island base, we built up a war fleet which escorts travelers and is slowly rooting out the corsairs. And in recent years under a younger and more vigorous Grand Master, the vice within the Order has been (God grant) eradicated.''

He contemplated Lucas more somberly than before. ''D'you take my meaning?'' he asked.

''Why—no. I fear not.''

''To be blunt, we've no place for you as a laborer. Even if we had not a superfluity of natives who need such posts more than you, I hope we'd be wiser than to hitch a warhorse to the plow. You could only be used for your subtler abilities. As swordsman, of course, where needful; as ancillary ship's officer; as a man who can read and write and calculate; as an interpreter; as a far-traveled advisor in our dealings with alien peoples. In short, a position of importance.''

At any other time, Lucas would have felt pleased. Now he said, low and afraid, ''Why can I not serve?''

''Perhaps you can. Perhaps you can.'' Brother Hugh struck the trestle table with his fist. ''And yet . . . can't you see, we who are so close to temptation—which many of us succumbed to in the near past—dare not make a confidant of someone who has, well, has lived by those very vices. The upshot would harm us and destroy you.''

Lucas felt himself flush. "That charge of witch-craft—"

"Oh, that!" Hugh brushed it away like an unclean insect. "Have no fear. Plainly enough, false witness was borne against you. The Aragonese Inquisition knows better than to meddle with our people!" Quickly curbing himself: "No, I mean this whole wild adventuring you've related. No doubt you softened it much for my ears."

"Frankly," said Lucas, "yes."

Hugh struggled with a smile and lost. After getting back his gravity, he said, almost pleading, "In large part you were the victim of circumstance. But not an unwilling victim . . . most of the time . . . were you? Interrupt me not! I know very well how many fanatical sophistries the Hispanic mind can produce to justify its own darkest wishes. I realize no one can say anything but that you aided the cause of the Holy Church, with a few minor fallings from grace as respects women and the like. And yet—"

He laid both hands on Lucas' shoulders, captured his glance and would not release it. "And yet, my friend," he said, "do you believe in your soul that Our Lord is pleased with you?"

Lucas fumbled after words. None came. He shook his head.

"You see," said Hugh. "I want to give you my recommendation for a post with us. My superiors will accept it without question. But therefore can you see how hard it is for me to do?"

Lucas had no answer.

Hugh released him. In a crisp, detached way, the knight said, "You mentioned having come here with a woman. Where is she?"

"I left her and her child in care of the nuns at Kyrenia."

"Your child, too?"

"Oh, no. Not that one." Lucas blinked hard, for his eyes had begun to smart.

"You can't leave her there forever."

"I know not what to do."

"Wed her."

"No!" Lucas said in haste. "She has a husband. He was taken as a slave. If he's still alive, he must be somewhere in the Turkish lands."

"Then without a miracle she'll never see him again. Under the circumstances, her marriage would be dissolved, if a special dispensation seems warranted. Think you she might agree? So she could have a protector and her child a stepfather?"

Lucas bit his lip, remembering nights and words whispered. "Yes. I believe so."

"Well, then?" Lucas hesitated. Hugh pressed his point: "I'm not only thinking of her welfare. Celibacy seems impossible for you, but as a wedded man you would be reasonably chaste, I hope. I could more readily accept you as a servant of the Order."

Lucas made his decision. "No. Forgive me, but no."

"Why? She can hardly be loathsome to you, if—"

"She isn't," he blurted. "But do you recall the Circassian slave girl? I hope to get her back. Somehow."

"Ah, so." Hugh stood quiet. Lucas tried to place his expression. It came to him. En Jaime de Caza had gazed that way across many years, at a lady who was dead.

231

"I wouldn't set that hope high," the knight mumbled.

"While the chance remains," Lucas answered, "I cannot take anyone else to wife."

"Well-a-day," capitulated Hugh, "we must do what we can for the other, then. There's a charitable sisterhood attached to this Order. I think I could find a place for her with them. Not as a novice, but as an indwelling helper. And perhaps, in the end, who knows? She might meet a worthy man. Of course, she'd have to embrace the true Church."

"That's no obstacle," said Lucas with relief. He forbore to explain that anybody prepared to leave Christendom altogether would find it a small step from one sect to another.

"This slave girl," Hugh said roughly. "Use your wits. She most likely was sold the day after you fled."

"I trust not. I left her with that grandee I spoke of, who was my own true friend. If I could only get back—"

"You'd hazard your life. The Order will not be sending ships to Gallipoli, and who else would protect you?"

Lucas shrugged.

"In no case could you depart before spring," said Hugh. "The equinoctial gales are here. You were fortunate to survive your own passage. No skippers I know of plan to leave harbor."

"Then I must wait till they do."

Hugh examined his fingertips as if seeing their loops and whorls for the first time. "I've sought out your old foe, the merchant Gasparo Reni," he said.

"He has a leading part in the Venetian factory. When I first came back here and heard the tale of your arrest and escape, I thought you most likely dead. I urged him for the sake of Our Redeemer and his own soul, as well as yours, to forgive and pray for you. He would not. He's wintering at Famagusta."

"Well?" said Lucas.

"Quite apart from seemliness," Hugh told him, "a factotum of the Order would have his usefulness impaired—would even be a detriment—if he was outlaw in Venice and at feud with a powerful man who's well thought of by the Cyprian nobles. Now I think I can, ah, arrange certain pressures. Reni might find it more convenient to swear peace with you and withdraw his charges, than not. Yet this would be a corrupt act of mine did it not work toward a genuine reconciliation. You have wronged him, Lucas. You must make amends. Are you willing?"

Lucas thought of a sword at his breast, of slander and machinations, but chiefly of Djansha in a slave pen. He needed a while to say, "Yes."

"Good!" Hugh smote his hands together. "God be praised!"

Eagerness jumped up in him. "I do want you," he said. "You're far from a saint, but you test true as I hoped. I think the whole Order will profit from your skill."

Somehow, Lucas could not respond with more than an outward smile. The end of unsureness made room for him to realize, in one wave, just how lonely he was for Djansha. But he compelled himself to listen. Hugh hobbled back and forth, striking fist in palm as he cried:

"Aye, indeed we can use you. We'll need many men, a few years hence, but you we need now. I may as well tell you the truth, under pledge of secrecy. You'd learn it as soon as you took up your duties. And by the angels, it boils in me!

"You can guess how little satisfied we are here in Cyprus. Not only are we hampered at every turn, mere guests of a king with scant interest in our purposes: a usurper, actually, since this year. No, for many of us, the compromise we must make, the shortsighted and unjust laws we must obey—must even help enforce—those are the worst things. Since William de Villaret was elected Grand Master, certain schemes have been debated among us. It'd be false modesty to deny that I myself have urged their acceptance, have traveled, worked, spied, intrigued, fought. My mission in Constantinople was a part of that: sounding out the Imperial attitude and capabilities. Other times I've taken ship, gone to the very place, sailed around it, made landings and short incursions. . . . I speak of Rhodes. The beautiful, unhappy island of Rhodes. D'you take my meaning, Lucas?

"Constantinople's suzerainty is a farce. Rhodes has become the haunt and booty of every pirate in Anatolia. Merely ridding its surviving people of those vultures would be a worthy deed in the sight of God. Would it not? But to keep the island! To make it our own! The dominion of the Knights of St. John, subject to none but the Holy Father. Governed as wisely as God will allow us poor fools to

234

do. A fortress of Christendom, at the very gates of the Turk!

"This year God took good Master William home to his rest. But already we've elected his brother Fulk, who is still more zealous. Our decision is made. We shall do it. A secret agreement has been reached with a Genoese corsair, Vignolo de' Vignoli. Call me not a hypocrite. We must use what instruments come to hand. We need ships and men. When the time comes for the grand assault, the Pope can preach a Crusade. But you'll understand there must first be scouting, probing, testing of defenses. Our true objective must not be revealed beforehand, lest the infidel strengthen his positions. For the task will be hard at best—but was there ever a more gallant one? In the next year or three, we must therefore practice guile, use agents . . . rogues, if need be, who'd fain win some remission of Purgatory by aiding our cause . . . rogues like Vignolo or yourself, my friend!

"And afterward, well, you spoke of desiring a country fit to dwell in as a man of peace. I should think a merchant could find ample profit in the course of helping to build a useful trade out of Rhodes.

"What say you, Lucas? Are you ready to lay the groundwork for a new Crusade?"

CHAPTER XVI

However late in the year, it seemed as if half the world were at Famagusta. As Lucas walked along the waterfront, he saw a variety and a magnificence such as Constantinople herself could scarcely boast.

The day was cold, wind driving low clouds like smoke over a dull sky. Beyond the sea wall, waves chopped gray-green. Yet the dressed stone of houses, sheds, defenses, held a glow. There were smells, not only paint and tar, but sandalwood, cinnamon, spikenard, pepper, ginger, a hint of baled silks, barreled wines and dyes, everything that was voluptuous, gathered here at the crossroads of three continents. A hundred ships lay at the docks—galleys, cogs, dromonds, dhows, feluccas, their yards rakish against heaven. The men who brawled and bustled through the streets were as mixed as their vessels: Iberian, Italian, French, German, Flemish, English, looked homelike among so many brown Moors, long-bearded Armenians, robed Syrians, stocky Turks, shy visitors from Tartary and the Indies. The bells of a dozen sects clanged through the wind; the talk, raucous, greedy, profane, torrented in more languages than Lucas could even recognize.

Despite the noise and brilliance around him, he drew his cloak tighter. The air bit with a chill that he knew was largely in his own soul. He found his attention dwelling less on walls and spires than on a Cypriote laborer who cringed like a beaten dog as the retinue of a Frankish baron passed by. When he came near a slave barracks, the sour smell drowned all spices.

He thought of Djansha in such a place, and his need of her clawed at him.

Trying to forget it, he directed his mind toward a number of ships along an outer wharf. They were lean, swift-looking galleys, worn with hard usage but carefully maintained, with catapults on deck and bronze beaks for ramming. Untrustful of the harbor guards, their captains left two men stationed on each. Even at this distance, Lucas could discern a certain gaudiness about those sailors. They swaggered.

The ships must be from Vignolo's fleet, he decided. Brother Hugh had said the corsair was wintering in Famagusta with a part of his band. Next spring he would again sail forth, to harass and probe the strongholds of the islands around Rhodes. Eventually, if all went well—

A war a man could fight in good conscience, Lucas thought, with chivalrous comrades against an enemy who was nothing but a bandit horde. Afterward, a realm where a man could live in peace, under the reign of justice.

But what is that to me, he thought, if I never see Djansha and our child?

He straightened. He would not admit the possibility. And meanwhile, his lack of her would mask the distastefulness of certain unavoidable tasks. Such as today's. If he held his mind on Djansha, perhaps he wouldn't feel too much sting at abasing himself before Gasparo.

The merchant's house came into view. He knew well the coat of arms painted above its door. It was a long, two-storied affair in the Venetian style. Doubtless it also held offices, though much of Gasparo's work must be done in the factory. As Lucas mounted the stairs, a footman asked his business.

"I was to see Messer Reni on a matter touching the Knights Hospitallers," he evaded.

"Ah." The fellow regarded him with an insolence so open that it must have been ordered. "Then you are Lucco of Candia." He rang a bell. Another man appeared. "Show this Greek to the master."

Lucas ate his pride and followed down a long, somberly wainscoted corridor. Cypriote servants, deferential to the Venetian who led him, scurried from room to room. An occasional clerk or apprentice gave the newcomer that cool, appraising stare he remembered from years past.

I will soon be finished here, he told himself.

Brother Hugh had insisted he come. Lucas Greco was bidden an excellent position as the knight's personal amanuensis—which meant everything from interpreter to warrior, with all the associated chances for profit and distinction. But first Lucas Greco must purge himself of that old offense which had made his persecution not wholly unjustified. Hugh himself was unsure why Gasparo was so embittered. To bring this meeting about had taken all the immense pressure which the Hospitaller could exert. "In the end he yielded," said Hugh. "He'll terminate his feud and see that the charges against you are dropped. But his acquiescence was grudging, and contingent on your humbling yourself to him—which is his right."

Recalling the hatred that had glared at him across a sword blade, Lucas wondered if matters were indeed that simple. And he was unarmed. As he walked farther down the tunnel of the hallway, among candle flames, his spine prickled.

The footman indicated a door, but did not move to open it. Lucas himself knocked, pulled the latchstring, stepped through and closed the door again.

Beyond was a small room, oak paneled and austerely furnished. Red velvet drapes were drawn across the glazed windows, so that all the light was from a chandelier and a marble hearth. An escritoire, littered with papers, stood beneath a crucifix in the grim Hispanic style. Gasparo Reni sat near the fire.

His gross form was clad in robe and hose of rich stuffs but dull brown hues. As Lucas bowed, the jowled, lumpnosed face remained expressionless.

"Good day, Messer," said Lucas.

Gasparo made no reply. The silence lengthened. The crackle of the fire began to seem very loud. Lucas was on the point of protesting when he realized Gasparo did this by plan, wanting to break his nerve. He took a long breath and made himself stand at ease. I can wait just as long as you, my friend, he thought, and the childishness of it all brought a heartening inward laugh.

Gasparo stirred. "I never expected we'd meet again like this," he said without welcome.

"Our past encounters were ill," said Lucas ingratiatingly. "I hope—Brother Hugh de Tourneville hopes—today will make a change."

"Aye, you always had a gift for worming your way into the favor of the great."

Lucas swallowed hard. He must not become angry. "I'm here at Brother Hugh's behest, to make amends for what is long past, Messer."

"As if you could!" Gasparo mastered himself. "You may as well sit down," he said. Lucas obeyed. They avoided each other's eyes.

Finally Lucas said, "See here, Messer Reni, I'm no more eager to stay than you are to have me. The wrongdoing is not all on my side, since the day you attacked me unprovoked in Constantinople. You know not how much you've cost me. But I ask no redress for that. I mention it only so you'll feel yourself even with me, and thus be more disposed to end this quarrel."

Gasparo sat up straight. It seemed as if a light flickered in him. "I caused you grief?"

"No matter."

"I want to know!"

Before that avidness, Lucas felt a quick horror. The sense was eerily familiar, and he could not think why, but chased a memory down dark byways. The answer came like a blow: thus had he felt when Violante spoke to him in madness under the walls of Gallipoli.

"What does it concern you?" he snapped. "You're quiet enough about your reason for wanting me dead."

Gasparo grew motionless. When at last he uttered words, they were unsteady: "You know what you did to the house that had sheltered you."

Loathing and anger shoved the imprudent retort out of Lucas' mouth: "Sheltered me? Made me an ill-paid servant! I owed you nothing except my labor. That you got, and your overseers cuffed me and insulted me into the bargain. As for your wife—when were you ever a husband to her? You and your Eastern trips! I can remember how young and merry she was when she came to your house. She'd laugh like a child at sight of a kitten with a thimble or my own poor playing on the cither. You took her for her dowry and her family connections, as you would acquire any useful article of commerce, and put her in your big dank house and went away. Month by month, I saw her fade. Sometimes she'd sit with an old rag doll in her arms—she hid it behind her back when anyone entered, but I was quick enough to notice things. Before God, you didn't even give her a baby to ease her loneliness! After we became acquainted, which happened because she'd nothing else to do than visit the countinghouse, she invited me to her home on various pretexts, and we'd talk at length in the presence of an old lady's maid who was stone deaf. But innocently as saints. For no other reason than that she could taste a moment's liberty to be herself, not your damned statue-wife!"

A weariness fell over him. He looked into the fire and said, with one corner of his mouth bent upward a little, but sadly, "Oh, I admit the innocence was hers. I was a hot-blooded boy who saw an opportunity and cultivated it. Yet sometimes when I held her in my arms she was weeping, for her lost girlhood and for the thoughts of you whom she feared. I wonder if you ought not to thank me, Gasparo, that I gave Moreta some warmth. You never did as much."

The flames sputtered and threw unrestful shadows into the corners. When he glanced up, Lucas was astonished, nearly dismayed, to see the look on Gasparo's face. It was as if the merchant were being scourged.

He crossed himself with a convulsive motion and said, "Moreta died many years ago."

"I'd heard that," said Lucas softly.

"But do you know how she died?"

"No."

"I'm not a man of fine words." Hairy fingers wrestled with each other. "I've had to work or fight all my life. I leave adornment of a tale to you silken dandies who've nothing better to do. But I'll tell you what you did to me, Lucco. You think dishonoring a man's bed was mere sport, a good jest. Venice taught you that, I admit—When you got away, I told myself I could not be the butt of laughter. My own apprentice putting horns on me! Nor could I afford to make enemies of Moreta's family. Especially since I needed her uncle's help in certain new enterprises. . . . But I told her, when we were alone, what she'd made herself into. Thereafter she slept in the inner suite, and I in the outer room."

Imagining a terrifed girl alone with Gasparo Reni,

Lucas dropped his gaze again. Merciful God, he thought, I never foresaw that.

The other man continued, low and flatly, "We went on thus for a few months. Then it became plain she was with child. I may be blaspheming, but sometimes I believe I've had my Purgatory during those weeks when first I knew. And must pretend I was the father.

"All this time she'd been so meek. Said almost nothing. Not just keeping out of my way, either. Even I could see she was unhappy, growing haggard, brooding alone. Sometimes lying awake at night, I'd hear her crying in there. At first that pleasured me. But then, I know not, except I couldn't lie night after night listening to her cry.

"When she took sick, the physicians said her case was grave. I went in and told her to take better care of herself. All this moping and eating naught would kill a horse. She looked at me—I can't ever forget how she looked at me—and asked why I cared. But she wasn't mocking me. She really wondered why I should care what happened to her. How tired she sounded!

"I heard myself tell her she had to get well because of the child. She turned her face away and said, 'It isn't yours. I've no way to tell you how much I wish it were.' Then I said, only it sounded like somebody else talking, I said, 'It is mine.'

"And the way she looked at me then—!

"She got well pretty quickly. We started learning how to be happy with each other. No easy task, that, but we both wanted to learn and we kept working at it. We were closer than most, I'd say, when time came for the brat to be born.

"It killed them both."

Lucas looked at his hands. They seemed as alien to him as Gasparo's voice had been to its throat. He sat in the skin of a murderer.

"God was good to me and sent the war with Genoa," Gasparo said. "You can forget a lot in time of war. I even married again. A sound marriage to bring in a big dowry. A fat woman who's quite happy I'm not often in Venice. But sometimes at night Moreta comes back."

"I never knew," Lucas said to hollowness.

Gasparo snorted a laugh. "I'm expected to forgive you! Now will you tell me what harm I did?"

Lucas made no reply. "Good saints," said Gasparo peevishly, "are you about to fall dead? You look it."

Lucas shook himself. A wave of cold went through him. He hugged his ribs and said, "I've long been in search of a just ruler."

"The least you can do is answer my question. Where've I hurt you? Because I sought your life? Nothing came of that. In fact, you've ended up with better prospects than you ever had before."

"But I can't use justice," said Lucas wildly. "Only forgiveness."

Gasparo controlled his eagerness enough to say, "Maybe I can, too. If we're to be friends, let's be honest with each other. What claim do you have on me?"

Lucas slumped. "You separated me from the one I care for," he said. "A fitting revenge, isn't it?"

"What d'you mean?"

"Do you remember the Circassian slave girl?"

"Yes, if that's the one you stole from me."

"I rescued her!" The flare died down; Moreta. "I'll repay your monetary loss. But we escaped together to the Catalan Company. She became dear to me. If she lives, she'll be the mother of my child next year. But I had to leave her behind when I fled, outlawed from the Company on a false charge. Now, at best, months must pass and great difficulties be overcome before I get her back. Perhaps I never will."

Gasparo raised a crook-fingered hand. "What's this you say?" he breathed. "You're in love with that heathen slave?"

Lucas had never readily shown his feelings to anyone. Even to himself. Surely, of all strange happenings on this strangest of days, he had least expected to tell Gasparo Reni what was in him. But the need to be understood and pardoned—an absolution beyond anything a priest could give—opened him up. "She's all I care about in the world," he said.

"What have the Catalans done with her by now? Sold her to the Turks or put her in a brothel of their own?"

Lucas could not acknowledge to himself how spiteful a grin Gasparo wore. He said frankly, "I'm more fortunate than I deserve. I left her in the care of a nobleman I know, who'll keep her as his ward until I can claim her again. I suppose the best thing is to send a letter to him, with a trusty messenger, by some ship in spring. . . . but so much could happen before then. And I not there!"

"I see." Gasparo stroked his chins. "Yes." He

pondered awhile, his muscles tensing under the robe. Offhandedly: "Who is this noble? I've dealt with many Catalans. Perhaps I know him too, and could tell you somewhat of him."

"I doubt that. He's no merchant, but a *rich hom* and a knight. En Jaime de Caza."

"No, I haven't met him. Is he very important in the Company?"

"Yes, he's on their governing council. Though they're so riddled with factions that I know not how much that weighs. Indeed, he finds the most careful course to be safeguarding his own treasures and his personal followers', rather than trusting the official vaults."

"If he should be killed by his rivals, then, or in battle—"

"I beg of you, do not voice my own worst terrors. But I think that's unlikely. At present, the Catalans have no serious opposition. I think they'll spend a quiet winter, for them. En Jaime isn't even prone to go on raids; he dislikes preying on helpless country folk. He has a villa outside Gallipoli, where he lives in peace."

Gasparo nodded. "And the girl is with child by you, eh?" He sat still for a while. Then he rose. "You may go," he said. "I've work to do."

Lucas stood up also. He could no longer evade seeing how Gasparo shivered with excitement, breathing hard, lips drawn wide. Unease pierced all desperate remorse, and he compelled himself to speak:

"Are you willing to make peace?"

"Oh, yes. Yes." Gasparo made an impatient

gesture. "Go where you wish. That was already settled, anyhow. Hugh de Tourneville made clear to me—more important, to my partners—what I must do to keep the good will of his Order. The necessary steps toward obtaining your pardon have been commenced before the Bailo of Famagusta. Your visit here was only an informal gesture. Go, I say."

"If you would give me your own pardon, as a man—"

The little eyes smoldered. "Isn't it enough that I renounce the vendetta?"

"I can offer monetary compensation—"

"I don't want any. I'd rather leave my claims wholly unencumbered before the law. Get out, now! I've much to do. It won't be easy, getting a ship to sail this time of year. I'll have to bully the captain and pay the crew double, no doubt."

Lucas shook his head in a stunned fashion. He had taken too many blows in this hour. He could not make sense of the words. "What's your plan?" he asked stupidly.

"To claim my rights. Nothing else. A quick voyage up to Gallipoli, to recover my property. I always keep papers, so I still have the bill of sale from Azov. I'm sure the Catalans will honor my claim. I shouldn't even have to bribe them. I know they're anxious to promote trade, and I'm a great merchant, and you're a wretch with a price on his head. If your En Jaime resists me, he'll be overruled. Don't you think so?"

Lucas took one step forward. Gasparo picked a bell off the escritoire and rang it. "As for what I'll do with my slave when I've reclaimed her," he said relishingly, "I don't know yet. Have you any suggestions, Lucco? She'll have to be kept alive till the baby's born, at least. Mustn't lose another little piece of merchandise, eh? But after that—"

The door opened. Two footmen bowed. "Show this man out," said Gasparo. "Then send for Captain Tommaso at the Sign of the Pied Dolphin."

CHAPTER XVII

Outside, the day was heartlessly bright, a breeze gusted from Limasol toward the watchtowers of St. John. Even the walls of this room, with its masonry designed to withstand battering rams, seemed to have become insubstantial. Brother Hugh sat on a bench in the middle like an old raven.

He crossed himself. "We're helpless," he said.

"In God's name!" exploded Lucas. "There must be a way!"

"We can go to the chapel and ask for a miracle."

Lucas struck the white wall with his fist, repeatedly. "If you could force him to withdraw his charges regarding me," he groaned, "when you knew they had substance, then why can't you protect a girl who never . . . never harmed, never gave pain . . . to anyone? What's the use of your damned Order?"

Pain twisted Hugh's mouth and he closed both hands around his walking stick. "You know how those concessions were gotten from Reni," he said. "I used many influences. The strongest, perhaps, was the promise to give his firm a larger share of the agency for the wine raised on our lands, versus the threat to withdraw the share they already have. Also, a contract to supply woolen goods to a large Commandery we have in Dalmatia. Even so, my task wasn't easy. Many brothers, the Grand Master himself, objected to such preferential offers. It smacked of bribery. I had to plead with them to agree, arguing that blessed are the peacemakers. Reni was practically forced by his partners to yield.

"Now we've shot our bolt. I have nothing more available to me, as punishment or reward. If Reni chooses to sail out on a lawful errand, how can the brotherhood, which exists to maintain Christian law, hinder him?"

"Do you call it law, or Christian, to take a woman and an unborn child for—" Lucas could not finish.

Hugh hung his grizzled head. "I myself can't believe God ever intended humans should be property. But the law is as it is, and the restrictions laid by Holy Church on the slave trade do not cover this kingdom. If you had been more zealous in seeing to her baptism. . . . No, forgive me, I didn't mean to play torturer. In all events, conversion doesn't mean automatic manumission. And you could not legally have freed her yourself, not having clear title."

"The child?"

"Aye, it has more rights, especially if christened and if proven to be fathered by a free man. Gasparo would do best not to bring the child here." Bleakly: "As for the mother, if he mistreats her within this jurisdiction, somewhat may perhaps be done."

"Yes," cried Lucas, "he may be given a fine and a few Aves to say. After Djansha is dead."

"I'll send an urgent letter to the Catholic bishop of Famagusta and ask him to remind Gasparo of the obligation of charity."

"Suppose Gasparo doesn't listen?"

"Then the church is powerless. The woman is his chattel, after all. But I'll make the attempt."

"Ha! Save your paper!"

Lucas laid his arm along the wall and leaned his forehead against it. The hand was bruised from striking the bricks. His shoulders trembled. Hugh rose with a muttered exclamation—his leg was troublesome today—and crossed the floor toward him.

"Do not be afraid to weep," he said.

Lucas shook his head, a violent motion. "I caused this," he answered, so harshly that it was difficult to understand him. "The punishment is for my own heedlessness. Which killed a woman. But why must Djansha suffer for it?"

"God's ways—"

"I told Gasparo we could go off alone and he could do anything to me he wished, if he'd let Djansha go free. He laughed and ordered his men to throw me out of the house."

Hugh made the sign of the cross again. "He's not right in his mind. God have pity on him."

"Let God first have pity on Djansha!"

"Watch yourself," said Hugh, growing stern. "According to your own account of what he told you, you woke that madness yourself."

Lucas turned about as if to meet an enemy. "And what must I do to make amends?" he shouted. "Walk barefoot to Jerusalem? Or fight for her?"

251

Hugh regarded him closely before saying, "How could you fight? The man has guards of his own, as well as being under the king's peace. You'd only get yourself arrested and imprisoned."

"You and I together—"

"No! I may not! I'm not my own man any longer. I'm bound to the Hospital. Be still!"

Lucas turned back to the wall. Hugh mastered himself and said more quietly, "You must not feel too deep a guilt. You were only a boy. No one could have foreseen what would happen."

"I knew a philosopher in Cathay," Lucas whispered, "who told me that because the future is hidden from us, the way of virtue is to do as little as possible—live alone and raise no more ripples on the pool of time than we can avoid. . . . Would I had been born a Cathayan!"

"You speak ill. Even those holy hermits who're called to withdraw from the world, are not freed of responsibility. As for the rest of us, it behooves us to act honorably and mercifully, and trust that the ultimate consequences of our deeds will be for better rather than worse. If you think you can, or must, do more, Lucas, you're guilty of spiritual pride."

"But what can I do now? Swim after his galley?"

"I fear you can only pray."

Hugh laid a hand on the other man's arm, and then released it as he felt the muscles go rigid under his palm.

"What's happened?" he asked, a little alarmed.

Lucas raised his head and stared into emptiness. The hair stirred on his scalp.

"Dear Mother Mary!" said Hugh. "What are you seeing?"

252

Lucas drew a slow breath. His eyes focused on the knight, as if he were awakening from dreams.

"But I can fight," he said.

"What do you mean? Are you possessed? There's no help for you on all this island."

"I think there is."

"Lucas, be yourself! Reni has armed retainers, I tell you. And the king's men—You could end on the scaffold! To no purpose!"

"The king's writ does not run beyond these shores."

"What devil is in you?"

"Only a recollection." Lucas felt his way, word by word. "Vignolo's captains. And the Catalan hoard."

Hugh smote the floor with his staff.

"Will you let me go?" asked Lucas.

The knight said something in English, half-challenge and half-despair. "Would God I could help," he answered. "There was a time— Aye. Go. I give you leave of absence. What you do beyond jurisdiction of the Hospital and the Cyprian crown does not concern either of them. I shall make it my business to see that neither takes any notice. And I'll pray for your success."

He lifted the staff. It looked like the truncated shaft of a spear, gripped in his hand. "Pray," he repeated bitterly.

The Sea Horse lay dingy near the warehouses, in sight of Famagusta harbor. Despite a bad reputation, it was much used by oarsmen and deckhands from Western countries, for it was cheap, and a rendezvous known over the entire Mediterranean. A man could always be sure to find someone there whom he knew, a friend to carouse with or an enemy to settle scores. The landlord looked the other way when a body was hustled out and thrown in the water. As for the rest of it, if the food was bad and the wine sour and the straw full of bedbugs, that was only what a common sailor man expected.

Lucas accompanied Earless Orio across the taproom to a corner where they could speak privately. Night had fallen. A dull heathfire and a few lamps did little to relieve the darknesses. The ceiling was so low that Lucas, who was not unduly tall, had to bend his head. The rushes on the floor should have been changed weeks ago. Dimly, through a haze of smoke and shifting shadows, a score or so of men could be seen at two long tables, drinking, dicing, yarning, squabbling. They were a rough lot, clad in dirty blouses and loose trousers, their hair pigtailed and their faces bearded: Genoese, Sclavonians, a few Frenchmen and Iberians, a stray Swede, the scourings of many ports. The landlord and a dispirited Greek boy were gathering up the trenchers off which supper had been eaten. A blowsy harlot sat in the inglenook, waiting for men to get drunk before she approached them.

Orio spat in her direction. "Reminds me of my mother," he said.

He clunked down the cups of wine which Lucas had bought and seated himself. His eyes were inflamed with smoke and many days' bousing, but they rested shrewdly on Lucas, who sat across the small table. Orio was a big man, hairy as a bear ex-

254

cept for his balding pate. His ears had been cropped for some offense, years ago. His beard swept to his waist, at which he bore an illegal dagger.

"Now," he said, "who d'you think you are, wanting me to take my ship out? And for what?"

"For a damned good plundering," said Lucas.

"Gold's no use to a drowned man."

"You know very well you can sail up the Aegean and back again, at this season or at midwinter. If heavy weather comes, there are plenty of islands to shelter at. You're no merchant captain, with an unwieldy ship and a cargo to lose."

"Nor's money any use to a man on the gallows," said Orio. "You've been asking around the harbor a couple o' days now, Messer Greco. I got wind of it even before you was led to seek me as the likeliest one to help you. I doubt you've a raid on any paynim town in mind. Nor even on Greeks. You're thinking of attacking the Christians. Eh?"

"I never thought the captains who follow Vignolo de' Vignoli made very finicking distinctions."

A louse crawled from Orio's beard. He caught it and cracked it between his teeth. "Well," he said, "in wartime, naturally, we take prizes. Other times—I don't admit anything. You know how gossip spreads. We never touched Genoese or Cypriote goods, I swear. Mostly we've gone after the paynim, and who can say a mucking word against that?"

"The foray I'm planning," said Lucas, "would get you in no trouble with the law. You've heard of the Grand Catalan Company?"

"Who hasn't?— Wait a bit! Wait one devil-buggered bit! You don't mean to raid them?"

"You are Genoese. Your own Commune is at odds with the Company: has ordered them out of the Empire, and sent Spinola to dislodge them."

"Aye. I heard what happened to Spinola, too. I'll not come near those hell-dogs."

"It would be a legitimate operation of war," said Lucas. "You'd win praise and honor from Genoa for avenging what your countrymen suffered. And the Catalans are nothing to Cyprus. So you can bring your booty here and dispose of it at the highest prices. What a winter you can spend then! Or would you rather keep on yawning the months away in this rathole, and sail out in spring with not a grosso in your purse?"

Orio gulped his wine and belched. "So one ship is to sack Gallipoli town? Haw!"

"Don't be stupid. Of course not!"

Orio dropped a hand to his knife. "What did you call me?"

"Stow it. Do you want to talk like a sensible man, or—"

Orio's huge left hand shot out and grabbed Lucas by the neck. Rising, the corsair growled, "You cojoneless popinjay! Down on your knees and kiss my feet! And then get out!"

Lucas chopped with the blade of his own hand. The blow cracked loud on Orio's wrist. With an obscenity, the mariner let go. His knife gleamed forth. Lucas stood up, reached across the table, got a wrestler's lock on that arm and threw his weight behind it. The dagger tinkled on the board. Orio gasped with pain.

"Will you sit and hear me," said Lucas, "or must I break a few bones?"

Orio wheezed something. Lucas applied more pressure. "I don't want to disable you," he said with a measured amount of cordiality. "This is a trick I learned in Cathay, among others less gentle. But Captain Orio, my enemy has already sailed. I have no time to haggle. Will you listen to me?"

He released the man. Orio sank shaking to the bench. Nobody had observed the brief struggle. "Drink your wine," said Lucas, and signaled for more.

The corsair eased. He looked ruefully at the purpling bruise on his left wrist, the right arm still lame. "I guess you're no eunuch at that," he said. "Were you indeed in Cathay?"

"Yes. And I fought this summer with the Grand Company, till I fell afoul of them. That's how I know about the treasure."

Orio watched him while the landlord refilled their cups. When they were alone again, the Genoese said: "You spoke of an enemy, and o' being in haste. What d'you really want from this scheme?"

"My woman. Nothing else." Orio looked skeptical. "I don't give a fig-plucking curse if you believe me or not!" snapped Lucas. "But the truth is, the Venetian merchant Gasparo Reni has sailed to get her. He claims she's his slave."

"Eh? The whole waterfront's been wondering why Tommaso, and Reni himself, should weigh anchor. For a woman? What kind o' bewitchment has she got?"

"She's a Circassian princess. Her family would

pay a very large ransom to get her back."

"Oh, so." The suspiciousness faded from Orio's visage. "I never heard Circassians valued their daughters that much. But a princess, aye, that might be different."

"She's mine," said Lucas. "I'll kill the first man who touches her. But you and your crew can pick up quite enough plunder in the course of helping me rescue her."

"Um-m-m. What about the Venetians?"

"I hope we can get there before they do. They've a head start, but your galley must be swifter than their dromond. If not, we'll have to attack them. I hardly think you, or the Commune of Genoa, or the Kingdom of Cyprus, will care if a little Venetian blood is shed. There'll be official protests, which will be pigeonholed. Confidentially, the Knights Hospitallers are in support of this enterprise. So no legal consequences will ensue."

"You're a Venetian yourself. I know the accent. Would you fight your own countrymen?"

"That's not my country. I only lived there a few years."

"What is your country, then? I know bloody damned little about you, Lucas Greco."

"You'll not learn much, either. The best proof of my faith is that I'll be on your ship. I think I've shown you I can fight."

Orio twisted his great beard. "Won't be any light task, getting a crew together in this season. Even for so short a voyage. And into the jaws o' the Catalans! Where's this treasure, anyhow?"

"On the estate where the Circassian princess is being held. It's a lonely place with a handful of men to guard it, and the loot of half the Empire in its vaults. We can seize the grounds, bear off the gold, and be on our way home within two hours." Lucas raised his cup. "But if we don't sail soon, I'll have no reason left to sail at all. You must decide tonight."

He drained the cup and banged it down on the table.

Orio leaned forward. "D'you know this estate well?" Caution was departing, shoved out by raw greed.

Lucas nodded.

Oh, very well, he thought in a hidden burst of anguish. Forgive me, Jaime. There's no blacker sin than betrayal. But whose Judas must I be, yours or Djansha's? Forgive me, my friend, for loving her above you.

If you draw sword on me, Jaime, I do not know if I will defend myself.

CHAPTER XVIII

When they passed Maditos castle, at the mouth of the Boca Daner, they saw campfire smoke to landward. A few horsemen trotted along the heights. Tiny at this distance, they reflected sparks off *jinete* corselets and the kettle helmets of mounted Almúgavares.

"So the Catalans have opened siege," Lucas murmured. "Not many here, judging from the smoke. But they'll keep ten times as many Imperialists bottled up."

"If they come out after us—" Orio said uneasily.

"No. They're too weak at sea. We've not been challenged yet, have we? I tell you, this will be a lazy man's pirating."

Inwardly, Lucas wondered. But he dared not show anything except confidence. The galley's crew were frightened enough at their own audacity. When a storm hit them on the way, they rode it out with small trouble; but wind and hail broke a badly strained courage and they demanded to turn home. Lucas and Orio had to put down a near mutiny with scornful talk and drawn swords.

And yet those men had warred all their lives, without bothering to reckon odds. Venetian, Pisan, Byzantine, Turk, Arab, Moor knew their pikes. Their reluctance now was a measure of that fear which radiated from the Grand Company.

Like the terror of lightning and earthquake, Lucas thought. Was that not, indeed, what the Grand Company was: a vast, roaring, brainless natural force? Were all war and conquest anything else?

He stiffened. The time was past for such questionings. If death and treachery were all the instruments he had, then let him use them, save what he held dear, and descend without complaint into Hell.

The galley rowed on. Near sunset, it passed En Jaime's home. The villa could barely be seen from the water, a glimpse of walls and tile roofs among trees; the landing, with a boat tied at the dock and a path winding upward, was not much different from any other. But Lucas would have recognized those steeps in worse light. His heart sprang and his hands grew cold. There was a buzzing deep in his head.

"They'll have seen us from above," said Orio. "If we turn inland now, they'll muster their folk."

Lucas had difficulty speaking. "Certainly. So we'll continue on out of sight. After dark we'll come back."

Orio grunted and gave orders to the steersmen. From the poop where they stood, they looked across decks less cluttered than on a merchantman. The craft was small for a fighting galley; it had not been easy to recruit mariners. But oars walked down the length of the hull and a good ten men sat in the open, whetting their weapons. When the palomer up in the crow's nest called down what he saw, another vessel or a hamlet, he larded the report with oaths and was apt to add, "Be simple to capture and strip 'em, skipper."

"What the blue-bottomed devils d'you want?" Orio retorted. "A few Greek coppers, or a houseful o' gold?"

His words were dissipated above rising waves, steel-colored and streaked with foam. The ship was headed directly into the weather, which came out of Asia with high, hasty clouds and a gathering chill. The mast rocked against sky and cliffs. A good omen—a useful one, at least—for it did not portend a real storm but did promise a full sail and swift escape once the raid was finished.

If it is, thought Lucas. Remembering how the Catalans fought, he wondered if he would not leave his bones here.

No matter, if only Djansha were freed.

Unless Gasparo had already arrived and taken her— No!

For the thousandth time, Lucas repeated his calculations. They had not spotted the Venetian dromond. He dared not assume they had passed it without seeing it. That was too unlikely, the coastwise route being so narrow a sea lane. By the same token, the other ship could not have completed its errand and started back without being seen. Therefore it was still hereabouts: doubtless at Gallipoli, where Gasparo would have to go first. He would need a while to discover Djansha's location and persuade the Catalan officials that she belonged to him. Muntaner would not willingly override En Jaime's opposition. Gasparo might well have to go over the governor's head, visiting Rocafort in Rhedestos . . . This would all take time. And allowing for the corsair galley's greater speed, Lucas was only two or three days behind.

So if Gasparo had not yet gotten possession of the girl, the task was to seize the villa and take her. If he already had, though, then somehow Orio must be persuaded to fall on him at sea.

Yet in that case, when the man he hated more than Satan came storming aboard, would Gasparo not thrust his sword into Djansha's womb?

Lucas jammed his teeth against each other till they ached.

At nightfall he forced down a little bread, entered the cabin and put on the equipment Hugh had found for him—conical helmet, with nose guard and cheekpieces; hauberk and breeches of mail, reinforced with plate at the critical points; steel-capped leather boots; a light strong targe to hang on his left arm; dagger and sword of Damascus work. When he stepped out on deck again, he heard an envious mutter. Orio had a morion helmet and a rusty corselet; the others were fortunate if they owned leather cap and three-ply doublet.

But their weapons were excellent.

"I think we can turn about now," said the captain.

Lucas agreed. The drumbeat changed pattern under him. Waves smacked and Lucas took a dash of salt spray in his face. Wind hooted in the shrouds; the waters rushed and rumbled; timbers creaked. A partial moon stood halfway toward the zenith, flying between clouds whose grayness it turned hoar. Europe and Asia were black walls on either side of the strait, which caught what light there was in metallic gleams. With all lanthorns doused, the ship became a well of night.

Human voices sounded long-drawn, lonesome, as steersmen, leadsman and lookouts fumbled half-blind among the waves. There was no danger they would be heard from shore. The wind devoured all sounds except itself and the waters.

Orio joined Lucas in the bows. "If we don't pile on any rocks, we'll soon be there," he rumbled.

He was a blocky animal shadow. Beyond him poised one of his men, lean, half-naked in this cold, clasping a pike whose head shimmered under the fugitive moon. Surely, thought Lucas with a flash of his old japery, no damosel ever had unlikelier rescuers.

He strained his vision ahead. "Lights up there." He pointed. "Must be from the house. Steer by them."

Orio bawled a command to the palomer, who directed the helmsmen. The galley bucked its way toward land.

Somehow, thought Lucas, a man gets through intervening time, until at last he sees the wished-for one. Or dies. He felt no eagerness, his mood was merely an unbendable resolution, he lacked the courage to hope.

"Hard a-port! Row, you bastards! Steady as she goes! Stand by the hawser! In, starboard oars!"

The boat boomed against the ship's prow. A sailor poised on the rail gauged his distance, sprang, and

264

made fast the line he carried to a bollard. The ship swung about, crunching against the piles. Other lines were tossed. Some dropped in the water; oaths fumed after them.

"Make fast, you whoresons!"

Up on the trail, a firefly light bobbed. Someone had heard and was coming to investigate.

"All ashore!"

In his armor, Lucas could not jump like the crewmen. He cut the gangplank lashings, dragged it to the rail and shoved it across. When he arrived on the dock, Orio had formed the two score mariners into a double line. Pikes slanted. The captain's own bordon sword flashed free. By a sudden shaft of moonlight, Lucas observed one man more closely: squat, barefoot, crouched in fluttering shirt and trousers, teeth grinning from a greasy beard, a light ax in his hand and two knives in a sash. He spat to leeward and hefted the ax with murderous pleasure.

Orio peered ahead. The lanthorn was closer now, but only one man could be seen, in cuirass and helmet, and a hint of others. "Shall we rush 'em?" he asked.

"Wait," said Lucas. "Let them debouch down here. The path's so narrow they could hold us off for a long while."

His glaive slid forth. He heard the clack of crossbows being wound.

The Catalans stepped onto the beach. Now Lucas could count six. The big man in the lead cupped hands to mouth and called, "Who are you? Why're you landing armed?"

"Fire!" cried Orio.

"Stop, you fool—!" Lucas' protest was too late. The bowstrings twanged at his back. He heard the quarrels go by.

Someone bellowed in pain. The leader's voice lifted: "You sneaking dogs! St. George for the right!"

"God's wounds!" Lucas yanked Orio around. "Have you a fever? Or did you never own any wits?"

"Should I stop and parley?"

"It'd be more honorable. . . . But did you think we could hit anything at this range in this murk? Your archers winged a single man. And now they're warned!"

Lucas raised his sword and broke into a run. "Charge!" he shouted. "Cut them down before they get away!"

The crew howled and swept after him.

The Catalan leader snatched the lanthorn from its bearer. Light streamed over his face, bearded, broken-nosed, scarred and pocked. So Asberto Cornel came back to the master I forsook, thought Lucas. Then there was no chance to think. Asberto flung the lanthorn. It struck one pirate on the breast. Burning oil splashed over his skin. He screamed. The moon burrowed into a cloud and darkness blew over the world.

Lucas reached the bottom of the path. Steel clashed above him. He lifted his targe. A blow shocked his arm. He struck back. One man stood across the trail, a vague hairy shape. Dimmer forms stirred behind. To the left the cliff rose straight; on the right side, a slope overgrown with brambles plunged downward.

"Desperta ferres!" shrieked the Almúgavare. Asberto rapped at his back: "Up to the house, Juan, and tell them. The rest of you, stand fast with me."

The Almúgavare dodged Lucas' sword and glided in. His knife flickered. Lucas had expected the tactic. He guarded himself with his buckler. His long blade chopped at a leg, struck leather and flesh and bone. The Almúgavare lurched off the path. Orio, pressing close behind Lucas, assailed him. The Almúgavare invoked his patron saint, stood swaying, and fought till he was killed.

Lucas was already beyond him, up to the next man. He couldn't make out that face either, but the size and the hoarse breathing told him who it was. A monstrous blow crashed on his shield. He felt his arm go numb, heard the wooden frame splinter. He staggered. The Catalan broadsword swung high again.

The moon broke free. "Do you know me, Asberto?" Lucas called.

It was done with unmerciful deliberation. Cornel almost dropped his sword. "Greco!"

In that unguarded moment, Lucas hewed, once, twice, thrice, with all the speed and power he owned. Blood sprang from Asberto's thigh and left arm. He stumbled backward, off the trail and down the throny slope. Lucas pursued, his iron belling on cuirass and helmet and defending sword.

"You swine of a sorcerer—!" Asberto groped with his feet, seeking a firm place to stand. "You put that spell on her!" he screamed. "You took away her soul! Satan rot me if I don't kill you!"

The mariners went past, thrusting with pikes, battering with axes, pushing back the last three Catalans by sheer weight. But the work was slow and savage.

Asberto recovered himself. His weapon blurred. The edge flew past Lucas' face, chopped at hands and knees, stabbed at his mouth. He parried, riposted, driven yard by yard down the hillside. Only his armor saved him. But when Asberto nearly fell in a rabbit hole, Lucas attacked once more. For a space their swords raged against each other.

They broke away, panting in the wind and the moonlight. Lucas dropped his ruined buckler. Asberto clutched his haft in both gashed hands; the blade trembled. "Where's Djansha?" Lucas demanded.

Asberto did not hear. "She gives herself to all who'll ask," he said. Tears mingled with the blood and sweat on him. "Violante who was so beautiful is any dirty soldier's who'll give her a bottle of wine. Each night when she's senseless drunk, she mumbles about her father. What have you done with her soul?"

"Where's Djansha, you creature?"

Asberto darted forward. His sword rose and fell. Lucas twisted aside. The steel buried itself in the ground. Lucas' glaive took Asberto across the wrists.

The Catalan fell on his face in the brambles. He rolled over, sat up, and raised his arms. Both hands were gone.

Lucas stood aside and sobbed for air. When he regained awareness, he saw Asberto still seated among the thorns, under the moon, rocking back and forth. Blood spurted from his arm stumps, which he had folded into a cross on his breast. He would quickly die, Lucas thought. Certainly that was best: death for the warrior who was crippled, and for the knight's daughter whose mind was drowning.

There was no more hatred in Lucas, nor even the revulsion he once knew. He thought, Christ have pity on them, whom the Grand Company also destroyed.

The path seemed empty. He plowed back through the brush and hurried upward.

The three Catalan guards had not had time to close the rear gates. The raiders forced them into the garden. But there they counterattacked so ferociously that forty corsairs scattered, giving them a chance to join their aroused comrades at the house.

Lucas followed the rising terraces to the court-yard. There was more light here, not only the weak moon but candlelight glowing in the villa windows. He could see a few men, hastily equipped, behind the colonnade at the top of the staircase. Orio's band had formed ranks. Just as Lucas arrived, the pirates charged.

"Stop!" yelled Lucas. "You utter idiot! Stop!"

None heard him above the war whoops. Orio's burly form got almost to the stairs. Pikes and axes seethed behind him.

Then the crossbows spoke.

A sailor, running, took a quarrel through the breast. The force raised him on his toes. He seemed to dance before he flopped over backward. His pike clattered down on top of him. Another man cursed, his collarbone shivered apart. A third fell with a pierced belly. The charge broke. The Catalan archers put down their bows, drew sword, and made a rush.

"God send the right!" En Jaime de Caza led them. No mistaking the tall spare form, the pointed beard and graying temples. He wore formal black clothes, but a shield was on his arm, its bearings weirdly gay-colored.

Orio met him. Their blades crossed. Sparks sleeted. Deadly fast, the *rich hom* eluded the captain's awkward defense. Red streaks appeared on Orio's face and arms. He turned and ran. His crew bolted with him, into the garden. Half a dozen of them lay dead or dying below the stairs. En Jaime took his own seven men back up onto the portico.

Lucas called from the hedges: "Will you parley?"

En Jaime's panther-like ease of posture turned rigid. "Who is that?" he answered uncertainly.

"Will you talk, Jaime?"

"Yes. I will. Hold your fire, lads. Come forth, out there."

Lucas came into view. En Jaime's weapon drooped in his grasp. "Is that indeed you?" he said, so low that the wind in the trees nearly smothered it. He came down the stairs and met Lucas on the flagstones.

They regarded each other, unspeaking. The moon vanished again. Lucas was glad of the dark across his countenance.

"I would not have expected you at the head of this gang," said the Catalan dully.

"I had no choice," said Lucas. "Is Djansha here?"

"Yes."

Lucas had never before been humble. "Father,"

he said, "I am not worthy."

En Jaime pondered until, with a sad little laugh: "I believe I understand. The Venetian is here too, did you know? He came by horse from Rhedestos this very evening. I had delayed and objected as long as possible, but En Berenguer Rocafort finally ordered me, on my oath as a soldier, to give the man his chattel. You see, Reni offered us valuable trade agreements."

"Would you indeed give her up to him? You promised me—"

En Jaime's interruption came strident. "I tell you, I was under orders! And the welfare of the Company was involved! I did all I could. Tried to buy her myself, bid ten prices, but Reni wouldn't sell. He said she'd taken the fancy of a nobleman in Constantinople whose good will was worth more to him than all my gold. I knew you were fond of her, but not that you cared this much. It was doubtful that you were even alive. Is the life of a pet concubine so bad?"

"Gasparo lies. He wants her simply as the means of his revenge on me."

Breath hissed between En Jaime's teeth. "Impossible!"

"Why else should I come to you like this, you who were always my friend? I could only get a crew by promising them loot. Djansha's life, and our child's, are worth more than some boxes of metal in your cellars."

"I didn't know! How could I? I'd have smuggled her away if—Were he not my guest, I'd kill that fat ruffian!"

"Well, then, yield to us. We'll do no further harm, only take the girl and the treasure and begone. I'll repay you someday, somehow."

The wind skirled.

"Well?" Lucas' voice cracked over.

"No, I cannot."

"In the name of mercy—!"

"Two faithful men are missing; slain, I have no doubt. They trusted me as their lord. The treasures of all my people are stored here, as well as my own. I cannot betray them."

"But let me have Djansha, and enough of your own wealth to satisfy the corsairs, and—"

"Now you are asking me to commit treason," said En Jaime. He drew a signet ring from his finger, put it back on, drew it off, put it on. "I'm to compromise our honor by yielding with no more fight than this, and our interests by surrendering one person who could buy supplies needed by our entire host. . . . No. If you don't care about me, Lucas, or my name, remember that I too have a woman and a child, who must also bear the consequences. The gold you may have, everything I possess. But as for the Circassian, all I can do is appeal once more to Rocafort."

"You know how little can be expected from that! You spoke of smuggling her away. Could you not—"

"Reni has already taken formal possession. He's returning to Gallipoli and his ship this morning. I believe he really is going on to Constantinople, even if his tale was a lie. But perhaps you could take him in the Marmora?"

"How should I persuade my men? They'll go straight home if they get the plunder, and slit my gullet if they don't. Jaime, you must let me have her, now! What's all your damned murdering company worth, against an evil such as this?"

"Silence!" the Catalan yelled. "Who are you to preach, you and your faithlessness?"

It was like a blow across the eyes.

"I am a captain of the Grand Company, sworn to the service of Aragon and my own honor," said En Jaime. "We do not yield."

Lucas found slow, clumsy words: "But I am in the service of my lady."

A warmth returned to the knight. "We've sent a horseman off to Muntaner," he said. "Troops should arrive in two or three hours. Your rabble can't take the house before then. Forget the woman. I've had her christened, her soul is safe, you've done what you can. Escape now while you're able."

"I never was able."

"Nor I. Well—" The moon came back. En Jaime extended his right hand. "So be it. I was happy to know you, Lucas."

"And I." The other went to his knees. "Master, give me your blessing."

The Catalan touched his helmet. They went their separate ways.

Lucas found the corsairs huddled behind the stables. Orio lumbered from their indistinct mass. "Well?" said the captain. "Will they make terms?"

"No. They'll stand us off. Help is expected from Gallipoli."

Oaths ripped through the wind. A few weapons were pointed at Lucas. "By the guts of Mahound," said Orio, "if you've led us here and gotten our friends killed for nothing—"

"Be still!" Lucas lifted his sword. Moonlight touched his mail; he stood as if clad in gray ice. The pack retreated from him, bristling.

"Your own slewfootedness brought this trouble to you," he told them. "But we've still two hours or more to capture the house, load the gold, and put out to sea. If you'll heed me, we can do it. Otherwise, you can skulk off without me, and Satan gobble you down!"

"Well," sulked Orio, "what d'you propose?"

Lucas went around the corner and looked across the yard to the villa. "Stout doors and shutters," he mused. "We outnumber the Catalans three or four to one, but they can defend any entrance with ease. Wherever we attack, even if it be on several fronts at once, a few crossbowmen can shoot us from the windows. Or they might sally. We couldn't stand against them in open combat between ordered ranks."

"If you're through proving how we can't get in, would your majesty please to tell us how we can?"

Lucas ignored that. All shutters had now been closed; the house was a pale block, with golden streaks where light seeped through the cracks in the wooden panels. Behind those walls, Djansha lay. And Gasparo. Lucas knew he was going to get in. As if it were some problem in planetary motions, he calculated how.

"Listen to me," he said.

He asked a few questions and gave rapid commands. Then he tood a pair of helpers into the stables. The air inside was warm, full of hay and horse smells. Briefly, dizzily, he was a boy again, riding across the Asiatic plains . . . summer, the sky enormous, raining sunlight, mile upon mile of grasslands rippling in the wind, like an ocean, like a heaven of stars, for the cornflowers were blooming and all the earth was blue with them. . . . Grunting and swearing, they bridled a dozen animals and led them out, strung together in a fan-shaped formation by cords between the harness.

A clangor lifted from the front side of the house, where Orio with ten men had started a diversionary assault. The horses skittered about, neighed and snorted. Lucas spoke to them, stroked a neck, smoothed a mane. "So, so, so. Easy, boy. There's a good boy. So-o-o-o." With a practiced tug on the lead horse's headstall, he brought them up to the villa.

The side door he had in mind opened directly on ground level, below the verandah, with the vaults behind it. He was almost there when a quarrel whined from the loophole in a window shutter. He laid a rope's end across the nearer animals and got them in front of the door.

"Break it down!" he ordered.

The two sailors' axes thudded. The horses shifted about, controlled by Lucas at the center of their arc. One fell dead, shaking the ground. The crossbow bolt had gone through its heart. *"Hurry, you apes!"*

The door sagged. A corsair threw his weight against it. Four Catalans blocked the entrance. Their bows snapped. Lucas had already ducked. The lead horse reared in agony. Lucas had a flicker of regret—but Djansha was in that house. He dodged under the bellies, among the hoofs, till he stood behind the herd. "Hee-ya!" His whip flew.

The horses were driven forward, into the cellar. The Catalans had to step aside or be trampled. Lucas came immediately behind. His sword flamed at the nearest man. They bounded through the vaults, seeking each other's lives. The defender made an awkward cut. Before he could recover, Lucas' point slipped into his neck. Not waiting to see if the wound was fatal, Lucas hurried back to the entrance. The main body of sailors, hidden in the garden, had rushed as soon as the door was forced. Most of the animals were still outside, milling about, offering cover for that dash. The pirates got into the vaults and overwhelmed the guards posted. They were already up the stairs, pouring onto the main floor.

Lucas followed. Lamps and candles seemed blindingly bright after the dimness outside. Silver, gold, silk and velvet, glowed in rooms where men trampled back and forth, thrusting, hewing, slipping in blood and going down under axes. Taken from the rear, the soldiers at the main portal were forced to turn about to fight. Orio's detachment chopped away that door and fell on them from behind.

Lucas glared around the atrium. One exit, leading to the entrance hall, boiled with combat.

Orio's heavy sword rose and fell, battering down the defense of a man-at-arms who retreated over the blood-soaked carpet. An Almúgavare stood above a slain pirate, defying three others to meet his knife. But they fell on him from three sides and killed him. In this situation, the Catalan discipline was of no avail; brute numbers smashed them.

An archway on the left showed a corridor where En Jaime and four men held fast. The *rich hom's* sword flashed and sang. It was beautiful to behold him. A clot of seamen made little snarling rushes, heard the steel whistle, and retreated again. He saw Lucas beyond them, and must have thought his old attendant was about to intervene. For he saluted once with his sword, then sprang from his defensible position, out into the middle of the corsairs.

He does not wish that I should be his slayer, thought Lucas.

It seemed far away, not very important. He ran down the opposite hall. "Djansha!"

Only the racket of battle anwered him. At the end of the passage was the bedchamber once given her. Presumably a man of Gasparo's had been stationed outside, but was now in the fight. Lucas flung the door open. Light seeped wanly into the room.

First he noticed her loosened hair. It turned the light copper. She wore a thin shift; he could see how she had gained bulk, but those curves brought a tenderness to him such as he had never known before. Her face had thinned. She sat on the floor, leaning against the couch, ankles bound together with rawhide—runaway slave!

"Djansha," he whispered.

She could not speak, only look at him. She tried to rise, sank down again, shuddered through her whole body. "L-l-lucas," she said like a prayer. He trod forward.

Her eyes went beyond him. She gasped. He spun on his heel.

Gasparo Reni stood in the door. He was dressed for battle, his ungainly form helmeted and corseleted. A sword was at his waist and a cocked crossbow in his hands.

"Drop your weapon," he said quietly.

Lucas moved to put his body in front of Djansha.

"Drop it, I say, or I'll kill you. And then her."

The sword fell to the carpet.

With an almost holy light in his eyes. Gasparo breathed, "This much I never dared pray for."

His bow pointed unwaveringly at Lucas' breast. This close, it would spit a quarrel through any armor ever forged.

"I helped the defense," Gasparo said. "My men and I were stationed at the rear entrance. We thought you were simple pirates. When you broke in at the front, we ran to defend it. But I glimpsed you going this way. There is indeed a just God."

Lucas made a step in his direction. "Stay where you are!" warned Gasparo. "I'll shoot if you don't."

The coldness in Lucas deepened. He saw this room— the folds of a drape, a crack in the plaster, the slightly obtuse angle of a corner—with supernatural clarity. He was not afraid. There seemed no emotion in him at all, except the will that Djansha should live. If he could prolong this talking, something might happen.

"Won't you shoot anyway?" he taunted.

"Oh, yes. But I want you to hate me first. So that you'll die not only unshriven, but in the sin of hatred," Gasparo explained earnestly. "Let me therefore explain what'll happen to the woman after you are dead."

"You'll die too. The corsairs will have this place in minutes."

"They'll take ransom for me. I know their breed. Now as to yonder slut of yours. I won't have much time, but I do have sharp knife. So—"

Djansha sprang from the floor.

Lucas knew, without time to reason, that she had cut her bonds with his sword while Gasparo's attention was diverted. The weapon was in her hands as she flung herself in front of her man. She threw it at Gasparo.

The blade clattered across his legs. He tripped. The bow fired. Lucas was already falling, arms around Djansha to drag her with him.

The bolt grazed his helmet. A crash went through his head, like a gong in Cathay. Darkness and meteors whirled upward.

Gasparo drew his sword. Lucas sprawled on the floor. Djansha wriggled free of his limp embrace. She yanked out his dagger. Gasparo raised his weapon above Lucas' neck. Djansha pounced. The knife entered Gasparo's throat.

His blade fell. He pawed at the steel in him. Blood pumped forth, splashing across his hands.

He buckled, went on all fours, down on his belly. With one red finger, he traced a cross. The life went out of him.

Djansha said like winter: "You would have killed my lord." When Lucas sat up, she knelt by him and the tears broke loose.

He held her close. "My darling, my darling." He shook his head, which ached but was otherwise clear again, and felt the dent in his helmet. She aided him to his feet. He picked up his own sword. For a little while he regarded Gasparo's body.

"I think we are even now," he said. "Let us forgive each other, as I hope Moreta forgave us both."

Turning to Djansha, he kissed her with enormous gentleness. "Dress yourself warmly," he told her, "then wait here. I'll come for you soon."

"But you have been gone so long!"

"Wait, I say. Afterward we'll have all our lifetimes."

He left the room and went back along the hall.

The fight was over. The Catalans lay dead among a heavy toll of enemies. Orio's jubilant men didn't care. They still had enough to get their ship home; and so much the more loot for the survivors! Most of them were already at plunder. It was a relief to Lucas that no women were about. En Jaime must have sent them beyond the wall, to the cottages, at the first sign of trouble, and now the victors would not have time to look for them.

Astonishingly, the *rich hom* remained. He sat in a chair, blood dripping from his scalp, staining the fine black clothes. Two pikemen guarded him. Lucas wondered in a dull, exhausted way whether to be glad for him or not.

Orio jerked a thumb at the prisoner. "He was a mucking tough one," said the captain. "But plainly enough, he's worth a pile o' ransom. So the men clubbed him down instead o' killing him. What d'you think we can get?"

"Nothing," said Lucas. "He goes free."

"What? Look here, you—"

"Silence," said Lucas without emphasis. Orio's mouth closed.

En Jaime climbed toilsomely to his feet and leaned on the chair back. "No," he muttered. "I do not yield."

"There's no question of surrender, Jaime," said Lucas. "Take a horse and sword. Go in honor."

"And afterward?"

"You fought as long as any man could. None can blame you. As for us, we'll be gone in an hour. I . . . I'll try to pay you back what I'm robbing."

The dark head lifted. "You steal nothing, Lucas. My men are fallen, so I their lord have disposition of their treasure, as well as my own. I give it to you, freely, as a gift."

"Oh, Jaime!"

The Catalan advanced unsteadily into the room, walking on blood and among his dead warriors, who stared at him. Lucas held out a timid right hand. En Jaime took it in his own.

"I've thought much since you fled, falsely accused by my nation and my Church," said the *rich hom*. "I kept remembering my vows when first I was made a knight, and then remembering what the Grand

281

Company has done. And now this— We, who made the world afraid, brought low for the sake of a slave girl! I think God is angry." With a bewildered hurt: "But how did we fail Him?"

Lucas could not bring himself to answer. En Jaime nodded. The madness and the nobleness of Catalonia spoke: "You would say that we were unjust and unmerciful. But do you really believe that nothing more is required of man than . . . than kindness?"

"I do not know," said Lucas.

"I cannot believe so. And yet I cannot think what else there may be. Everything I imagine seems false. I'm only certain that the truth is not here."

"How then will you seek it?"

"I know not. Search I must, but search is useless. He will come to me if He chooses. But I don't think He ever will. I am not worthy, and don't know how to make myself worthy."

En Jaime rubbed his eyes. It left a red mask. "No one remains to me," he said on a thin, rising note of terror. "No one but God, who will not show Himself."

He dropped Lucas' hand and walked from the room, out through the entrance hall and the broken main door. Lucas listened for the sound of hoofs, but there was none. En Jaime had gone from the house on foot.

Orio shivered. "Move along, you scuts," he barked to his men. "Let's get loaded and away."

There was too much death in this place. Lucas went out onto the portico. The wind bit and whistled. Weariness dragged at him. A long way back, he thought; will it be as hurtful to as many as were all the miles which led me here? He leaned on a column and wished he could weep.

A footfall sounded behind him. He turned with the jerkiness of worn-out nerves. Djansha stood there in a woolen gown and cloak.

The clouds were breaking up. Moonlight streamed across her. "I could not wait any longer for you," she said.

If a man is fortunate, there are a few pure moments in his life. They do not last; the doubts and fears, guilt, loneliness, all the grubby little weaknesses return; but he has had those instants and knows life is joyous.

The wind filled his lungs and blew the ache from his head. A good wind for their voyage. Northward glittered his oldest friend, Polaris, the wander-star. But I am bound the other way, he thought. I am going home.

He took her arm and they walked down toward their ship, the victorious knight and his lady.

HAVE YOU READ THESE BEST-SELLING
SCIENCE FICTION/SCIENCE FANTASY ANTHOLOGIES?